THE FISHERMAN'S SECRET

A Story of Forbidden Knowledge

THE FISHERMAN'S SECRET

A Story of Forbidden Knowledge

G. KIM BLANK

SUNSTONE
PRESS

SANTA FE

In memory of Lynnie and Doug—and for my children, for reminding me ...

Sunstone books may be purchased for educational, business, or sales promotional use.
For information please write: Special Markets Department, Sunstone Press,
P.O. Box 2321, Santa Fe, New Mexico 87504-2321.
Printed on acid-free paper
∞

Library of Congress Cataloging-in-Publication Data

Names: Blank, G. Kim, 1952- author.
Title: The fisherman's secret : a story of forbidden knowledge : a novel /
    G. Kim Blank.
Description: Santa Fe : Sunstone Press, [2024] | Includes readers guide. |
    Summary: "A coming-of-age novel set in the 1960s, about how deep family
    secrets and the secrets held by nature collapse into an unthinkable
    tragedy, revolving around a commercial fishman, the disturbing discovery
    by his precocious son, his young daughter, and the sinking hopes of a
    First Nations woman"-- Provided by publisher.
Identifiers: LCCN 2024011372 | ISBN 9781632936639 (paperback) | ISBN
    9781632936691 (hardcover) | ISBN 9781611397390 (epub)
Subjects: LCGFT: Bildungsromans. | Novels.
Classification: LCC PR9199.4.B575 F57 2024 | DDC 813.6--dc23/eng/20240325
LC record available at https://lccn.loc.gov/2024011372

WWW.SUNSTONEPRESS.COM
SUNSTONE PRESS / POST OFFICE BOX 2321 / SANTA FE, NM 87504-2321 /USA
(505) 988-4418

Bye bye love
Bye bye sweet caress
Hello emptiness
I feel like I could to die
Bye bye my love
Good-bye

—"Bye Bye Love," The Everly Brothers, 1957

PREFACE

It applies to *The Watchers' Club* and now to *The Fisherman's Secret*: one third is true; one third is not true; and one third falls somewhere in-between.

This, of course, may be the case with more than just fiction, but we'll leave it to philosophers to parse the connections between perception, experience, the will, and (often unnoticed) the imagination. Arguably, and paradoxically, the imagination might be the faculty by which we construct "reality" and the meanings of our lives.

Here, though, an attempt should be made to draw out a few things from the more confined imaginative space of this new novel.

First, there's the connection with *The Watchers' Club* as the presumed sequel to *The Fisherman's Secret*. Indeed, *The Fisherman's Secret* is set in the same place (the Pacific Northwest) and the same neighborhood (Eastfield); likewise, it is close to the same era, but six years earlier, caught between the late 1950s and early 1960s.

Second, the story also calls upon the seemingly indelible recollection of the same narrator; but this becomes blurred when a complementary yet competing narrative emerges within the tale, an account fashioned by the narrator's older brother, Simon, who claims to know things beyond the narrator's direct experience from all those years ago. In particular, Simon's tale seems to hold the hidden record of a young First Nations woman up the coast in a remote village, which, I hope, profitably complicates and expands the narrator's central story.

Third, as a prequel, some of the same characters in *The Watchers' Club* appear in *The Fisherman's Secret*. Most interestingly, Mrs. Raskolnikov ("the old witch-lady down the road") is now, six years earlier, alive; via a single tarot card, she mysteriously predicts what will come, and what she foresees is not good.

And finally, fourth, we move into knowledge about the family across the street, the Caines, who (for dark causes) are not there in *The Watchers' Club*. The idea is to uncover things hidden in plain sight within that family's history—secrets within secrets. And in that family we encounter the main character, twelve-year-old Daniel Caine, whose "found" knowledge causes the unthinkable collapse of (revenge upon?) his world. His extraordinary attempts to connect the balanced laws of nature with scripture and myth are at moments disturbing, and he does so while filling the heads of two six-year-olds, one of them being his sister, Rebecca.

The Fisherman's Secret is neither a true nor false prequel to *The Watchers' Club*. In a measured way, it predicts it, commingles with it, but does not solve it. Both novels mark moments of childhood's end, which suggests new beginnings. But what about Daniel Caine, who slowly, then suddenly, falls to an ending so absolute?

A bottom line remains: Every life is secret, but some lives more than others.

—G.K.B.

THE PRELUDE

The trouble must have started earlier than I can recall—the trouble, I mean, that led to what happened at the end of that hot summer, the summer I tagged around with the kid from across the road.

My brother, Simon, tells me as much. But here's the kicker: he also told me that he spent some time "looking into things," though he's a bit cagey about what he was up to, about exactly what he "followed up on"—and why. Older brothers can be like that. Cagey, that is.

Back then, how could I have figured out what was going on? And even if I did know, what would it have meant in my six-year-old head, a head in which rubber balls, mud puddles, dead insects, and stinging nettles held prominent places?

How do you know that the family you see almost every day could be so hidden, so complex—and then, in a flash, so broken and gone?

But I'm not going to change a word below despite what Simon just told me, though it was not much. I shrug off his idea to "ramp up" what I remember. I tell him I can't stand the phrase, "ramp up."

I point out to Simon that what I have written—the story below—does head toward a moment at the end of that long-ago summer when things fell apart, when the center did not hold. Isn't that enough? Though recollections are never perfect, and words, exchanges, and events are rounded out, the easiness of imagination has been thoroughly tempered by what happened—by what I saw, by what I heard, and by what I felt, or at least what I think I felt.

And nostalgia's fuzzy lens? Hardly. In fact, the amount remembered amazes me. No—frightens me. Nothing needs ramping up. At all.

Okay. Simon's story should be somewhere. In fact, we've struck a deal: he will write out what he has told me, and add much more—what, he says, he knows, and what, those years ago, I did not know. He adds, "Not in any particular order." Simon's words, then, will come to be set between mine, without, at this point, me fully knowing his or him knowing mine. Brotherly love? Maybe, but perhaps more likely sibling rivalry. I know him well enough to keep both eyes open.

The vague hope is that the two stories complement rather than compete with each other. I, at least, enter this knowing that no story is ever complete.

But this, too, unsettles me, especially since Simon reminds me he's a professional who, for a living, tackles facts. From me, he says, readers might instead prefer an unstable situation, spiked-up plot, rising action, and all that sort of literary stuff. Things to tease them out of thought. "Speed toward the ka-boom," he urges. What a way to put it, given what happened! But I can't. There's just too much in the way—creeping, critical, confused, connected moments. Yet I know I have begun with it, and will have to then begin again. Unstable? Yes. Rising? Sure, I guess. Spiked-up? No, never—what happened, and the way it happened, is more than enough.

For those of you who want the picture of that time as clearly as a fixed memory can render it, perhaps don't read Simon's inserts—*the other story, the so-called facts*—that you will find between my chaptered account. He at least kept his part of the bargain shorter than mine—the story behind and, now, embedded within mine. I have to remind myself that I saw more than Simon could ever find out, though understanding may be a different matter.

Sorry. One other thing: despite what Simon says, he does hint that his story, at moments, does venture beyond the facts. He admits that he sometimes represents unknowable intimacies, that he has had to imagine or at least presume some things, things that he carries forward to judgements and conclusions that at moments do sound big. He also hints that he has seen some letters and checked some documents; I'm not going to ask, though I think I can guess what they might contain, given what I remember seeing and hearing. Maybe I'm just a little jealous, in that brother Simon seems able to round out a story that simply held me—and holds me—captivated yet captive.

And so I can hardly believe it: I will give Simon the final word in what I thought was my story to tell. You owe me, Simon. Big time.

FIRST, THE END

He ran toward the car—shouting, running, stumbling, getting up, running again. I had never seen him run before. When you plan everything, when you seem to know all things, you don't have to run. That's what he said. But now he was shouting, running, stumbling.

The sound of that dreadful crack and the picture of the sudden, rising, yellow flame on that hot summer day doesn't go away. Now and then it thumps away through uneasy dreams, and sometimes it's triggered by chance associations that might otherwise have been innocent enough. And, with each trigger, more comes back.

And that's fine. Time's ticking buffer should not soften everything that falls from childhood. Memory should not treat all things equally. Memory is not always a safe place. Or a place to hide.

From other youthful seasons there are hazy, blended moments in backyards and fields and woods. They carry something comforting in their vagueness. Those kinds of moments don't, years later, get caught in your throat. They seldom surround themselves with indelible details, especially like those from that one summer. And we all know what's supposed to lurk in the details.

But now I am almost lying, since, six years after that hot summer, in that same landscape, and among other kids who formed a club for plain mischief, there was yet another uncertain, dark moment of the unthinkable, when being out there at the wrong time and the wrong place meant childhood's real end, as innocence spilled over into guilt—and the memory of that, too, is hardly vague. For now, though, that has to be a different story, but it does make you wonder. Uneasy questions rise so easily. Things happen, but for a reason? But what would that reason be? To learn? To learn what? Or do things merely roll out from chaos, which, at best, we attempt to slow down with order? Let's leave that to Hamlet, who is the expert on uncertain meaning and dark confusion, as well as being the master of questions.

NOURISHMENT

The poisoned buttercups that reflected the sun beneath our chins. The vines we used as handcuffs. The limbs of young maples that became arrows. The precious, breathing creatures that surrounded our every move. Nature provided all we needed in our quest for play and power.

Over forbidden fences and through unfriendly bushes we made our way, carrying plans in every pocket that could hold a marble or rubber band or bit of twisted wire—or, even if we were careful, razorblades cased in folded cardboard. Our unthinking joy was to wander through the woods and hollows and trails, to where cat robins shuffled among the dry leaves, to set bird traps and, with anxious expectation, return to collect the living spoils for further examination. There were always specimens to collect. Jars and discarded match boxes were never wasted—they acted as tiny examination rooms, holding tanks, and, often enough, little coffins. Sometimes, when we strayed far from domestic turf, when we were up to no good, or we were late to return home, we were chased to our houses by the long, guilty shadows of coming evening. The low breathings of the forest and bushes sometimes followed our quick steps and pounding hearts. We dare not turn around to see what followed us.

Eastfield, my birthplace and only childhood home, composed all the pictures and sounds of those early years. Here, in this rural community, with the nearby town of Silverford creeping toward us, we were daily nourished by these scenes of wonder and fear until, in weariness, we went separate ways to our homes, and we fell into the sinking twilight of sheets and blankets—tucked in and, we hoped, protected by the fading sounds of kitchens being cleaned up, and by the murmur of voices we knew would be there in the morning. There was always another tomorrow, another day beneath the sun, behind the garages, in deserted shacks, and up The Trail.

For most of one young summer, everything seemed balanced and controlled and forever as we named what had to be named, collected what needed safekeeping, and used what might be needed for purposes great and small. There was no such thing as childhood's end. We were green, and Nature's secrets were rendered by comingled curiosity and awe. Science would help. Instruments would assist. Myths would explain. Sometimes living creatures would give up their lives for those purposes. We were to be given demonstrations and explanations and new words; and I was, in the beginning of this hot summer, ready for knowledge and its forbidden fruits. I was, it seems, ready for Danny, though I had no idea—no one had any idea—what Danny was ready for.

FEARFUL RATIOS

Daniel. That's what his mom called him. His dad usually called him Dan. For us, he was Danny. His last name was Caine. "Not the sugar kind," he liked to say.

Danny was our mentor. Our guide. Our window and mirror to a world that, without him, might not have held so much purpose and clarity—and so many secrets. He knew exactly where the largest garter snakes warmed themselves in the noonday heat. He knew how to make a carpenter ant attack—and eventually kill—itself. What a leech could do to a tadpole. How a magnifying glass could focus sunshine into a smoking needle of death. Where to find mushrooms that bleed—the devil's tooth. And he knew how—and once showed me—how to make gunpowder, though he used it twice.

For parts of that one hot summer, I was Danny's sidekick, maybe because I lived almost right across Eastfield Road from him. I came to feel I was special, chosen to share all that wealth that held me in thrall. After all, Danny didn't need my company. There were other kids around Eastfield closer to his age—kids smarter and faster and stronger than me. And more experienced. Like my older brother, Simon, who was about Danny's age, but for reasons I am only beginning to understand, didn't mix with Danny that much. Danny, anyway, welcomed me as his second shadow. Maybe he fed off my guiltless curiosity. Or what I didn't know. Sometimes, too, I was Danny's tool; other times, his assistant; and always his audience. I was there to watch—and, though I didn't know it, to record, to attempt to find something in what remained behind from what seemed to be an endless summer that ended in one blinding instant.

Danny's other follower that summer was his younger sister, Rebecca. She was, I admit, my best friend, which says a lot for

Rebecca. I mean, she *was* a girl, but that didn't really mean so much—that is, before the confusion of adolescence set in. It might have meant more to Danny. At a certain point, it may have opened up, well, certain confused possibilities that Danny attempted to explore and, on one day, have us act out in a garden scene.

Up until that summer there are quite a few photos of Rebecca and me: at the beach; in the snow; on our tricycles. We were, it seems, a cute couple. She was dark, smooth-skinned, and just a little round. I was blond, freckled, and skinny. Despite being on different sides of chromosome thing, we got along, her with her plastic dolls and me with my wooden swords. She played hopscotch; I threw rocks. She liked birds' nests; I liked wasp nests. She had a jumping rope; I had a rope whip. She liked pussy willows; I liked prickles. She cats, me dogs. And so, fulfilling the truism of the rhyme my grandma Maxine used to repeat, Rebecca tended to sugar and spice and everything nice, while I was attuned to slugs and snails and puppy dogs' tails. Yet though Rebecca was drawn to that other side, she was game for just about anything her older brother Danny could conjure up and dish out, which, on one occasion, did in fact involve sugar and slugs.

At the beginning of that summer, when Rebecca and I were six years old, Danny Caine was twelve. He crafted what that meant while he examined an earthworm he'd put into a jar of salt water:

"How old you two?" he asked.

"Six years old," we answered together.

"How old am I?"

We knew he was twelve and said so.

"Now, what's six plus six?"

Twelve, of course. A dozen. We knew that. Well, Rebecca knew it more quickly than me. The simple equation: Rebecca + me = Danny. We could, sort of, get that, whether it meant height or weight or smartness—or, in this case, years. For Danny, however, the calculation carried more.

Danny proceeded to give us a discourse on doubleness and twiceness and pairings, with examples beyond the realm of common numbers and the simple logic of measurement. He explained how dogs are twice as strong as cats, how chickens are half as smart as foxes. Wasps cause twice the pain of bees. Razor blades are twice as sharp as knives. Revolvers pack twice as much power as pellet guns, rifles have double the blast of revolvers, and shotguns double the blast of rifles.

Danny, it seemed, could keep this kind of talk going and going, though he concluded with a pairing he seemed to like best: "Baby blackbirds drown in half the time of snakes."

Danny paused to look deeply into us, then to his jar with the earthworm suspended in salt water. "But remember," he added, "one is not twice as much as none. It's only one on top of nothing, just like one thousand is just one more than nine-hundred-and-ninety-nine, not twice as much. Life isn't twice as important as death. Without death, no life. Zero plus zero equals zero."

Some small part of this philosophical figuring perhaps soaked into our unsubtle six-year-old heads. But, as with all things that came from Danny that summer, we were caught somewhere between blind wonder and enthusiastic confusion.

These fearful ratios weren't neat or tricky. Danny did not use sleight of hand to keep our attention. He instead used what he called "the Hand of Nature" to show us what was there, what was always-already true, though if necessary he was prepared to help. "Sometimes," he said, "we need to push things—to see the truth." Yes: The Truth. The absolute we knew absolutely nothing about, making ignorance our bliss.

Danny rendered harmony in our summer world, despite the compelling and sometimes cruel connectedness of all we touched and pondered and collected in the fields and ponds, in the soil and trees. Our Danny was playing with power and balance and control—and precision. Danny's gifts and Nature's boon were hard to tell apart—until, that is, that day it all went unspeakably wrong, but I don't want to get ahead of all that fell in-between.

Well, we two, Rebecca and I, were momentarily privileged, and we inwardly sang in the kingdom of our innocence. Danny made our minds leap up at all we beheld. And we beheld much. But how much is too much?

Danny hadn't finished. He wanted to define the moment:

"And now, I'm twice as old as you two—but this will only happen once, and just for bit. That time is now. By the end of this summer, I'll be thirteen, the unluckiest of all the numbers. The unluckiest. You pipsqueaks will still be six. Six plus six does not make thirteen. Later this year, you two will both be seven, the luckiest of all numbers. Thirteen divided in half does not make seven. Bad luck divided in two does not make good luck. It makes twice as much bad luck. "Like they say in Bingo, 'Under the B, unlucky thirteen.' B, I, N, G, O. Rearrange the letters, Big No."

Danny clearly knew drama as well as philosophy and math—and spelling—as we tried our best to catch up to his words and his numbers. Ending talks with a semi-magical word like "Bingo" gave him center stage.

For much of those few summer months, then, Danny sustained this role with us. This job as witness, student, lab assistant, audience, supporting cast, and accomplice was easy, and we assumed it with naive willingness, tinged with fascination and awe. What he played out in front of us, out there in the basements, backyards, and bushes, made some basic sense, even if we didn't always understand the chemistry or logic or the sources of his attending stories. Everything had a place and purpose. Everything—forces big or small, sweet or sour, sticky or smooth, sharp or dull, living or dead, good or evil— seemed to hold the promise of balance and explanation in the clear, hot air of that summer.

In the end, though, there were questions that we couldn't yet articulate or weigh: Did Danny break the balance, or did some imbalance break Danny?

But the deeper facts remain. With the fuse of summer lit, Danny made many things possible—and he was gravely marked to make one impossible act true.

§

West-coast commercial fisherman like Mr. Joseph Abel Caine lived divided lives. When the fishing season opened, there were intense and extended periods away from home, sometimes over a month at a time, out on the waters between the Queen Charlotte Islands and the Alaska panhandle. The times were testing and sometimes dangerous—and always unpredictable. There was also much down time at home when the fisheries were closed. In some ways, these were the toughest moments: men with too much time sometimes turn to darker activities, thoughts, and longings to mask or funnel their energies. Then, too, their lives were divided between good seasons with plenty of fish and plenty of profit, and those barren seasons when the salmon seemed to disappear, and no one knew why. Hard times meant tightening belts and somehow getting through. The stress of poor seasons led some men to abandon commercial fishing altogether, and in a few cases to turn to ruinous ways. The life of a fisherman was all they knew, and if they couldn't fish, what was there?

It was well known that some commercial fishermen had women up the coast. Tucked away at the end of forest-lined inlets in tiny, isolated fishing villages, in and around places like Ketchikan, Kake, Tlell, and Klawak, the fisherman found more than safe harbor and places to refuel, and this was another division in their lives. A few fishermen had relationships that covered years, seeing the same women season after season, often bringing gifts from and intimations of another world. In almost all cases, these women were natives—from various small and scattered First-Nations communities.

This, then, was a secret kept among some salmon fishermen. Even those who did not have women understood how loneliness, long hours, and the unforgiving, uncertain open sea could tempt a man too long away from his home. When the fishing season was over, these women, with their own longings, were left behind. Part of the secret stayed, but the other part was taken away, lodged within the fishermen, brought in silence into their homes, where, they hoped, nobody knew. The women of the villages carried on, in their own ways, with, perhaps, some kind of formless wish tucked away.

OPEN-MITT SURGERY

Danny was a little chubby. His pale face—his round cheeks and small nose—appeared too young for his soft body. His quick eyes seemed small, but maybe this was because they were always so focused. His hair was somewhere between curly and wavy, and the color somewhere between brown and blond. It always seemed little greasy, even when he had just taken a shower.

In fact, Danny took many showers, and often at peculiar times. Sometimes, right in the middle of something important, like the discovery of the stiffened corpse of a mole on The Trail, he would put us on hold—"*don't* move and *don't* touch anything"—while he rushed off for a shower. He would come back, looking much the same as when he left, except that his hair would be combed back and flat. He would then continue his particular business: dissections, burials, burnings, explanations—whatever. Whether his showery baptisms were preparatory or some kind of other secret ritual we never knew. Rebecca said that Danny showered with some strong-smelling green soap, and that the shampoo he used was green too, and it smelled like disinfectant. Cleanliness—scrubbed, clinical cleanliness—was important for Danny and his work. He once told us that he liked to use toothpaste to wash his hands. He'd show us his hands before he'd begin his work. "Look," he'd smile, "no cavities." Danny could be pretty funny sometimes.

Unlike most of the kids his age around Eastfield, Danny wore sensible clothes: buttoned shirts instead of t-shirts, khaki pants instead of jeans, and brown oxfords instead of running shoes. Danny didn't like to run. It was, he said, a sign of weakness, of failing to see what was to come.

His fine fingers on the ends of those plumpish hands could manipulate the most delicate of things. His fingernails were perfect, and he often cleaned them with the manicure tool from his fantastic Swiss Army knife, which he enjoyed advertising to us: "Not one, not two, but three mini screwdrivers—and two blades, one saw blade, tweezers, scissors, toothpick, punch, cork screw, bottle opener, can opener, reamer." No matter how many times he flipped the parts in and out and listed the various blades, bits, and mini-bits, it was amazing, like they appeared out of nowhere. All in one impossible tool!

Despite his clinical cleanliness, Danny recently had begun to get pimples and pockmarks on his face. Not tiny ones, but sometimes large, open ones, as if his skin had been stretched, torn a bit, then sucked in. He told us that at any given time these pimples were at various stages: some beginning to rise; some risen that were red and sore; others with small, fiery heads; after that they became brownish-purple scabs. Danny, ever the opportunist, knew the right time in the life-cycle of a scab to pick it off so that there was dry but slightly scarred skin beneath. Sometimes he collected these little flakes of dead blood in clear, plastic pill bottles. "Ant food," he called it. And the ants did indeed seem to like it. So, too, did Rebecca's two swollen goldfish, Henny and Penny. The first time we sprinkled a few bits in the fish bowl, they flashed to the surface to gobble the little scab bits; Rebecca and I looked at each other and then to Henny and Penny with smiles of surprise. We weren't, of course, to tell our parents. Danny made us pinky swear in the spirit of scientific secrecy and absolute loyalty.

Danny in fact talked about how he had started to change, evolving from kid to adult, and how this caused confusion in his body that showed up in the pimples. A boy's body and an adult's body fighting it out. "The pimples," he said, "are signs of the struggle. A kid's body is not always ready to change—to grow up. It's the big change, you know. Deep voice, bigger body, hair growing in...in new places."

Hair in random places was not an altogether pleasant prospect. Danny, not unusually, crafted a correspondent story from nature: "Like a caterpillar not ready to be—something else. Has to be a pupa first—the in-between stage, the chrysalis or cocoon, before becoming adult. Inside a dark shell, while it changes. What goes on inside, no one knows. A fight to hold back, maybe—before ripping its way out."

My vague thought—or my thought now?—was that maybe Danny was holding back while in his own pupa stage. Fighting against something before "ripping" out. Danny had explained the full life cycle to us more than once, and it was always mysteriously good.

Danny worked it out a little more: "Sometimes the change is Dr. Jekyll becoming Mr. Hyde." We didn't know these people, though Danny's nodding expression suggested he knew them quite well.

Danny sometimes popped a few of his pimples for us. Milky fluid burst between his index fingers, followed by watery blood with a hard, small white nub. Under a magnifying glass, it looked like a tiny white tadpole. I once noted this, but Danny said it look more like a very large sperm. We took his word for it, given that, for the moment, sperms would remain something that we didn't understand in much detail, though during the course of the summer we would learn a little more.

Danny explained that the little white hard bit was the center of things, and that if it doesn't gush out with the rest of the watery stuff, you really haven't squeezed out all of what's in there. "It may rise up again," he pointed out. "Not in the same way, but as a sore."

Danny controlled the direction of the squirted fluid so that it landed on one of his fingernails. He transferred it from his fingernail onto a piece of broken glass for closer examination.

He explained that the white fluid was a kind of poison, locked into tiny pockets beneath his skin. "Soon under your skin, too—when you start growing up and your body changes in ways you don't want to think about. Jekyll and Hyde," he again reminded us, repeating their names while slightly raising his eyebrows in our direction.

The one thing we could not imagine was growing up. We may not have known Jekyll and Hyde's particular issues, but we did have a great deal of admiration for Peter Pan, who, as far as we knew, had solved the growing-up problem.

Danny drew us in to look at the milky fluid. He noted that when the poison beneath his skin reached a certain point, it boiled up and made the red marks on his face. "A war," he said. "Good things in the blood against bad things in the skin. The body wins the war against the bad stuff, but not without a fight, not without little scars. Yep, but sometimes the other side wins. Infections. If infections win the bigger battle, you die."

Danny often took advantage of any reference to death, upon which he could expand endlessly. "An infection," Danny repeated and expanded, "is nature battling things out—good guys don't always win, you know."

One thing about Danny, and what we liked: he often favored bad guys, bandits, crooks, villains, aliens, monsters, outsiders. Danny once said, "There should a story where a drooling dragon burns a goody-goody knight into a crisp and then eats him like a potato chip." We agreed. That would be good. "The dragon would live happily ever after, surrounded by sheepish villagers that he could snack on when feeling a bit hungry."

Another thing: Danny never ever talked down to us, even in his most creative and scholarly moments. But this is what seemed to challenge some of the parents when we overheard them speak about Danny: that he spoke beyond his age, that he didn't have the same interests as most kids. One of the parents called him "a little professor," whatever that meant. They seemed to doubt Danny in some way, while for us, he offered pure wonder, understood or not. My own Mom seemed split: as she once said to my Dad, "You know, Danny's mom told me he's read most of the *World Book Encyclopedia*." Mom was really into reading, so that was something. "He even underlines places in the Bible," she added. Dad was not so convinced or impressed by any of this, so he kept his thoughts to himself.

For us—well, we could care less about Danny's reading list. We could look upon Danny's face and see the rise and fall of epidermal empires, an evolving laboratory wherein and whereon the forces of good and evil and life and death battled each other with blood, water, pus, and poison. Danny's face was the history—his story—of the natural world: a map, a battleground, a hatchery, a laboratory, an excavation site, a graveyard—and sometimes a food source for goldfish and ants. His eyes could see right through this scene, straight into us—his little mirrors wherein he may have seen his own passing innocence, but maybe that's too much thinking. For a second, Danny really did seem to be a pupa, with some kind of hidden change going on inside. What would be become?

This lesson was not finished.

"Want to watch the power of the poison?"

Was there any doubt?

Danny took us over to our favorite spider, which at the moment was a large brownish one whose web was in the corner of the open garage down along the side of his house. For some reason, he called her Charlotte. He put down the glass with the pimple fluid on it.

We hadn't thrown any insects into the web for a few days, so we expected some kind of action. Even when the spider had had its fill, it was always ready to wrap up some new victim for leaner times and for the end of the summer, though it might die after leaving its sac in some corner. Spiders, Danny said, never wasted meals, just like he never missed opportunities.

"First, we need two tiny victims."

Rebecca and I looked at each other.

"No, not you two. Though that's a nice idea." Danny flashed a smile. "A couple of juicy bugs to throw in."

We hunted around for couple of minutes—we knew where to find such creatures, as well as how to capture them with minimal damage—and soon we each came up with a damsel fly.

"Nice," said Danny. "Just what the doctor ordered."

I passed him one of the flies. He held it by its wings while its spindly legs frantically spun. Danny noted as much: "Like it's treading water to no use—drowning. But in a moment it will drown in reverse. Fluid will leave its body—not fill it."

Danny smiled and let this picture settle into our imaginations.

"May I have the poison, please."

Rebecca handed Danny the piece of broken glass with the pimple fluid on it. With one of the tiny blades from his knife he delicately scrapped the pimple fluid from the glass onto the fly. He tossed away the glass and put away his knife.

"That should do it. Fly A, we'll call it. Now, pass me the other. I'll rub nothing on it. Fly B."

Once more, he looked intently at the flies, one in each hand. Both were still scrambling.

"Now, watch this. Let's take Fly B, *au natural.*" It sounded like he said, "oh natural," which seemed like a pleasant declaration.

Danny flicked the damselfly that was not signed with his poison into the web, and for just a fleeting moment the fly must have felt like it was free. But now it was caught in the web and making a commotion. Charlotte bolted for its vibrating victim and quickly made contact. In just a few seconds the spider had paralyzed Fly B with a little bite and spun it up securely in a white, silk coffin. Charlotte was quick and efficient.

"Nighty-night, little fly," Danny murmured. "*Au revoir.*"

Meanwhile, back at the web, to which we again turned our attention, Charlotte had retreated to its trap lines at the edge of the web just as quickly as she had come.

"Fly B, the one we just saw get wrapped up, is to see what happens when things are normal," Danny said. He looked at our questioning faces. "To compare what happens, I mean. Fly B was definitely something lovely Charlotte liked, right?" We nodded. "Now watch."

Danny took Fly A, the one marked with his pimple poison, and tossed it into the web. Once more Charlotte sprinted tip-toe for her new potential victim. It made contact for a split second, but instead of paralyzing it and wrapping it up for later on, the spider sped back to the edge of its web and remained there, nervously flexing her front legs. The damselfly continued to shake the web.

What happened?

Danny explained that the juice from beneath his skin, and made in his body—the pus—did not taste very good for the spider, "Just as if someone sprayed rat poison on a hot dog and offered it to you." We definitely related. Gross. "Just because a spider has its own poison doesn't mean it likes poison."

Danny told us that Fly A would die slowly for other kinds of reasons, and that Charlotte had no choice but to watch a death that she won't have anything to do with. He also told us that Flay A might prefer to die by the bite of the spider rather than from slowly drying out on the web. "You know, the bite of the spider is like what happens when the dentist gives you a shot. The fly doesn't have to think about these kinds of things. Just wants to get away. That's all it knows. For Charlotte, there will be other things to suck life fluids from. Maybe even another spider."

Danny raised his eyebrows. He could tell we didn't get it. He explained that sometimes women spiders eat guy spiders just after the guy spider gets the sex-stuff done with the woman spider. "He gives her the curse of having babies—he gets what he deserves. When you get, something has to give. Both got, and both gave."

This was still pretty vague, but it was one of Danny's favorite themes, how Nature kept Balance, how it never wasted anything or took more than it needed. "Only people are that dumb—in the end it gets them." That didn't sound good. "Some more than others." That sounded even worse, like a warning, though we weren't sure where it was directed.

We nevertheless took note as we struggled to get our little heads around time and fate and consciousness and suffering and matrimonial cannibalism and giving and getting. Whew! What we lacked in knowledge, though, our imagination would no doubt make up—eventually. The best part was that we didn't have to understand to be impressed or to remember. We were happy, though, that at least Charlotte had prepared a meal.

While we finished up with all of this, we were aware that a car was coming down the long, bumpy driveway beside the house and making its way to the garage. The car stopped just before it entered. It was Danny and Rebecca's father, Mr. Caine. "Joe," my Dad called him.

Rebecca ran around to the side of the car as he was getting out.

"Hi Daddy, hi Daddy!" she shouted. He swept her off her feet and swung her fully around once. She put her arms around his neck and he held her with one arm. In the other arm he had a shopping bag. Mr. Caine handled Rebecca like she weighed nothing. He was not that big, but his sunburnt arms, with a few sea-serpent tattoos, betrayed muscle and sinew that flexed from every movement of his wrist.

"Well hi there yourself, little monkey! Think I got anything for you in this bag? You think? Some old gumboots, maybe?"

"Oh, come on, Daddy, please, what's in the bag? Something for me? I just know it—you said so! You promised!"

"I did, did I? Let's see, hmm."

Mr. Caine let Rebecca down and purposefully spent much too long foraging around the bag. "Well, not much interesting in here..."

"I know you got—you said you would!"

Rebecca was just at the end of the teasing stage and about to enter the huffing stage. Mr. Caine relented just in time.

"Oh—oh, what's this?"

With mock surprise, he pulled a rectangular package out of the shopping bag and gave it to her.

"Oh thanks, Dad! Thanks!" She stole a kiss and ran off into her house.

She knew it was this certain kind of doll—a "Barbie," I found out later—that she had been pleading for ever since her Dad got back from fishing up north a few days ago.

Mr. Caine stood awkwardly for a second before walking the few steps toward Danny and me.

"So, what trouble you boys up to, eh?" Mr. Caine turned and gave me a pat on the head, sizing me up. "Starting to sprout up there, eh—still skinny as ever, though. Muscles like a sparrow's kneecap, eh. How's your mom and dad? Tell them I got a couple of salmon for them."

I said I would, nodding.

Mr. Caine was sort of nice to me, but I didn't really like being called "skinny." I thought of myself as "slim." At least my Mom would back me up on this: "Better to be a racehorse than a workhorse, right?"

Mr. Caine stood there for a moment or two before clearing his throat.

"For you, Dan. Here."

Danny seemed like he wasn't paying much attention to what was going on. He had his Swiss Army knife out and was intent upon sharpening a stick. Danny turned and took the package without much enthusiasm. He barely looked at his Dad.

"Yeah. Thanks." He put the package on the hood of the car.

Mr. Caine stood there, as if waiting for something more. "Well, gotta be going in now. Supper time. You'll be coming in soon to get cleaned up, Dan. Don't be late."

Danny continued to work on the stick, which was quickly being whittled down to nothing but a long, sharp point.

"Well, I'll see you around, too," Mr. Caine said to me. And make sure ya tell your parents about the salmon. Right?"

I nodded again.

With this, Mr. Caine picked up some other shopping bags from the back seat of the car and went into the house.

Danny threw the remainder of the pointed stick into a bush. He carefully cleaned the blade of his knife with his handkerchief and returned it to his back pocket, which also had his magnifying glass in it. The unopened parcel remained on the hood of the car.

"You gonna open it?" I asked.

"No. You," he said. "Go ahead."

I ripped open the parcel. Wow! It was a beautiful baseball mitt, jet black, the kind with silver and gold lettering.

"Nice, huh," I said. I had just started Little League, and so I appreciated the good-looking hardware. Danny took little interest in my praise, which carried a touch of envy, since I had unhappily inherited my older brother's mitt with my Dad's reasoning: "It's all worn in and ready to go."

This was a strange present, given that Danny didn't like sports much—or at all—and he never played on any ball teams. It wasn't that Danny was clumsy. With a BB gun he could knock the eye out of a sparrow from fifteen feet. He could even pull the antennae off a bee with some tweezers without the bee seeming to notice.

But the baseball mitt: Danny barely looked at it.

"Well, here, I guess." I handed it to him.

Danny looked at it like it was an odd specimen that carried some scorn.

"He's not my keeper," Danny said in a low voice.

I didn't know what this meant, but it was clearly something directed to his father.

He finally added, "Make a sacrifice. Maybe some of the leather will come in handy. Bring it 'round back."

We walked behind the garage to where we often sat to perform many of our more secret jobs. And there, nested at the base of some fir trees, and using the smallest blade on his knife, Danny amazingly, carefully, shockingly began to dissemble and disembowel the beautiful mitt, bit by bit, piece by piece. Precise, open-mitt surgery.

He sliced and slit and carved and cut until twenty or thirty perfect pieces of black and tan leather in all possible shapes lay before us, some of them as thin and long as shoe laces, others square or triangular. After fifteen or so minutes, there was not even a hint that what we once had before us was a singular object with special purpose—to catch baseballs.

I had no idea what to say or even think.

Danny surveyed the scene before him. "Just goes to show," he said. "Parts are greater than the whole. Each part is a whole, and every whole the part of something else."

Who could disagree with the evidence spread out so perfectly! I had begun watching what he did with the new mitt with horror, but now, in the end, with wonder—of how it ever became or was a baseball glove in the first place. "Like a...like a jigsaw puzzle, sort of," I added, not knowing whether this was a lame comment, given the marvelous dismembering.

Danny stopped for second or two and looked at me. I held my breath and let it out when Danny at last nodded his approval.

"Yeah," he added, "Like a jig-saw puzzle. Like everything. Some known things are known better when they are taken apart."

Danny kept going: "And sometimes when you try to put something back together that you've taken apart, it turns out to be something different—good things taken apart and then put together can become bad things. But you don't know until—until the end, and sometimes when it's too late. But you've already started. And you may have to get rid of it—or try."

For a second Danny turned to me more directly as his complicating words pushed my understanding: "You heard of Frankenstein?"

I squinted a "Nope," but it sounded familiar. Was it a hotdog or something? A kind of cow?

"Well, he was a guy, a scientist. A doctor. He took some parts, and he hoped to make something new from them."

I asked what happened.

"In the end...not so good."

"What kind of parts did he put together—after things were taken apart?"

Danny gave me a smile, as if he had been working the conversation for my question.

"Body parts. Human body parts. Pieced together. Put them together to make a new human. Well, sort of human. It became alive. Off it went, but not real happy about things."

Body parts? I wasn't sure what more to ask, so I nodded like I understood. I wondered how this Frankenstein guy put the body parts together. Glue?

I watched Danny to see what came next or what he might add. But he returned to the leather shapes in front of us. Then I sorted of wondered where Frankenstein got the parts, but Danny was now going in a different direction.

"We'll save the bigger leather pieces for branding. The smaller pieces we'll burn and bury tomorrow, maybe. A couple of pieces will work for slingshots. Longer bits, the cords, can be used for tying things up."

Indeed: some of the bits were perfectly supple squares and rectangles. One of them was the piece with a silken label sewed on to it. Danny gave it to me in a ceremonial kind of way. "Something to remember me by," he pronounced. He smiled just a little. "A body part."

I took it. It was like a medal, in way. A secret badge. I'd keep it, for sure, and it made its way to the bottom of one of my pockets—*a body part.*

"Remember," Danny said, picking one of the larger triangular leather bits, "this used to be a cow, walking 'round eating grass, chewing its cud, swinging its tail at flies, making poo pies and mooing at the moon. Might have given milk. Maybe you drank some of this baseball mitt's milk. After that, it was probably meat. A burger. Maybe you ate that, too. The leftover skin turned into shoes, coats, car seats—or a baseball mitt. Now, just bits of cow on the ground. Never forget what things used to be before they were taken apart. Part of a story is nothing. A lie, really. Know the whole story. How things got where they are. And why. You never really know." Danny stopped, only to add something more: "Some try to keep it a secret."

Yep, it was easy to forget what things once were, how they were, where they came from, or what things might become. Part of a story is not a story. I thought to myself something I knew: a book was once a tree, made from paper and all that. Should I say this to Danny? He didn't mind my earlier jigsaw puzzle idea.

Before I could get it out, Danny continued: "Remember, the story never ends, 'cause if we, say, burn some of the pieces here, they turn into something else—to ashes and dust. Or if we bury these cowskin bits, they turn into something different again, part of the soil, which feeds the grass, which cows eat. The cows grow, get whacked with a bolt to the head, gets sliced into steaks, and turned into baseball gloves that some kids might return into pieces." He looked at me, and I might have blinked back. "And," he said, looking around, "here we are, sons under the sun." Danny tensed just a little. "And we don't know—"

Danny stopped there. His thoughts must have run too deep for me, or to something so sideways that he didn't want to speak of.

Then, in the quiet of the day, in the shade of the tall trees, he confirmed the lesson and sealed the conversation with something I was on the verge of understanding: "Everything used to be something else. All things in Nature break down, fall apart, to become something else. That is the law."

This moment was tempered by uncertainty that Danny put slowly, almost slyly: "But you never know what. There's always sacrifice, a loss. And some try to break the law."

The moment passed into more stillness.

"Leave this stuff here," Danny said.

We got up and made our way toward the back of his house. I left him at his back door, and as he opened it, I could hear his mom and dad talking loudly with each other. Arguing, maybe. There seemed to be some trouble when they were together, which meant those stretches between fishing trips. I didn't like witnessing any of this. Danny's face tightened. *But you never know what. There's always sacrifice, a loss.*

"See ya," I said. Danny didn't say anything. He stood by the back door, frozen by the voices of his parents lashing out at each other. He looked back toward the garage and the car.

I didn't wait to see if Danny went in or not. Maybe he went back to the baseball glove. I ran off toward my house across the road, jumping over the ditch, leaving the Caine property behind as fast as I could, barely looking to see if there were any cars, which I would have heard anyway. I was hungry. I hoped we weren't having any boiled vegetables. And I didn't feel much like eating anything that had to do with cows that night, though a cheese bacon burger could easily make you forget that breathing, mooing, pooing, peeing, cud-chewing, fly-swatting, grass-eating, leather-bearing cows even existed, especially ones that might get made into baseball mitts.

§

Not so long after their marriage, word drifted back to Mrs. Joseph Caine that her husband may have been spreading himself around up north during the fishing season. At smoke-filled bingo nights she gossiped with the wives of other fisherman, who likely got snippets from their husbands who knew about such things, though maybe a few of these husbands also fell into the easiness of finding a place for their temptations when away during the fishing season. Maybe hinting at what other fishermen did were attempts to disguise their own guilty acts.

Hannah Caine did not know if such rumors about her husband were true, though such doubts and thoughts often begin to work away in hidden corners. She did not know that there was just one woman, a young native woman, who pulled on her husband's passions. She had thought she was enough, that she gave enough. Hannah did not know that this woman's name was Emily Cooday.

Hannah would not have known the way that Emily Cooday wanted her husband. How much Emily knew of her husband's ways. That Emily hoped beyond hope that at some point Joseph Caine would leave his world down the coast, though she knew little about his life beyond her own small world. But he couldn't—or wouldn't, even if Emily expressed desires and attentions in every way she could think of. Mr. Caine had no trouble taking in those desires, but he had no emerging resolve to take them away along with her, or to stay behind with her in some sort of new life.

Did Joseph Caine love Emily Cooday? No doubt, and in ways that made both his body sear and, for moments, his mind rest. When he was with her there was nothing else, and it was simple. But it was a love that had meaning at a particular place and at particular times. For Emily, time and place rolled into one thing only, and that one thing was Joseph Caine. He was a dream of and a feeling for something she did not know, and because this rose from unseeing hope, it was crossed through in necessary disappointment, the kind that could, left to itself, perhaps end in darkness.

THE TREE OF SACRED RUBBERS

Summer meant no school. No school meant being outside all day. And being outside all day that summer often meant following Danny's explorations into the deepest and darkest parts of our backyards, bushes, and beyond.

Although Eastfield was a rural community, not much more than a rough area defined by a few secondary roads, we were within walking distance to our school. Most people had at least a few acres of undeveloped bush, old pasture land, and patches of evergreens. The properties tended to be long rather than wide, in strips off Eastfield Road.

The dominant feature were those evergreens—Douglas firs and a few tall red cedars. Here and there a maple. These trees were vantage points for crows, ravens, and the occasional eagle. I, too, sometimes used the tops of lesser trees as a perch, and there was this free and scary feeling while clinging to the slightly swaying trunks and bending branches. Then there was the smell of pitch on your hands, which Mom did not care for. She showed me how to remove it by rubbing butter between my hands, which was magic, since regular soap had no effect on the pitch. Pitch, though, was incriminating evidence of climbing, which brought warnings to be careful. While buttering my hands for me, Mom always said that if you rubbed butter on the paws of a new cat, it will always find its way home. She added, smiling just a little, "And so you'll always be able to find your way home, too." This would be proved true some years later, when we adopted a little stray cat, who helped to solve an unthinkable mystery that forced innocence to collide with guilt.

My parents had one of the average-sized, long properties along Eastfield Road: a number of acres of fairly heavy bush, lots of evergreens, thick salal, and few small clearings here and there. Once upon a time my great grandfather owned much of the land in this area, and Dad ended up with a strip of this property after the war. His brothers and sisters got rid of their inherited land in order to be closer to the city. But after not too many years, the city of Silverford was slowly coming to us. Dad said that one day the property would be worth something. Mom wasn't so certain. Adults were obsessed with such things as subdivisions and property prices. There were even rumors of plans for a modest shopping mall a mile or two away, just past the bottom of Eastfield Road, but most of the adults doubted it. "That'll be the day," they said. We kids let the parents have their dreams, predictions, and fears. We had our own pressing business.

Running through our property from top to bottom was something we called The Trail, a well-worn path that was older than our being there. At the top, The Trail emptied out not too far from the dead end of an isolated secondary road where guys and gals would have their weekend amorous adventures in their parked cars or, in the summer, in the fields and bushes not far from where they parked. Often a Saturday or Sunday morning reconnaissance mission turned up odd remnants of their close encounters of a weird kind: empty whisky or beer bottles, garters, stockings, underclothes, an old blanket, lighters, matches, cigarettes, sometimes a little change, and so on. This area came to be known as Lovers' Lane. Danny never called it that. About six later it would the scene of something that shocked the community and that, for a while, took over my life and the lives of my friends, but, once more, that's another story.

When we were up past The Trail with Danny, close to Lovers' Lane, he would have us search for the used rubber things he called Sperm Traps. He called them by other names, which he rattled off like a poem: rubbers, French letters, jock sock, condos, pecker pockets, willy wrappers, wiener warmers, donk zeps, cock corks, jack sacks, bone domes, oven mittens, horn hoods, and so on. If we could find one, it was often lying soggy and limp somewhere close to the struggle nest, or close to where a car had parked. We would poke it with a stick and then place it on our secret and sacred Rubber Tree, as Danny christened it. In truth, it was an old thorn bush. We would hang it on the bush with the other rubbery carcasses from previous searches, so that the whole thing looked a little like a scrawny Christmas tree decorated with a bunch of pale, deflated, dried out balloons. When we didn't find a rubber, Danny would mutter something like, "Hmm...with nothing to stop them, they must have escaped. Escaped, up, into the Mother of All Caves, where all evil begins. Where evil began."

Again, mainly through bits and pieces of what Danny told us about couples "Doing It," we had come to almost understand what he was talking about—about what was in the Sperm Trap, about where the sperm had come from and where they were trying to go, and even about what they were going to do when they got there. It didn't make much sense, or sense to think about it too much, even if Danny thought about the birds and the bees stuff a lot—in his own way, of course. In fact, sometimes the whole thing seemed to make him a little upset. One time he broke off a small branch of the Rubber Tree and set it alight. He stood before the little burning bush: "So much for the Tree of Knowledge," was the only line he tossed to us. We had no idea what the tree knew, or what it could teach. But Danny knew, and that was enough for us.

Danny did tell us, and made us promise, not ever to discuss any of this sperm stuff with our parents. "They wouldn't understand," he said, confirming that Danny knew much more about things than our parents, which was hardly surprising.

At the moment we had to deal with that haphazard nest pressed into the tall grass—the sign of the struggle between the male and female of the species. Danny, massaging our imagination, rolled out a tale that, instead of marking the inexperienced rolling around of two excited teenagers, pictured some large snake-like beast of prey making a kill in this spot: "Waiting in the night for some young animal to stumble upon its waiting place, the beast rears up its cyclops head to jump on its innocent prey, with one well-directed blow that spills the blood from the victim while the beast drools, and then—then nothing. Only darkness. Darkness and waiting."

We didn't get the heavy-duty symbolism, but, oddly enough, it was a lot easier to picture Danny's invented story than what had really been going on there.

This summer we thrived on these tales and parables and scenes without particular human faces, where, once more, the balanced forces—of good and evil, light and dark, life and death, water and blood—surrendered to and merged with the laws and jaws of Nature—and to Danny's discourse that moved between and merged the mythic with the scientific. "The Super Natural," Danny would say.

As monitors, maybe one day it would be our job to pass on these parables, and thus become Danny's disciples. But the last time we went to the Rubber Tree area, about halfway through the summer, the lesson took an uneasy turn when Danny pulled out a flat, little square out of his pocket. It looked an individually wrapped candy or gum. Danny unwrapped it. We closed in.

"What is it?" asked Rebecca.

"One of those," Danny replied, pointing to a sagging sperm trap hanging on the ragged thorn bush. "Unused."

We had never seen one before in this unused state. Danny quickly had it out, and he unrolled it over his thumb. It was weird in its flabbiness, with the little thimble shape on the end. Rebecca and I were fascinated but wary, given what we could almost imagine it was used for.

"Casper," I mumbled, almost to myself.

"Huh?" Danny and Rebecca looked at me.

"Casper," I said again. "Casper the Friendly Ghost. Kinda looks like him."

We all looked at the rubber again, sitting there on Danny's up-turned thumb.

"I can see that," he said.

Rebecca nodded, too. I felt better about my observation, until Danny suddenly moved it toward me and blurted, "Boo!"

I recoiled just a bit, tried a smile, trying to remain unphased, especially because Rebecca laughed. Danny added, "Casper the Friendly Condom...ha!"

The joke sat for second until Danny directed us: "Touch it," he said. "It won't bite—or," he said leering slightly at me, "spoo-ooook you."

Rebecca and I had only prodded and lifted them with sticks before, holding them at arm's length like they might infect us, so this was a testing moment. We reached out. It had a damp, cold, flaccid feel, kind of like kelp or jello.

"Here," Danny said, looking at me only. "Stick out your, uh—." He stopped, looked around, and got closer. "Stick out your..." He looked at me. "Your finger."

Danny gently slipped it over my index finger. It felt moist, though it was not wet.

Then Danny, almost as suddenly as he had booed me, pulled it off and flung it toward the Rubber Tree, marking, it seemed, the end of this lesson. We began to walk away toward The Trail, but without the satisfaction of some conclusion. Instead, Danny somehow darkened.

We walked on in silence, until Rebecca spoke out to Danny: "Where'd you get it, anyway?"

We walked for a few more seconds through the high grass.

Danny finally answered, sped up, leaving us behind. "On dad's boat."

§

How do you make time go by in a world where the only light that shines comes from uncertain moments with the one you love? What do you do if the single word your body speaks out is a question—"When?"

These were the vague thoughts that passed through Emily Cooday over the few seasons since she had met Joseph Caine.

What Emily did do was to try to improve herself by reading, and also by writing to Joseph. She started out with skills not much better than an elementary school student. But she worked at it, tracing letters carefully, curving and joining them as best she could. She read stories, some over and over again—paperback novels and the occasional classic that came her way. She heavily fell into these fictional places, plots, persons, and sentiments. They were at once real and impossible, and she could never tell which. She was at once the little mermaid, Cinderella, Snow White, Anne of Green Gables; or, more difficult for her to understand, Hester, with her scarlet letter, and a troubling line that stayed with her: "She could no longer borrow from the future to ease her present grief." *These stories were worlds far beyond her own, yet they had become part of her, perhaps, in some cases, as possible endings. Maybe she could become a princess; after all, she had her prince.*

Most of all, Emily wanted Joseph to see that she was not just some chug woman, some squaw without a thought in her head. She could move into another world, if only he would take her, try her. She sent away for special lavender stationary with matching envelopes, and she spent much time trying to find the right words, the right expressions, to correspond to what she felt in her body, to what she felt for Joseph. She also ordered a fancy fountain pen and some ink, though at first it horrified her that her permanent writing mistakes might flaw the refinement and feeling and correctness she sorely sought. The pen, she hoped, held some magic hope.

Emily pondered and repeated each word before her pen touched the paper. An old, battered red paperback dictionary was her only help. She felt she had no grand experience of her own to give her words shape and depth; she had no sense of any tradition that permitted her to say what went through her, though she was haunted by some of those stories she had read. What did Joseph need to hear? What did he want to hear? Her words. Words only for him. She often pictured herself for him, sitting on the hillside beyond her grandparents' home, writing to him, waiting for him, sometimes surrounded by the small wild flowers that climbed the hill.

And so she spent many evenings trying to find—desperately trying to find—a language that might win Joseph's heart and attention. And to make time speed forward. When—when will he come again? When will he take me away?

Just before Joseph would leave her and return to the waters, to his other world, she would slip him letters she had been writing while he was away, each letter with a separate envelope. Though awkwardly, she tried to offer every bit of herself in those letters. She wanted to somehow sound better than she was. She feared, too, that she might push him away by being too forward.

Joseph read her letters in those still moments out on the rolling waters, and though he wanted to dismiss them as the misty outpourings a young, inexperienced woman who was in love with being in love, he did come to feel her words in ways that both excited and frightened and touched him. And at moments sadden him. My Emily, he would think. My Emily...

How was Joseph Caine supposed be with this woman—this young, strangely beautiful woman with floating thoughts, who made it as clear as a cold Pacific night that she wanted him more than anything that the rest of the world could give her?

FIRE, EARTH, WATER, AIR

Dad said it was late for tent caterpillar nests to appear, but suddenly there seemed to be more than usual. Maybe it was the wet spring followed abruptly by such hot, dry weather.

The nests appeared as grayish-white webs at the end of branches, like small clumps of dirty cotton candy. After a few weeks, hundreds of black and brown fuzzy tent caterpillars covered each nest. A few weeks later, if undisturbed, the tiny creepy-crawly things would become an inch or two long. Their hunger could quickly reduce large parts of trees to shabby, barren wrecks. Dad had some work to do. He took good care of the yard immediately around our house, though he was not like cranky Mr. Bryer up the road, whose place and property looked like it was out of some magazine.

We had about ten fruit trees—mostly apple and cherry, and a couple of pear trees that never did very well. There were a few more very old apple trees halfway up The Trail in a small clearing among in the bush and trees, known as the Old Orchard, but Dad didn't tend these. They were apparently planted by my grandfather, who had ideas to turn our acreage into an orchard. World War I stopped his plans by confining him to a bed for most of the rest of his life—"mustard gas did it," so my Dad told me at one point when I was older.

The caterpillars seemed most abundant on the apple trees—sometimes six or seven nests in a tree. You could get rid of them a couple of ways: smoke the trees and basically try to choke them into falling off; spray the trees with nasty chemicals; or cut out the nests as they appeared. Dad preferred cutting out the nests and the branches they were attached to with his pruning pole, and that's what he was doing with me on this early evening when Danny joined us. He had probably just finished supper.

"Where's Rebecca?" I asked.

"At home." Danny answered. "With her Daddy-Daddy-o."

My job was to take the cut-out nests as they fell to the ground and to throw them on a small fire that Dad had started. I was constantly cautioned not to get too close to the fire. It was sort of fun—but, more than anything else, fascinating. The nests were almost immediately eaten by the flames. The caterpillars waved one of their ends frantically before they crisped and blackened. Some immediately fell off into the hot ashes below. Some hung on and burned away to nothing.

The crackling fire grew as the burning nests and branches piled up faster than the flames could level them.

Danny knew right away what we were doing. He politely asked if he could help. Dad said it was okay.

"Your dad back from fishing yet?" Dad asked Danny.

"A day or two ago."

"Good fishing?"

"Yeah, I think so."

I suddenly remembered the message Mr. Caine had wanted me to pass on to my Dad, that he had a couple of salmon for him. Danny saved me from my forgetfulness: "My Dad has some fish for you. He wanted me to tell you."

"Great," said Dad. Danny gave me a quick look.

"And your dad?" asked Dad. "Don't see him as much as we used to. Away with the fishing season, and up the coast a lot now, huh. How's he doing, anyway? Guess he's busy, keeping up his boat and all."

Danny didn't answer right away. "Yes, busy."

Danny gathered a couple of fallen branches loaded with caterpillars and gave me one. Dad got back to work, angling to prune out more infested branches.

Danny, meanwhile, suggested that we not throw the branches straight into the fire, but instead hold the branch a couple of feet above the flame. He said the smoke would get them. He held one of the branches like he was conducting an orchestra, and he murmured a few lines from a song we all knew, though he said them rather than sing them: "On top of Old Smokey, all covered with—" Danny stopped and looked at me to complete the line.

I finally came up with "flames," though I said it more like a question than an answer.

Danny thought for a second: "Yeah. 'Flames' is good."

He delivered the new line: "On top of Old Smokey, all covered with flames, I lost my true—" Again, Danny looked to me for completion.

"Caterpillar?"

"I lost my poor caterpillar...it burned—what a shame."

I smiled, and together we approved of our new version.

Danny held his branch steady. The caterpillars soon began to drop off into the fire. "Souls falling into the flaming jaws of hell," he noted. The caterpillars on my branch began falling off as well, although it was harder for me to hold the branch as high and as steadily as Danny.

After the caterpillars all dropped away, we tossed our branches into the fire and went to get more before returning to the flames.

"Now, lower it a bit." We put our branches just below the smoke level, but just above the tip of the flames. "The heat gets them— fast—not the smoke. They broil and boil before they have a chance to choke in the smoke."

The caterpillars shriveled to the size of uncooked macaroni. Their orange and black furry coverings disappeared immediately. In hardly any time, the branches were in flames, and we dropped them into the fire.

We watched the nests burn away into ashes, and Danny asked me, "So, which way would you like to go: smoked slowly or burned quickly? I mean, if you were going to have to die by fire?"

"The quick way, I guess."

"You're a quick sizzler, hmm?"

"Guess so." The choices didn't seem all that great.

Danny thought for a while, and he poked the edges of the fire with his shoe. "I'd like to be put right into the fire, have a chance to feel what it was like to be taken up by the flames, to see myself burst into flames. Explode with heat."

I didn't fancy this myself, but I appreciated his want of experience. Danny somehow knew what I was thinking. We picked up a few more nests: "In death, you learn something." He thought for a second more: "Especially in death." Then he added, as if he were reading from somewhere: "Just as the weeds are gathered and burned with fire, so will it be at the end of days."

Dad continued to prune away. He must have had one ear on us all along, picking up on bits and pieces of our conversation. His unmoving face suggested he wasn't altogether pleased or comfortable with Danny's words about death by fire, or "the end of days," whatever that meant—summer days?

Dad in his way didn't care for Danny that much, though he wouldn't say so in so many words. Like Mom, he would have preferred I play with kids more my age. It wasn't just that Danny was older. Some adults thought he was "smart beyond his years." I'd even heard it whispered that he was "gifted," which, for me, back then, meant that Danny *gave* plenty—that was true. What was clear is that what was said about him was not full of neutral acceptance, let alone praise. Of course adults tried to keep this kind of talk from us. It was not, as they would say, "for our ears." But children hear, even when adults think that they aren't listening. Kids are always around the corner or up the stairs or near the window or just on the other side of the door, listening, taking it in. I didn't know exactly why adults were so wary of Danny. He led, he amazed, he entertained, he taught—and even if he sometimes confused us, it was a celebrated confusion of wonder. No dull moments. What else could we ask for?

Danny asked me, "Want to do something else now, I mean, with the caterpillars? See if your Dad will give us a part of a nest that he's cut out."

"Sure."

We walked over to Dad. "Can I go and play with Danny now? You're almost done, sort of, right?" I forgot to add something, but remembered quickly. "Please?"

Dad said it was okay. I asked, "Oh, and—can we take a bit of a nest, of caterpillars, with us?"

Dad didn't like this idea much, but I promised we wouldn't take them in the house or leave them around the fruit trees. He gave us two bits of nests wrapped around small branches.

We were just about to set off and go up The Trail when Rebecca joined us.

She filled us in: "Dad's going down to the boat now."

Danny countered with a mumble: "So?"

Between fishing trips, Mr. Caine went down to his boat every night after dinner, about seven o'clock, and sometimes during the day as well. There seemed to be much work to prepare for his fishing trips up the coast, and he had to be ready when they opened the fisheries. It was easy to tell how important the boat was for him.

I was happy to give Rebecca the details: "We were burning up caterpillars. Smoking them up over the fire and cooking them up." Rebecca nodded with both interest and knowledge. Not much grossed out Rebecca.

Danny provided some background about the caterpillars as we three made our way up The Trail. That caterpillars didn't have too many enemies, and that, like Monarch butterflies, they don't taste very good for the birds. "Their real enemies are wasps, which feed them to their own young. Some wasps lay their eggs inside living caterpillars. When the eggs hatch, the little wasp larvae start eating away at the caterpillar guts—from the inside out."

I thought that being born inside your food was weird, but a good idea, and I said so as fast as I could while we were walking. "You mean, it would be like being born inside a big box of—of a big box of corn flakes."

This was meant as enthusiastic confirmation, but Danny, whose rhythm was interrupted, took it more as a question. "No," he said, barely scowling at me. "It would be more like being born inside a cow. A live one."

I thought of the dismembered baseball glove.

Danny continued: "You can't say that tent caterpillars and wasps are enemies." Wasps, he noted, needed the caterpillars to eat and to hatch their young, and that caterpillars needed the wasps to kill off some of them so that there will be enough food for the remaining caterpillars. "Too many caterpillars and they eat themselves out of the picture. Nature's Balanced Eating Plan: eat and get eaten, but don't eat too much, and don't get eaten too much. You are either looking for food, or you are food being looked for. Likely you're both. If we were in the jungle now—for lions or tigers, we're in the meat section of the supermarket."

Rebecca and I glanced around just a little nervously into the thick bushes and trees surrounding The Trail. Danny, smiling a little, added, "You're just a couple of pork chops with legs and hair on top."

We weren't sure if this was a good thing.

Danny got more serious: "What makes this weird are people, because when they see wasp nests, people get rid of them. Then wonder why they have so many caterpillars. People take the salmon, and nothing takes the people, except a war once in a while, or a plague. So you'll end up with no salmon and lots of hungry people killing each other. That's the way the world ends. Amen."

Rebecca took this seriously. "But our dad doesn't take too many salmon. There'll always be fish for him."

Danny wouldn't have it. "No," he flatly said. "There won't. And we're kind of burning up the earth, too, with all the stuff we use. Oil. Coal. Gas. Not a good idea. We're just dumbots."

Dumbots? What was that? Sounded cool and somehow right.

Rebecca, meanwhile, tossed an unseen glance to Danny, but rather than thinking of the apocalypse or some weird roboty things, I was thinking of my own Dad. When there were wasp nests around our house, he got rid of them. But I couldn't really imagine him trying to mess up Nature's Balanced Eating Plan. I thought of my Dad in the war, too—in the big World War, the second one. He said he was in a tank some of the time, but most of the time he was a foot soldier. He didn't say too much about it. Did he help keep the number of people down so that the number of caterpillars, wasps, salmon, and people would be balanced? This was getting a bit deep. Thankfully, pressing business moved us up into The Trail. I asked what we would do with the caterpillars.

"A couple of things. One of them is both the same and the opposite of burning them." We walked on.

"First stop we make—a wasps' nest."

Danny always knew where such things were. He did a lot of solitary reconnaissance work. We stopped at a small clearing a little off to the left of The Trail, about midway up, not far from the Old Orchard.

Danny warned us. "Careful. A ground wasps' nest. Just over there. See it?"

We stopped. Danny pointed to a patch on the ground about ten feet in front of us. We didn't see anything at first, but after a while we could trace a steady movement of wasps coming and going and circling from a small hole in the ground. We knew these were nasty wasps. Very nasty. With their upper body connected to their lower body by an impossibly narrow stalk, and their harsh yellow and black markings, they had an exaggerated, jagged, dangerous look. We'd had heard about people digging in the ground and discovering these nests by accident. The wasps rampaged, attacked. We heard of smaller animals being stung to death. So when Danny warned us to be careful, Rebecca and I held our breath.

I had to ask Danny one question, which I whispered without taking my eye off the parade of wasps: "Do they sting or bite you?"

Danny nodded. "Both."

"Geez."

We edged up. You could see that some of the returning wasps carried bits of things. Danny told us that many of the wasps were returning with small, newly hatched caterpillars and bugs to feed to their own young.

"They stun the caterpillars with a sting before carrying them off to their underground homes. The young wasps are puffy—white, like plucked marshmallowy chickens. Waiting for their meal, below, down in the earth. They've never seen the sun. They eat the caterpillars up, bit by bit—bite by bite—while the caterpillars are still alive." We weren't at all surprised. "The caterpillars are food made by sunshine, since they fed on the leaves, which are grown by the sun." Made perfect sense.

Danny said he was going toss a part of the caterpillar nest on top of the wasp nest opening. The wasps, he predicted, will sense danger and attack, and they will immediately try to find the intruders.

"Here's the good part." Danny paused, which brought us into his words. "The wasps might believe that the caterpillar nest—and the caterpillars—are a threat—an enemy—and they will go after the nest. But what will happen when they find out that the danger is also a meal that their young ones can munch on?"

Danny's point wasn't clear—but no doubt it would be. He stepped a few feet closer to the nest. We followed closely, carefully, behind.

"I'll throw the nest on to the wasp nest. Don't move. If you do, the wasps might think that we're the attackers. The message will be passed to the whole nest. They'll look around like crazy, so if you move and you are close by, they'll think that you are the enemy and go right after you like fire coming from a hose."

We didn't move. The thought about being food for baby wasps was not comforting.

When Danny was about five or six feet away from the wasp nest, he threw part of one of the caterpillar nests on top of the opening. We backed up a little and froze. The wasps went on immediate buzzing-about alert and increased their number and their intensity. They quickly set upon the caterpillar nest.

Danny whispered back to us: "We want to see if the wasps kill the caterpillars. Will they figure out that the caterpillar nest is not an enemy, but really just a home delivery of one their favorite foods?"

Danny got closer. Rebecca and I stayed put. We would trust Danny's eyes. We stayed like this for a very long minute or two, but it seemed that the wasps had tuned into our presence. A couple buzzed by close to us. Maybe it was our smell. Danny once told us that most creatures can smell fear. He carefully backed up, and so did we. Luckily, the wasps did not follow.

When we got back to The Trail, we continued on. We still had one caterpillar nest left. We waited for Danny to tell us what happened.

Danny told us matter-of-factly that the wasps attacked the caterpillars right away, and that they didn't care whether the caterpillars were food or not. What they cared about first was protecting themselves, their nest. "Kill, then think," Danny said. And then Danny himself thought some more: "Ask questions later. Protect your home from harm-doers at all costs. The wasps are one family. When the queen, the mother of every single one of them, is in danger, they are all in danger. Her children give their lives to protect her. That," he added with a certainty that sounded personal, "is what they must do."

This might have made us feel reassured, that this was Nature's way, but translating this into anything larger was beyond my years, though perhaps not Danny's. Danny had a way of having Nature speak for him when he spoke of it.

Our next stop was further up The Trail. A watery place close to our neighbor's property. There was a small permanent spring nearby, and water collected in a tiny small pond before it seeped away back into the earth. A foot or two deep. As Danny had noted more than once before, the dimensions of the pond were about the same as a coffin. In fact, Danny called it Dead Man's Pond. Rebecca didn't like the name very much, mainly because of the little bunches of wild strawberries that grew nearby. She preferred to call the place Strawberry Fields.

Danny alluded to the name he had given the place: "Now we'll find out it if it also Dead Caterpillars Pond."

He took the branch with the nest on it that I had been carrying, and we knelt beside him at the edge of the little pond. "Let's see what the caterpillars do when they are put under water."

Danny slowly submerged the nest. A few bubbles rose: "Air trapped inside the nest," Danny informed us. With six-year-old male sophistication, I thought of farts in a bathtub. I kept the thought to myself.

When the nest was fully under water, Danny told us that the caterpillars have a choice. Let go of their nest, and then float up to the surface and take their chances. Or hang on to the nest that has always been their home—die a watery death. "Certain death in your home or likely death but no home?" Danny placed a couple of larger stones on the branch in order to hold it down so that he could take his hand out of the pond.

We tried to see what the caterpillars were doing. They wiggled back and forth, but it might have been the slight play of light and shadows through the water. After a few minutes, a couple of caterpillars surfaced. Danny scooped them out with his hand and looked at them carefully. Perhaps they had run out of air and let go to avoid drowning. Danny noted otherwise: "Dead—or almost dead." He tossed them over his shoulder into the bush. "Flying compost," he said with a bit of a smile.

A few minutes later, Danny pulled out the nest. We inspected it. All appeared to be drowned. Danny tossed the nest back in Dead Man's Pond, and we started back down The Trail toward civilization.

Danny provided more commentary: caterpillars who stayed with their nest, their home, faced certain death, but letting go of their home was almost impossible. He added that, for the wasps, concern for the safety of their home is the most important thing for them, too. "True for all living things. Home must be safe—kept safe. If it's not, then there's trouble that can become—not natural at all. Terrible things can happen. Will happen."

Danny continued with his more serious tone. "Creatures, all creatures, all do what they need to do." Danny stopped to deliver his final line on the subject: "To protect their homes—their nests, their hives—their queen mothers."

Danny must have been right, mainly because he sounded right—sounded determined to be right. If such big pictures were somehow tied to his own picture was not clear, though, again, it often somehow seemed so.

We three walked in silence down The Trail. Rebecca pulled out a couple of sword ferns and waved them around as we walked. I swiped at some of the bushes with a pretty good stick I found. Danny kept a few feet in front.

As we approached the back of my backyard at the base of The Trail, I thought about what Danny said about protecting home. I imagined hitting intruders with my stick if anyone attacked where I lived. Or if I had a bazooka, then I could really do the job. Then I wondered out loud if *The Rifleman* was on TV tonight. Everyone loved the way he shot his gun, except my Mom, who said more than once that there was too much violence on TV. Danny said that the Rifleman—the cowboy named Lucas—could fire off rounds of his special Winchester rifle "almost like a machine gun." Wow, I thought. Like a machine gun. Yea.

§

For Emily Cooday, Joseph Caine was that prince who arrived from the sea, not just with his gifts and his rum and his passions, but with the shapeless hope of passage elsewhere, to somehow rescue her. To live happily ever after, she dreamed.

Secretly, Emily prayed for storms after he arrived. Joseph would then be unable to leave the safety of the harbor, and they could spend more time with each other before he returned to the fishing grounds or to the other home he had, a home she could not imagine. When these storms peeled off the Gulf of Alaska, the howling winds and rains allowed him to retreat further into and longer with her. She was his warm, safe port that could close around him. The salt spray from the ocean mixed with the sweat of their passions. They clung tightly those nights that, with the shaking and rolling of the boat, would otherwise have been uneasy, but uneasiness only came with the calm. That meant he would be leaving.

Emily would remain behind in her desolate, defeated community, trapped by poverty and the legacy of a pitiless reservation system that did little to nurture hope or dignity, let alone satisfy something she knew must exist beyond her small world. Once, when Emily managed to say something about how cut-off she felt, and when she hinted at her loneliness, he could only say that the sky and land and ocean around her were large, not small. She groped to think that he did not understand that her world was only big when he was with her, that the landscape had come to mean nothing when he was gone, but she could not find the right words to tell him, words that could hold him.

What she could not say to his face or explain to him, she tried to express in her letters. Most made their crumpled way into the wastebasket beside her small bed, and then into the woodstove.

Beyond a voice that spoke to her passion for Joseph, and expressions of how she would wait forever for him, the elements she could almost master were vague, enclosed descriptions of her eventless, empty time. What could anything mean without him? Without the possibility of him? She also sometimes placed pressed wild flowers into the letters. She believed— she hoped—these flowers gathered from the hillside behind the house of her grandparents might carry something of what she felt, something of where she was, something of why she wanted him to come back. She often prayed to baby Jesus that, one day, Joseph Caine would take her away on his boat, to some kind of life beyond her tiny, broken-down village. She often found herself looking down the inlet for his boat. It was the most she had. It was the only looking-forward she possessed, and she had fears that it might become narrow.

She waited, and words she recalled from the Bible often fought from within her. 'I shall not want. He makes me lie down in green pastures. He leads me beside still waters.'

WE WATCHED, AMAZED

Rebecca and I were around the front of my house, sitting in the shade and eating penny candies—jujubes—out of two little brown bags. For Rebecca, they were gummies. Little matter. We savored and considered each candy before it disappeared into our mouths. I preferred the black and red; Rebecca was partial to the green and yellow ones; we both liked orange. And so we negotiated:

Me: "I'll give you one yellow for one black." Done deal.

Rebecca: "One red for one yellow." Done deal.

Me: "I'll give you one orange and one green for two blacks."

Rebecca needed to weigh this up. I didn't want to appear too anxious. But shortly it too was a deal. Rebecca, who was a tough negotiator when it came to the candy trade, knew my weaknesses.

Rebecca: "One red and one black for two yellows and a green." She had me. I barely hesitated.

While we carried on, Danny wandered over and watched us barter and chew. Our haggling interested him. He gave us ideas about the pleasure in trading sweet treasures, that there is balance in giving and taking so that they become the same thing. "Loss and gain must be equal," he said, "if you want things to carry on, live on."

It felt good to be part of something that confirmed balance in the world. Danny was right: the best exchanges took place when Rebecca and I both felt we were getting a good deal. If Rebecca made an exchange she thought was great, but it didn't seem so good for me, others deals seemed to lose their goodwill. Danny showed us how this worked by focusing on me:

"Say Rebecca got two greens and one orange from you in

trading for one black. You might feel cheated. She might feel okay, but not you." Danny was right. I wouldn't. He asked me what I would do.

I thought. "Maybe want to trade back, I guess?"

"What if Rebecca didn't want to?"

"Then I might not want to trade anymore."

"Right," Danny said. "Balance gone. Things stop. Two losses." I nodded. Danny added: "The death of a deal—for *both* sides."

Our faces asked Danny a question: For both sides? He explained that even the person or thing that gets a great deal to begin with will lose out later. "Because if you got a bad deal from 'Becca, you said you might not want to trade any more. That's her loss, too. Too much of a good thing becomes a bad thing. Too much good on one side can make one side bad." He went on to tell us that people can't always take what they want just because they want it. Someone, or something, might want to stop them.

We young ones chewed on this conflict theory while chewing on our colored sweets, but now we both figured to save some for later. We didn't want to eat ourselves out of possible future good deals. We didn't want to make *one side bad.*

I asked Danny if he wanted a candy. I held out a black jube-jube. At first Danny declined. But then, on second thought, he accepted. He didn't pop it in his mouth, but instead began looking around on the ground. We could tell he was going to show us something. We followed him around as he searched beside our sidewalk. When he found what he wanted, he sat down. We sat beside him, clutching our little bags.

"Take this candy. It has something all creatures, including people, need: energy. In sugar. Made out of three basic things all around and in you, what you are made of. Carbon, hydrogen, oxygen."

These were big words, but they all sounded familiar. We even knew a little bit about them, especially about oxygen, which was in the air we all needed. What we had also heard is that hydrogen was in big bombs. We had seen films of the huge mushroom explosions, and there was even a guy in Eastfield who had a bomb shelter that could protect him just in case someone dropped a bomb on him. At school we were told that if a bomb warning came, we were to go under our desks, close our eyes, and cover our ears. It was clearly going to be really bright and really loud.

Danny continued. He held the candy in front of us: "Sugar is all over the place, you know, but usually not in a super-concentrated clump like this."

Rebecca and I looked at the candy as if it was something we had never seen before. *Carbon, oxygen, hydrogen, energy.* I blurted out, "A little sugar bomb."

Danny and Rebecca stopped and looked at me, and then Rebecca looked at Danny to see if I would be rewarded, ignored, or chastised for my observation.

Danny at last managed a nod. "A bomb...right...a bomb." This seemed to stop him, as if it was a seed for a plan.

He continued: "Okay. You like candies, right? Well, guess what: so do little black ants."

Danny licked the candy and then placed it on the ground in a particular place. He had found a trail of little black ants doing their daily foraging. He placed the candy in their path.

Rebecca and I bent forward to watch. In very little time, one curious ant managed to partially crawl up on to the candy.

"Watch what happens when you get more than you need, or know. A good thing becomes a bad thing, when you—when you bite off more than you can chew."

Danny smiled, maybe to congratulate himself for his own wit. He told us you have to be careful if you want something badly, but you don't know what it means, really means, to have it. You could lose by favoring some short gain.

We watched. The ant meanwhile had become stuck on the licked candy.

He repeated: "With much to gain, there must be much to lose. The ant will die right there on the candy, gripped by the sticky sugar—energy—that it wants so badly. That all things need."

We looked carefully at the ant. Once in a while it managed to lift one of its legs, but it wasn't going anywhere. Its antennae continued to twitch, as if trying to know or say something

"A couple of ants dying on this black lump of energy won't really make too much difference in the history of the world, or to the ant nest that's probably underneath the sidewalk. But a little bad thing has happened, changed by something being where it shouldn't be. Gone. Balance gone."

Danny looked at me and raised an eyebrow, thinking, as if I was somehow responsible. "Changed by a—by a little bomb," he said, now sounding serious. "The wrong place at the wrong time. Highest price paid. Boom!"

Danny paused to look more closely. We bent even more forward along with him. "Don't mess with balance," he added. "Or something—or someone—will get you."

We didn't need convincing—the evidence was right there. But Danny had a provision that had to do with proportion and the scope of change. "Don't mess around too much unless you plan to make a big change, a quick shift. The kind where things—where things can't go back to how they were."

We watched a few more ants climb on and also get stuck. A couple of others, gathered around the candy's edges like little black cows at a water trough, were now barely touching it with their feelers. Maybe they were learning. We watched, but not much more seem to be happening, and so for the moment we left the candied ants and Nature to their own devices.

What next?

Danny: "Slugs. We need slugs."

Slugs were not our favorite things. My Dad didn't like them because they managed to munch on his lettuce and some of the other veggies in his garden. Besides, they were slimy, slow, and not exciting. They didn't wiggle like snakes, squirm like worms, or fight like wasps.

"Slugs like darkness," said Danny as we began to look around. "They're creatures of the night, like vampires. While you're sleepy-byes in dreamland, they're chewing away, leaving sparkling, silvery, ghostly gooey lines all over the place. When the sun comes up, they disappear. If you want to find them, you have to find their dark, wet sleeping places, just like you would have to find Count Dracula's sleeping place underground, in a coffin or tomb."

Slugs and vampires. Who would have thought? Well, Danny.

We managed to find a couple good-sized slugs underneath some rotting boards close to where my Dad had recently done some watering. When the board was turned over and brought out of the shadow, the few slugs there slowly moved away, shunning the light.

Danny took two things out of his pocket: a double-edged razor blade wrapped in thin carboard and a sachet of salt, like the kind you get at take-out restaurants.

"Okay. Which, do you think, is most dangerous, I mean, if you were a slug? The razor blade or the salt?"

Rebecca answered. "The razor. Razors are the sharpest things in the world. They use razor blades in brain surgery."

Danny nodded and looked at me. Even though I knew that easy answers to Danny's questions were not usually the right answers, I also had to believe it was the razor blade, and I said so: "Yeah. They're super sharp." This sounded too simple, so I offered a little more: "A razor blade can probably cut through jello without the jello even moving."

Danny nodded to me as well, and replied, "Good, good. Well, we'd better see, then, shouldn't we. Slice some slug jello, or jello slug. And," he added, "Some surprising slug blood."

I hadn't meant that my answer should become a suggestion for action, but it somehow seemed to be. Or, more likely, it happened to align with Danny's planned demonstration.

Danny picked the razor blade, unwrapped it, and we expected that he would simply slice the slug in half. The only issue would be if he planned to separate the head from the body, or one side of the body from the other. Two slugs out of one. Yes, it would be like slicing jello, which made me feel both better and worse. But instead, Danny stuck the razor in the ground, so that while one of its two edges was lodged in the soil, the other was exposed and upright. He made certain it stood firm.

"Razors are so sharp that when they cut you, you don't feel it at first."

Danny picked up the larger of the two slugs, held it up to us for a moment, and then draped it, not even that delicately, over the razor. He took his hand away, and we watched, expecting a gooey, cruel cut. But the slug slowly, slowly dragged the front of its body over the blade, and the rest of it followed over the razor's edge until it had climbed over.

"Not even a scratch," Danny stated, flipping the slug over to inspect its wet, jello belly.

No! Not a mark! No cut! No slug blood, whatever that might be like. The slug slowly turned itself over like a fat corkscrew and began to ooze along the ground toward the cool shade of the grass. We watched it leisurely ripple away, with something like admiration.

"The slug had no fear of the razor blade. It is—its body is—a dull balance to a razor's sharp blade."

Yes, the blue blade and the dull, gray slug seemed, somehow, to work with but not against each other, with, as Danny pointed out, their measured, balanced differences in hardness and softness and sharpness and roundness and dryness and wetness.

"Giving, taking. Give and take. The slug gives in to the razor's sharpness, instead of fighting against it. Fight against the blade and it fights you. Think of those guys who sleep on beds made of nails. They don't try to go against them. If you go against the sharpness of the nails, you end up being a bleeding pin cushion."

He added more, bringing back the slug blood he'd mentioned: "And if the blade would have cut or killed the slug, spilling blood, what'd you suppose it would be like?"

"Red gooey," I answered, a little happily but much more hopefully. "Really gooey, like red syrup."

Having heard my answer, Rebecca was thinking. "Well, I bet—I bet it doesn't even have blood. Just slime."

Danny looked at both of us. "Good answers, but both wrong, I'm afraid."

What might it be then?

Danny put us straight without much waiting. "Slug blood is green."

Well, who would have thought?

He added: "And their whole body is a nose. And they solved a big problem: there are no male or female slugs. They are all both male and female. Too bad for us, eh?"

We could only nod with a bit of wonder, but without much a picture in our minds. What if your mom was your mom and dad, and your dad your dad and mom? How would that...?

Danny seemed not to have time to give us any explanation, and so he turned his attention to the little package of salt. He ripped it open, poured a little into the palm of his hand, and put the package down.

"Just a little salt. What harm can it do? It's everywhere. On your skin. In your tears. In the ocean. More importantly, on potato chips and popcorn. Basic—like oxygen, hydrogen, and carbon—and sugar. What is it, what could salt do—compared to a slicing and dicing razor blade?"

Very little, we thought. But we knew something was up.

Danny added a little phrase, that somehow seemed familiar. "The salt of the earth." And then something less familiar: "Some use salt to get rid of evil spirts. It makes things pure. And once upon a time a person was turned into salt—like a statue of salt, a pillar—for looking back on something bad."

Danny looked at the salt in his palm, looked at us, looked to the slug, and then took a pinch of it and sprinkled it onto our remaining slug. It settled like a little flurry of hail. A few grains seemed to dissolve on the slug's sticky back. The slug stopped and began to shudder and curl around itself. We had never seen a slug do this. We had never seen a slug move so quickly. It was amazing and weird and freaky.

"The salt will kill the slug—even this bit of salt. It will take a little while, but the salt will kind of burn the slug in reverse. And melt it—like the witch in *The Wizard of Oz* when she got the bucket of water thrown on her."

This image sunk in: the evil slug witch, melting, melting...

Danny brought us back from our daydream: "What seems harmless can be most dangerous. Everything in Nature can kill or give life. The salt sucks the water right out of the slug—the very opposite of drowning."

We watched, amazed.

The slug rose up a little and swayed back upon itself like a giant sea beast with an unwanted rider. It turned over and writhed. And after a few minutes, it slipped on to its side and stopped moving as it shuddered to a slow-motion, slimy death. It seemed to ooze some mucus stuff as it died.

Danny filled us in: "So what we got? Sugar for the ants. Salt for the slug. Harmless, little white crystals. Natural stuff. Stuff you need the day you're born. Stuff in your cupboard. But both killers when used in a certain way. Natural born killers."

Whether Danny's logic or natural philosophy was impeccable

didn't matter. Danny words were for taking in, and not for questioning. Sugar and salt. The stuff of life—and death.

On that day, a slug in the grass lay motionless in the slick of its own slime, and a couple of little black ants along a sidewalk got a life sentence—both the result of what they could not resist.

Danny wiped his brow. "See," he said, showing us his sweat. "Because I used up energy—sugar—I ended up with sweat. Salt water. I could have sweat all over the slug to kill it. That would be something." Yes, we thought. It would. Danny added, "I could have cried tears of sadness or joy on it, and it would have died."

Having let the silence of sweat, blood, and tears sit long enough, Danny at once got up. A few bees buzzed by at the speed of light. He said he was going to take a shower: "A shower a day keeps the bad things at bay." He also mentioned that he might get some stuff for his chemistry set. He looked at me: "And thank you for the sugar bomb idea." He added, "You'll see."

But just before Danny went on his way, he told us that beyond the little things we had just seen, and could see, there was more. There was, he said, "Super Tiny Nature. Stuff that's really, really small," he said. "Germs. Bacteria. Worse yet, viruses. They come around for a visit after changing themselves from the last visit. You don't see them coming. No way to stop them at first."

This made us want to look around a little nervously—but at what?

Danny kept going. "These can do more bad stuff than the big things that you see. A grizzly bear comes—you run away, climb a tree, bark like a dog. But a virus comes—there's nowhere to run. It moves, fast, looking for a place to live so that it can grow and grow and take and take, then change and take more."

Again, this didn't sound good. We could tell Danny needed to go, but I had to ask: "Where do they live? The tiny stuff."

Danny answered, "In you. Or at least they want to."

"What do they want?" Rebecca asked.

"You."

This sounded even worse. Danny let the idea settle, though of course we had no idea at all. Danny did add some hope, though it sounded weird: "If you want protection from a virus, sometimes you can take a bit of it into body, and it will make your body better. It will make," he said slowly, "anti-bodies. In you. Other super tiny stuff."

Aunty Bodies, I thought. This was weird.

"Or you could live in a bubble. Never touch anything or anyone. Never go anywhere."

Becoming bubble people did not seem like a great option.

But we could tell Danny had something else before ending our session.

"There's one more. One more Nature," he added. He said this like some kind of warning, but also like a riddle. "And this Nature is worse—the worst of all. And you can't see it in a clear way. It hides but is always seen. It can even destroy itself in seeing itself."

Danny's questions were often bait. We were the fish. This time Rebeca had to ask.

"What, then? What Nature is that?"

Danny looked at his hands, then swiped them together, like he was brushing something off. He took a slow breath. He wanted to go, but we also knew he held the moment for us. We waited. The question hung: *What Nature is that, the worst of all?*

"Human Nature," he announced. "Us. You. Me. All confused. All dangerous. All the time."

Danny turned and left.

Rebecca and I, now somehow surrounded by kinds of Nature we could neither really see nor understand, didn't feel like eating or trading our way through any more candy business.

We decided to finish off the afternoon in the coolness of my basement. We would build a fort out of boxes and blankets, and we would, at least for a few hours, ward off whatever might attempt to enter or even take our world. We hope we would survive our own natures. Until tomorrow, at least.

The years bring back this seemingly small moment with force, confusion, and, oddly, nostalgia. Somewhere down deep and way back into that summer, beyond the mysteries and understandings that were rendered, was the mystery and understanding of Daniel Caine himself that he had now named—his human nature. Given where things would go, his words remain, as a poet might say, too deep for tears: *It hides but is always seen. It can even destroy itself.*

§

Joseph Caine's family life fell into a vague pattern of regularity determined by the openings in the fishing season. Home and away, away and home.

When Joseph was at home, he often thought about how he met Emily, about how he and Emily fell so easily together one late, windy afternoon after he chugged into her village for diesel fuel and few supplies. His forwardness even surprised him. What was he thinking? She was down at the wharf to check her grandfather's crab traps, which was one of the few things that gave her pleasure. She took an old, scarred rowboat a hundred or so yards off into the bay to check the traps. She told Joseph, who asked her, that her grandfather said she had the spirit-gift of beckoning creatures, and the old man teased her with the name Híntu Nakws'aatí—"Witch of the Sea." Seldom did she come home empty-handed. The old man would touch her head, as if to make sure that her magic would continue.

Joseph did not know much more about Emily's life. He did not know that Emily's father had deserted the village and her mother for somewhere up north when Emily was almost too young to remember. That she was brought up in the makeshift household of her grandparents. Emily's mother suffered long bouts with the bottle and with her own pained darkness. Emily's mother harbored secret hopes that one day her husband would return. Some of this hidden yet failing desire was passed on to Emily's bearing—it was the unforgiving trick of grief. The endurance of disguised sadness and loss clung to almost every motion of both mother and daughter. Emily channeled some of this look when she gazed down the inlet. She kept some of this disguise when she met Joseph Caine, though he offered a distant glint of light.

Thus it began: Joseph Caine looked at Emily Cooday that windy summer afternoon when first he saw her on the wharf and invited her on to his boat. As he felt something inevitable approaching, any second thoughts fell to his singular, simple desire. The impulse hardened for him. He first thought it would be a passing moment fueled by a little rum and blind passion. There was, he felt, nothing more that he wanted—innocent desire riddled by hidden then passing guilt. For Emily, she was less sure of what she wanted, but it was something that until this point had been both unknown and missing.

WHAT THE STARS CAN TELL

Rebecca and I carried on a piecemeal conversation as we walked, skipped, jumped, and occasionally stopped beside the fairly deep ditch flowing along the side of Eastfield Road. Even though it hadn't rained lately, there was still a good flow of water coming through, mainly because the ditch took some of the runoff from a large swamp a mile or so up at the top of Eastfield Road, and a permanent spring fed into the swamp.

We had each put a wooden popsicle stick in the ditch almost in front of Rebecca's house, and we were following their downstream progress, prodding them along with our own stick when they got snagged up by rocks or plants or shallow waters. It was a race between our two pretend boats. Which one would make it down the stream the fastest? Rebecca was winning by a few feet.

Rebecca: "How old do you think she is?"

"I bet she's a hundred years old."

"Do you think she's really a witch?"

Most of the kids around where we lived referred to the old lady who lived down the road as The Witch Lady. With six-year-old emerging rationalism, I sort of knew that witches didn't really exist—maybe—yet if ever there was such a thing as a witch, the subject of our conversation, old Mrs. Raskolnikov, had all the qualifications for the job, which Rebecca and I noted as we formulated our witch profiling.

First of all, yes, the witch lady was old—very old. She was all stooped over, and she used a strange knotted cane to get around. Her face was very wrinkled, and she might have even had a front tooth or two missing. She may also have had a wart on her face, or at least a few bumps. Second, she lived in a tall, spooky-looking run-down shack—an old farmhouse—and, except for her animals, she lived alone. Third, there was always smoke coming out of her chimney. Fourth, she had no car, so she might must relied on a broomstick for getting around. Fifth, she had lots of cats, some of them black. Sixth, she talked with a strange kind of accent, not unlike the way that vampires talked in the movies and on TV. Sixth, she dressed in a weird way, with layers of old shawls or capes, with a kerchief around her head. Finally, she was known to use strange cures or potions for her animals when they were sick. Some people even brought their animals to her when they had problems the vet couldn't sort out. It also seemed, sometimes, that people came by to get potions or medicines for themselves. It was easy to picture her, hunched over a boiling cauldron, chanting strange, magic words, tossing in eye of newt, toe of frog, tongue of dog...

Besides living from food her farm produced—she planted corn, lots of potatoes, masses of cabbage, and other vegetables, and there were also a few cows, some geese, and chickens wandering around all over the place—Mrs. Raskolnikov supported herself by occasionally repairing fur coats. Mom once said that Mrs. Raskolnikov was the only person around these parts who really knew how to tailor and repair furs, as well as how to clean them.

It was strange, then, to think that a person who was so poor knew so much about things that were so valuable. Medicines and furs. For us kids, though, the fame of Mrs. Raskolnikov remained that she might be a real witch, and also because she was strangely generous at Halloween—if, that is, you were brave enough to knock on her door, which did not have a light to guide you. Some said that she gave a lot because she wanted the kids to come back so that she could cook them up. That's why her chimney was always smoking: the fire was ever-ready to bake up a couple of careless kids who may have lost their way.

This scary idea was exciting to hold. Even though I had hardly had a conversation with her, I secretly liked Mrs. Raskolnikov for one enormous reason: Danny liked her.

Danny told us that the old woman knew how to use plants to fix and cure about everything, and how crystals could be used, too. She could see into the future. She could predict the weather better than the best weatherman. She knew how to find water in the ground by using sticks as pointers. She knew when a long, cold winter was coming, and she had told Danny that this, right now, would be the hottest, driest summer in memory—and, so far, this was true. Bees, Danny said, didn't bother her. Or wasps, even. Her farm animals surrounded her when she walked around her property. Like Dr. Dolittle, she talked to them, only in a strange language—and they seemed to understand. In a way, then, Danny was under her spell. In a way, she was to Danny as Danny was to us: a guide, a reader of things strange and wonderful in Nature—a supernatural Nature.

I finally had to answer Rebecca's question about whether I thought Mrs. Raskolnikov was a witch or not, though I was more interested in my popsicle stick boat catching up and passing hers.

"Maybe, but maybe no. No such thing as witches—well, not around here, anyway. But, you know, she came here from somewhere else, far away, from a weird place." I wanted to leave the possibility open, so maybe, just maybe...

I continued to hurry my boat along with my guide stick, even though the unspoken rule was that you couldn't touch your boat unless it was stuck. Rebecca didn't notice.

After my boat started moving decently, I thought that it wasn't much fun to say that there was no such thing as witches around here, so I added a more exciting idea, though it didn't make much sense: "She could be a witch if she wanted to be. She's not from around here. And she does know how to do things that nobody else knows about. She knows a lot about special weird things." This didn't seem to impress Rebecca. I added, "Danny said so."

Rebecca added flatly, "My dad says she's an odd one. That's why she does weird stuff. That's what my dad says."

Rebecca said this in a way that sounded like it must be the-whole-truth-and-nothing-but-the-truth-so-help-me-god.

She continued: "My dad told Danny to stay away from her."

I couldn't let this go.

I told Rebecca what my Mom told me, that old Mrs. Raskolnikov came here because there was a war where she used to live, and if she didn't come here, she would be in danger. She escaped what bad people were doing. They took all her things away from her. She had to leave her family there, or they were killed. And now she doesn't have any family or anything. When she got here she only had one suitcase. My Mom knew more about the neighborhood and everyone in it than anyone else, mainly because she volunteered for just about anything and she wrote the community newsletter. She was also the president of the local Welcome Wagon.

I felt good about being able to stick up for Mrs. Raskolnikov as well as for Danny and my Mom. Rebecca, it seemed, wasn't that impressed with my humanitarian speechifying. She happily trotted along, humming and singing, "Row, row, row your boat, gently down the stream—Merrily, merrily, merrily, merrily, life is but a dream," watching her boat float down the ditch, unimpeded by the hazards in the watery landscape.

I, meanwhile, had to keep unhooking my boat from the snags. But Rebecca broke her tune to get the last word in: "But she is a weirdo. My dad said that she brought bad luck with her, when she came here. I bet you anything that there's smoke coming right out of her chimney right now, even though it's hot out."

I let this go to concentrate on trying to get my popsicle-stick boat past hers.

By this time, we were some ways down the road, and, in fact, not that far from being across the road from Mrs. Raskolnikov's spooky place. We would see for ourselves whether or not smoke rose from her chimney.

My boat was beginning to catch up, and so I said, "Okay, the race ends when we get down to her house. The loser has to drink some ditch water." Somehow this challenge had to do with disagreeing with Rebecca's words about Mrs. Raskolnikov.

Rebecca happily agreed. "Okay."

And off we went. Anyway, drinking ditch water was not such a big deal, even if it would have horrified our parents.

I continued to have to run around like crazy in order to get my boat moving along. It still seemed to get hung up on every rock or plant or ditch debris, while Rebecca's boat merrily merrily merrily did most of the work on its own. I was behind by a few feet. In order to curse her boat, I frantically sang the counter-song to Rebecca's: "Row, row, row your boat, gently down the stream—Ha, ha, fooled you all, mine's a submarine!" In a few minutes we would be in front of Mrs. Raskolnikov's house. If I could just prod my boat on a little more, a little faster...

"There," said Rebecca. "I won." She turned to me and then looked to Mrs. Raskolnikov's house, across the road from where we now were. I still pushed my boat along. Rebecca immediately quit paying attention to hers, and it drifted away, merrily.

"No way," I said. "The race isn't over until we get *past* her property."

Rebecca turned to me with a little scowl. "You didn't say that."

Well, in truth maybe I didn't. But I didn't *not* say it, and so I said, "But that's what I meant."

"But you didn't say that!"

I quickly turned my attention back to my boat and ran further ahead, and, with a bit of help from the guiding stick, my boat overtook Rebecca's. At this point she didn't care. She was still looking at Mrs. Raskolnikov's old house. When my boat was way out in front, I ran back to her.

"There. I won!"

Rebecca ignored me. We both knew that a true winner—or loser—would never be declared. In the heat of play such things were quickly forgotten.

"See," she said, "there is smoke coming right out of her chimney. White. You probably get white smoke when you burn bones, you know."

She was right. White smoke rose and disappeared into the blue sky. We toddled up across the road to the edge of her property. There was always something worth seeing, even if it was only a couple of chickens running about and pecking at the grass. Maybe a cow would saunter up to the fence and we could inspect the goo that came out of its nose. Maybe, if we were lucky, we could even get a glimpse of old Mrs. Raskolnikov herself, out in her yard, maybe looking for stray chicken eggs.

After we scouted out Mrs. Raskolnikov's property, the front door to her house began to open. Maybe she saw us from one of her dark windows and was going to shush us away, or maybe invite us in to be an ingredient in her stew or gingerbread cookies, or—. But instead of Mrs. Raskolnikov's shriveled figure emerging, it was Danny! Danny? What? He closed the door behind him, and made his way through her front yard past a large, sprawling growth of blackberries to where we were lurking. Around the back of Mrs. Raskolnikov's house some crows seemed to be madly caw-cawing over something.

Danny didn't seem surprised to see us, but both Rebecca and I were quietly stunned. We knew that once in a while he had talked to the old lady when she had been around the front of her property, but we didn't think that he had been inside her house—alone! In the witch's house! We could hardly imagine what it must have been like in there. Cobwebs and cauldrons, potions and broomsticks? Bats? Piles of bones and rags? Snakeskin powder? Bottles with weird things in them, like the brain of a rat? My estimation of Danny suddenly went even higher than it already was. Rebecca didn't see it this way, and she said so to Danny: "You know, you could be in really big trouble, you know, if dad found out you were in there with her, all by yourself, too."

Danny had a pointed response: "And how would he find out?"

Rebecca kept secrets about Danny's goings-on without any pressure from Danny, since she often liked being part of what he was up to. But something now rose between older brother and younger sister.

Danny added more: "And besides, who really cares if he knows?"

This was even more challenging, especially given Rebecca's unconditional regard for her father. We all knew she was Daddy's Girl. Daddy's Doll. Princes 'Becca.

This left Rebecca quiet as we three headed back up Eastfield Road. But I needed to know what Danny learned from the strange, old witch lady, what it was like inside her broken, old house. This was legendary stuff.

"What d'ya see? In there, I mean."

Danny took a little breath and then answered, "Many wonderful things..."

This was not good enough. "Like what?"

"She has a lot of different kinds of plants in there. Healing plants. Plants you can rub on to your skin to keep mosquitoes or any kind of bugs away, or heal wounds. Candles that she makes. Fossils from animals that don't exist anymore. Pieces from a strange object that landed in her country fifty years ago and made a hole a mile wide and knocked down every tree as far as you could see. She showed me some old pictures of what it did. An explosion. Some people said it—the bomb or meteor or whatever—came from outer space."

This was good. Magic plants, fossils, an explosion from outer space.

Danny added more: "She makes pottery, then fires it. She also does lots of drawings, of flowers and things. She draws them with charcoal sticks or crayons, which she makes herself. They're good. Like you see in books or on cards."

This was less exciting, but still, strange.

"She also had a room full of bread crumbs. Jars and pots and piles of bread crumbs."

"What for?" Rebecca asked.

"Don't know."

I waited a moment before asking: "She say anything more?"

"Yeah," and here Danny seemed careful, like it was important to get it right. "She said that every chapter tells the whole story in a different way, but you can't tell this until the end, when you look back." Danny thought for a bit, like it meant something big. "Then she told me how you could read the stars so that you can tell what is going to happen in the future."

Danny waited, then added. "And she has cards, too, that help her, help her see the future. Cards of the sun, the fool, the devil, fortune, the hanged man, more."

This sounded pretty good, though I was hoping for news of broomsticks or jars labeled "eye of newt."

I thought I might be bugging Danny with the questions, but he added more without being asked:

"Other things, too. Her first name is Anna. That her name is the same spelled backwards or forwards. She said she very old, that it would be the hottest summer ever—and," here Danny paused a bit, "that a death would be near and soon—her own. And also others near, too. Also, some unlucky animal. And then, in a few years, with a light in the forest, more again. She pointed to a picture of that huge, mysterious explosion, and said it would be one of the coming moments."

This was almost too much to hold, yet even in its abstract picturing it kept us in full, quiet attention, although I was still trying work on the spelling of "Anna." Rebecca finally piped in as if to test Danny: "And how would, like, anyone know any of that stuff?"

Danny lifted his gaze to the sky: "She looked into the stars—and through the cards."

This was good and mysterious, and then he pulled out a card from his back pocket. "She gave me this," Danny said. We stopped beside the ditch. It was a card with, it looked like, some guys with wings in the clouds, blowing horns. Some naked people below looking up, with raised arms, coming out of darkened spaces, like graves or something.

"What is it," I asked. "One of her cards?"

"Yea," Danny said. "She asked me to pull it out from a deck she had spread out. She gave it to me. Tarot. A Tarot card. She said it was a future card, to read the future. My future."

It looked old and wonderful and strange. Angels, I wondered. The wings. Maybe angels looking down. There were two letters at the top of the card, letters that I knew: 'XX'

I had a question, though I was not sure if Danny wanted it.

"What does it mean? The card."

Danny took it from our gaze and put it back into his pocket. As we began to walk back up Eastfield Road beside the ditch, he gave his answer: "It's a future card. Judgement. The card for Judgement."

§

Emily Cooday did not know how she knew how to take on Joseph Caine's body. But almost from the first, their love-making felt like a slight unlocking, an opening-up of sorts—something that seemed to be already with her, inside her to be touched, something in her that had been waiting, for him. Was it real, or something she had somehow invented?

Emily could feel that when he gave his body over to her, she owned him. She had never owned much, but now she owned this man from another world, an outside world, a world where he had power and knowledge.

She somehow knew how to use every part of her body on every part of his. She mastered; he surrendered. Her strength, the will and way of her body, seemed greater than his: she pulled him to her, and he gave in. He *quivered and folded and rose up and fell, and he was hers. His unconnected words at those deepest moments when his eyes rolled back sounded like prayer, or agony and joy, and she tried to hold him still, almost calm him, so that the moment might last, so that she could own him longer, and longer still. Then she, too, could find those spots that, at moments, made her warm yet shivering. To pull away from what was between them was to fall back into her narrow, tight world—a world she didn't own. How, she thought? How might he be held so that they, together, could become something more?*

THE MIND OF AN ANT NEST

Danny observed Big Nature's goings-on, but he also felt that it was his duty to add to or, as he put it, "fiddle with" Nature's fine balancing act, which often meant more than offering a benevolent, nurturing hand.

One ritual on our excursions up The Trail was a quick pee on the Ant Nest. Well, Rebecca didn't usually pee there, since squatting so close to the nest was neither comfortable nor safe. Not that she didn't try. Of course for Danny and me it was just a matter of aiming our peckers and hosing where we felt like it. Sometimes I imagined I was a giant, sometimes a fireman. Sometimes firing lasers at insect aliens. I don't know what Danny imagined, but he once told us he was like this guy called Gulliver who peed on a castle fire to put it out. So pee we did, and during that summer the ants had to cope with at least a couple of quarts of kid piss soaking through their nest. Danny's comment: "If it doesn't kill them, it'll make them stronger." And there was no doubt that this was the Mother of all Ant Nests. It was almost chest high, and growing, spreading.

These were red ants, with brownish-red front ends and black rear ends, not the tiny black or brown ones that lived underground around the foundation of houses and along sidewalks. They were quick, and there were zillions of them in this massive mound, which was mainly made from fir needles and bits of dried wood and grasses. Danny said they were really called thatching ants, but red ants sounded better.

Danny told us that at the center of the nest, a foot or two below the ground, there was a lumpy, oozing, pulsating Queen Ant whose only job was to produce egg after egg. He described how male nurse ants would gently take these away to nursery rooms where they would be kept safe and clean and moist—and fed the moment they hatched. After that, alongside their siblings, it would be a lifetime of busy service for their mother, their Queen.

Besides the Nurses, who never came to the surface, there were the Worker Ants, the backbone of the Nest—endlessly gathering, hunting, building, foraging, exploring, warning. Then there were the Soldiers, fewer in number, equipped with oversized jaws to protect the Nest, ready to give up their lives in defense of that quiet, royal chamber of birth. We loved to think about this feudal world. Danny knew every part of ant life, and it was amazing. "We could learn something," he'd said, more than once.

If you were quiet, you could, from a few feet away, just hear the rustling and shuffling of the Nest as hordes of Workers built up and rearranged their fortress mound, all for the greater good, and to keep themselves warm in the winter. When we peed on the anthill, Danny pointed out how the Nest instantly responded, communicating the disturbance in every direction: one ant turning to the next and passing on a chemical message of warning and assault. *Intruders! Intruders! We're getting wizzed on!* The surface reaction was, first of all, an increase in the pace of activity as the ants aggressively sought out the source of the disturbance, and second, the acid smell that the Nest gave out as a deterrent for intruders. Danny especially liked the idea of the Nest giving out a smell as a warning.

He told us that if they get a chance to bite you, they'd spray some of their stinging acid on the puncture they make—"just for good measure." He added, "The chemical the ants give out is almost the same as the kind of acid we have in our wizz. Except theirs is stronger. For defense. Ours is just waste coming out of our body, though maybe we should never waste it."

He was right. Whenever we were outside and had to take a pee, we would often try to find some use for it, even it just meant hosing down some wild flowers while a bee was making a pollen stop. Dandelions gone to seed were favorite targets, since you could knock off and disperse those little parachute seeds with a well-aimed blast.

Peeing on the giant nest gave Danny another moment to frame the Big Picture: "It's chemistry. Life, nature—chemicals balancing.

We take them in through our spongy lungs, into our stomachs—oxygen and sugar, proteins, minerals. Breathing. Digesting. What gets left over—more chemicals. Ideas going across our brains are passed on by chemicals, like the chemical message that moves across and through the Nest. Your mind: just like this ant nest, you know—messages passed along your brain cells, just like the Nest passes on messages, ant to ant to ant. God—he made all the stuff—was a chemist. We're just his test-tube. Hell—a Bunsen burner that heats it all up and burns the waste. The bottom side of heaven, not its opposite."

Wow.

Danny repeated something like story of All Things more than once during the first part of the summer, so it began to sink in, despite how he moved from the little that we could understand to the big we could only imagine. Sure, we didn't get everything, like "brain cells" and the like. On the other hand, how could we forget? Our minds *were* like an ant nests. We *were* chemicals. We *did* burn up chemicals inside us in order to make energy. God as the maker *did* try to make sure the chemicals get balanced. Hell *was* the furnace for all things. Take this summer, for instance—"Hot as hell," people said over and over. Which, according to what Danny said, meant something more than they knew.

But yes: we sacrificed more than just our pee to the Ant Nest that operated much like a brain.

§

The commercial fishermen who harbored at places like Emily Cooday's village were cut up by time, the open sea, and a tough, haphazard job that often glazed them with cynicism and, too often, crudeness. They arrived in their boats, got a few supplies and the shelter of the harbor, and then they were gone, leaving behind their empty bottles and some garbage. They were not always liked by the First-Nations people, but the fishermen represented one of the few ways that extra money came into these poor, isolated communities.

Emily seldom noticed these passing white men, though, as she became a teen, and as her body and her walk took on proportions and a gait that men see only in terms of their own lusts, they often noticed her. She was barely aware of their gaze. Neither did she recognize her own hidden and growing longings.

Until, that is, she met Joseph Caine.

Emily had never encountered a fisherman quite like Joseph. He was younger and tight, with something more vital and controlled. Clean-shaven over an angular face. Once on his boat, she fell to having a drink with him. Little was said, maybe something about crab traps, her grandfather, something about the weather—a coming storm. There were looks. It surprised them both that it took little to bring them together and to find each other, and then to fade into that place where the outside fell away and the approaching storm unnoticed.

Joseph was not Emily's first man—her other encounter was a few years earlier: a minute or two with a native boy from up the coast, a second or third cousin, and it felt like nothing. This cousin forced his brief, frenzied way into her, and dropped away with blank disregard. And it meant nothing more to her than a submerged, sad feeling that the sex of a man was something passing and incomplete and weak. His only mark was an unmeaning patch of sticky fluid on her stomach.

So Joseph was not her first, but it felt like he was. Her only man, and the only man for her. He was at once foreign to and familiar with her, and she for him. Their smells, their textures, his hard body and her soft shape. His face, reddened neck, and arms toughened by the sun and wind and the salt water, and, for him, her brown skin like velvet.

Emily was quiet as they pulled together that first time, though her body spoke in ways she was unaware of. It was a confused revelation for her—a new world that folded all things together, hinting of something more that existed not just within, but beyond. A way, perhaps, of looking forward. A way out, perhaps.

For Joseph, it began as a passing night in an obscure fishing village, and at first he thought little about it. But when he was out on his boat over the next few days, hauling in those cold, hard, silver salmon, Emily Cooday crept, unannounced, back into his thoughts and desires. She was young and beautiful. Her touch made him rise and dissolve at the same time. She moved around and over him in ways that did not fully register that first night. But it soon did, and there was something more about her, too.

And so, first chance he had, he went back to her, back into her, and their love-making took him to a place of passionate easiness that was urgent yet simple. His body and his thoughts pulled to her when he was away, and when he returned to his wife and to being with her, it was Emily that played in his imagination, and he had to stop himself from saying her name when he shuddered into his wife.

BLACKBIRD, BYE BYE

Thus spake Danny: "Death is life's best friend. Its twin. No death, no life. No life, no death. They have the same mother. It all makes perfect sense, really. Death, life, nature. How it goes."

It did, it seemed.

Danny went on to preach about how we were—or at least he was—meant to work with these things. Speed them up. Slow them down. Try new combinations. "New paths for Nature to follow so that we get a bit deeper into"—and here Danny paused to get phrasing he must have been working on, or that he read somewhere— "evolutionary consumerism."

Whoa! What? Danny lost us—or at least me. His big words were, like our parents said, sometimes beyond his years; you could tell they did not really know what to think about what he sometimes said. Maybe it scared them. But there was a more immediate problem for us, his two six-year-old observers and minions. Well, there were actually four problems beyond the vocabulary, especially for the male of the species, that being me: 1) information overload; 2) attention span; 3) abstract thinking; and 4) believing just about anything you hear, even if you don't understand it. *Evolutionary consumerism* bounced right off that part of my frontal lobes that attempted to turn words into images. Danny, of course, knew this. He could, he once said, "read me like a book."

"Okay." He gathered and reformulated. "It's like the snake with its tail in its mouth. The picture I showed you in the *Encyclopedia*."

Yes, the snake with its tail in its mouth.

"It eats itself. Lives off its own death, forever and ever, round and round. It eats and grows, and eats as much as it grows. No more, no less. And it never dies, though it eats itself, and by eating itself it gains strength in its life through its death. Like seasons. Trees growing, falling, rotting—then new trees growing. So goes life. *Evolutionary consumerism* means that, for life to go on and change, it must feed off itself. The snake eating itself."

Okay. We were still a little left behind by his mini-lecture, but by Danny's tone we knew it meant it was time to put theory into practice.

His summing-up was basic: "Everything more or less becomes compost—including you and me." Compost I knew all about, since Dad at moments was almost possessed in making sure our big vegetable garden was full of it, feeding the garden with itself. Yes, the snake eating itself! I got it!

This particular morning we were about to feed the Ant Nest something it probably hadn't eaten before. Bugs and worms and caterpillars were easy pickings, and part of the diet we regularly sacrificed to the Ant Nest. Danny had something else in mind. Something to put new life into the Nest's jaws and gullet.

"How about...a baby blackbird?"

There were lots of nests around, especially in some of the low evergreens down the road. The doting, cheeky blackbird parents often dove at us when we got close to or passed by their nests, so they were probably doing more harm than good in giving away nest locations.

"Their squawks are bigger than their pecks," Danny assured us as we made our way.

I, of course, blithe climber, was to get up into the branches to pluck out a choice young bird from its nest. I relished the climb and Danny's need for my skill. Danny did not climb trees, just like he never ran.

"Leave climbing to monkeys," he said as I made my way up. "You know, evolution took higher species out of the trees. That's why I'm down here and you're up there." I didn't get it (there was that word again, *evolution*), but what he said did motivate a monkey howl on my way up, perhaps confirming Danny's comment.

He wanted a very young bird. "Not one with too many feathers. Get one with its eyes not opened yet."

The first nest had two small birds that cheep-cheeped noisily when I got close. Their red mouths stabbed into the air. They thought my commotion meant feeding time. Well, in a sense, it was. But these particular siblings were too developed for Danny's tastes, with feathers just beginning to show along their backs and stunted wings.

A couple of trees down I found another nest with three hatchlings. One was smaller and probably a day or two younger than the other two. Its eyelids were not yet opened, though through the transparent membrane you could see its oversized eyes. This little family also cheeped hungrily at my presence as their parents squawked overhead.

I plucked the little thing out of its nest and climbed down to show Danny. I told him it was by far the smallest. He scrutinized it, and with a nod pronounced it suitable. "Out of the pot and into the frying pan," he said, smiling. "If it was the smallest, likely it wouldn't survive. The older, bigger ones often kick the smallest out of the nest. More food for them, more chance for them. Perfect, natural sense."

Rebecca's task was to carry the chick carefully. She cupped in her hands as we made our way to the Ant Nest.

The baby blackbird was as ugly as it was unaware of its fate. It looked like a miniature plucked chicken. Its bulging, black, membraned eyes seemed ready to burst. Its skin was pale pink and blemished.

The bird was not making much noise as we approached the Ant Nest. It may have been calmed by the warmth and gentleness of Rebecca's cupped hands. Or just confused into silence.

"First, we stir up a little trouble—get the ants in the mood. Any ideas?"

"Want me to pee on the nest?" I asked.

"No—not the right message."

I had another suggestion: "Maybe get a stick and stick it in a few times? That'll get them running around like crazy!"

"Better. Yes, do bit of ant poking. Anger them a bit."

I found a broken branch and, within seconds of jabbing it into the Nest a few times, the ants switched to panic-alert mode, collectively and frantically looking for the source of the attack. We couldn't wait too long, for we knew that after a while the Nest would recover its composure and begin to repair damage. I broke the stick in half and dropped one piece on top of the Nest. They would soon build over it. In fact, lots of stuff built within that nest had come out own hands: glass, nails, paperclips, snail shells, matches, chunks of Drano, iron filings (this was an interesting experiment, which also included magnets, fish food, and honey), hair, string—even hot wax drops from a burning candle. (Danny sang "Happy Birthday" to that one.)

"And may I have the birdie, please."

Danny liked saying this. He was indeed a master—no, THE Master—of Ceremonies.

Rebecca passed him the chick, to which she sweetly whispered, "Bye-bye little bird."

Danny looked into its blind eye, and it seemed to look back at him, quizzically, though it could hardly have seen him. There was, though, something unusual in seeing the tiny bird so close to Danny's face, and the strangeness took a second or two to register. But there it was: the color of the bird and the texture of its skin were not unlike that of Danny's face. Danny didn't see this—himself, that is, reflected in the doomed little creature—or did he? Even in the two pairs of eyes, in the bird's blindness and Danny's insight, there was some joining. But who knows? It remained a passing, unsettling sight. The little blind bird and the all-seeing big bird-boy.

"Just so we can get some idea of this poor pilgrim's progress into—into who knows where, we will use some string." He added that if we just tossed the bird onto the nest, it might simply get covered with ants without being subject to observation and due process.

Danny had some string in his pocket. He made a little noose that he slipped and tightened around the chick's scrawny legs. The branch of an arbutus tree extended over top of the nest. All was ready.

The baby bird, being upside-down, suspended, and swinging slightly, was distressed. The ants were still frantically searching out the source of the threat made by the stick. The bird began to make a quiet but high-pitched cheeping. Danny mocked the sound in his own tiny words, "Help me! Help me!", which we knew was from some movie he had seen and told us about in detail: an insect-size half-fly, half-man gets trapped in spider's web, and he pathetically squawks out, "Help me! Help me!" before someone dashes it with boulder. Danny gloated in the re-telling of this scene. "Best movie ever," he said. "All about science. About how anyone can become a monster. Anyone." We believed him, even though it sounded a little scary. *Anyone?* Really?

Danny slowly lowered the bird so that its head just touched the top of the Nest, swaying barely an inch or two, back and forth, roughing up the fir needles that composed it. In a few seconds, the word was out across the colony's collective mind, and the bird was quickly swarmed with ants that acted with one, clear purpose. Within a minute or two, hundreds of frantic, biting ants took the bird as the source of the disturbance, as a threat to the safety of the Queen. The smell of their acid rose, like rancid smoke over an altar. Danny gave us his sermon from the Nest.

"In its short life," said Danny, "this bird has been twice a victim, which is more than most of us ever achieve."

This was so: as Danny explained, the bird had unfortunately fallen into our hands, and now into the crawling grasp of the Nest.

The bird twisted and shuddered. The ants fed off its panic, and reinforcements soon covered most of its featherless, pink-skinned surface, biting and pulling. The ants were one jaw with thousands of little teeth.

Danny touched his face and watched. "A life inside and a life on the outside. Direct action. Protecting, destroying, consuming."

Without the picture in front of us, these words would have meant nothing. Danny could go on like this forever. He took stock of the results of our plans. He noted that the parents of this bird did not know that the bit of energy they spent in feeding its offspring would be changed into energy to feed the Ant Nest. He said that even if the bird became an adult and died in just a normal, regular way, it would eventually become some kind of energy. "We're just the getting the energy transfer started a little early."

After a few more minutes, the bird was still, though it seemed to move in the way its crawly surface shifted with the frenetic activity of the ants. Rebecca and I wondered aloud if the bird was dead. Danny thought that it might be, but added that at this point it may have been shocked into stillness. The ants kept a furious pace for a bit longer, but now they explored more than they attacked. Some entered the mouth of the bird and disappeared down its throat. They may have been satisfied that the threat was over. Now it was time for them to scout what had been conquered. "To the victor, the spoils," said Danny, nodding over the scene. "Vanquishing point."

Danny pointed to the ants entering the little bird's mouth: "The ants may be looking for a way in, into the bird's heart of darkness. Ants, you know, love little holes. They're at home without light."

I imagined the ants as mini-miners, going down into this ruby-red fleshy tunnel, chipping and cutting away, taking out precious parts of the bird's guts: bits of tiny lungs and livers and whatever else was down in that tiny gullet.

As we watched, Danny spoke a few lines from a poem, though they sounded sing-songy:

"Pack up all your cares and woe,
Here I go, swinging low,
Bye bye blackbird.
No one here can love or understand me,
Oh, what hard luck stories they all hand me.
Make my bed and light the light,
I'll arrive late tonight,
Blackbird, bye bye."

Danny did usually entertain like this, and at so much length. It was like Danny had pulled these words right out the still, hot afternoon. Were they his words? Yes: it was indeed bye-bye time for the swinging, bald blackbird that looked a little like Danny. He began to whistle a familiar-sounding tune.

His final word was there again: "Amen."

A decent morning's work. Without much more to see, lunch whispered to us. Danny, suddenly more somber, must have noted as much: "Our bodies always call out for something. Food. We do as it says. But listening to your brain? That's confusing, 'cause sometimes your body says one thing and your brain says something else, or more than one thing. Makes some people nuts. Or," he added, "maybe all of us."

We may have looked a bit surprised by this, but Danny seemed not to mind. In fact, he upped the idea with something we could picture: "An angel sits on one shoulder, whispering into your ear. A devil sits on the other, whispering into the other. Who do you listen to?"

As we walked down The Trail toward my house, Danny was a little ahead of Rebecca and me. *Whispering angels, whispering devils.* We all went quiet for a few minutes. Danny's words eventually slipped away, but the tune he whistled stayed a little longer.

When we broke into the clearing where the back of my house came into sight, I could only utter what was upon me: "What you having for lunch?" I asked.

Rebecca thought they would likely have sandwiches. Danny grumbled: "Probably salmon sandwiches."

I knew Danny hated salmon, which was too bad since his dad was a commercial salmon fisherman. Mr. Caine had his own troller, called the *Miss E. D. Pussy*. My Mom thought it must have been hard for Mr. Caine to manage his fishing boat on his own, but Dad said that Mr. Caine was a bit of a loner, and besides, he wouldn't have to divide what profit he would make. "He's a good fisherman," my Dad always said. "Hard working."

Danny seemed touchy about things that had to do with his own dad, especially lately. I thought of the amazing baseball mitt that his dad gave him, but also how Danny could hardly wait to dismember it. But who, especially a hungry six-year-old, could solve such mysteries? Only one thing was on my mind—well, two things: what was for lunch, and how fast I could eat it so that I could get out playing again. After all, it was about mid-way through summer, and time, though of the essence, could only be made to slow down by hurrying up. Visions of alphabet soup and grilled-cheese sandwiches danced in my head, all washed down with glasses and glasses of anything cold.

"See ya after lunch," I said, and I started to run for the backdoor. At my flying start, Rebecca too began to dash toward her home. Danny walked on down the driveway and across Eastfield Road, slowly, maybe with thoughts of lunch, but, perhaps, with something else eating away in him that might not be satisfied by salmon sandwiches.

§

Hannah Caine did not like getting gossipy hints from others about her husband's possible affairs up the coast. She was not prepared to sit back while her husband, Joseph, carried on up north. So she sometimes got around when he was away. She came to believe that she wanted to have her body flattered by and filled with the attentions of other men. Nothing serious, she would say to herself. Was it anger or resentment? Spite? Revenge? Her own needs? This worked away within her and her family in hidden and then bad ways. A way that everyone would eventually see, and then try very hard to forget.

HOME, SWEET HOME

Indeed, I probably had grilled-cheese sandwich and alphabet soup for lunch that particular bye-bye blackbird day. And glasses of some cold, colorful drink. A cookie or an apple often ended off such hurried lunches, though these were, with some pleading, taken outside and on the run, barely chewed, swallowed in chunks, with apple cores chucked who-knows-where. This run-and-eat didn't go over too well with parents who believed you were supposed to sit peacefully, have conversation, and chew things thirty-two times before swallowing.

Motherly medical advice was often offered: "You're going to give yourself a tummy ache. You've got all day, you know. It's not a race."

Little did she know. All day? Days were short. They could fly by with games incomplete, goals not scored, nails not driven, traps not checked, holes not dug, ropes not climbed, swings not swung, bugs not collected.

Mom usually had just long enough with me to ask about what I had been up to. My answers about were usually as vague as possible, especially when it involved Danny: "Oh, just playing around." "Oh, nothing, really." "Oh, just horsing around." "Oh, just playing up The Trail." The "Oh" represented all the good stuff that had to be left out.

Knowing that she could get little else out of me, she inevitably replied, "Well, just be careful. Careful when you cross the road. And be good."

My "I will" never completely reassured her. She knew there was little she could do to keep me completely safe or good, save keeping me home, which would have driven her more nuts than me. Bee stings, stinging nettles, broken branches, bike wipeouts, slivers, dirt in the eye, knee scrapes, blackberry-bush scratches, rope burns, baseballs in the nose—just a few of the daily hazards of pre-adolescent play; and given the amount of territory we covered, there was never a way for Mom to keep me safe, clean, or on time. She was always just slightly relieved to have me home and in her clutches. She trusted me as much as a mother could trust a curious and energetic six-year-old boy with long summer days ahead and too many acres at his disposal—and this was the first summer where there was some sense of granted independence.

On the day of our bye-bye blackbird, she once more attempted to search for specifics: "I saw Rebecca come by. Were you playing with Danny this morning? I think I just saw him come past."

"Yeah, well, sort of," I mumbled. She didn't disapprove of Danny as much as Dad, who in fact just came in the back door. He was home for lunch.

Danny was, as Mom said more than once, maybe a little too old for me. I also knew from stolen conversations that my parents thought he was a "too smart by half—odd." I didn't have a problem with that. If "odd" meant knowing The Complete Works of Nature, A-Z, then such oddness was next to godliness. Sometimes, though, when the Caine family was mentioned, my parents exchanged a look that signaled *say no more* or *we'll take about this later.* I would say, "What?" Of course they'd say, "Nothing," which even then I knew meant something. What could they not say about the Caines in front of me?

"Oh, we were just up The Trail, by the Ant Nest. Doing nothing, I guess."

Mom didn't like the Ant Nest, but she probably resisted saying so since she had made this clear a couple times already.

"Nothing?" she said, hoping for a little more.

"Looking at stuff."

She knew this was the limit of her information-gathering, and so the subject was changed: "I see Mr. Caine is home from fishing."

"Yeah." I was a bundle of information. "Any cookies?"

"Did you talk to him? How was the fishing?"

"Yeah. He said it was good, I guess. Juice?"

Mom offered some correction: "*May* I have more juice, *please*. But you've had enough. If you're still thirsty, have some water."

Water?

I gave out a little information, but I was suddenly inspired: "Mr. Caine bought Rebecca a brand-new doll. And he got Danny a real nice baseball mitt. Black leather. And you should see it!" Well, actually maybe she shouldn't, given its new, discombobulated state. But I thought I could soften Mom up with a bit of guilt—keeping up with the Caines—so that I might get something out of her, like a new bicycle before the summer was over. We had recently talked about it, but the conversation went nowhere.

"Does Danny play baseball?" Dad asked.

"Not sure." But I was. He didn't. Not even close.

Mom and Dad exchanged one of those glances.

"What?" I asked.

"Nothing," Mom answered. Dad settled into his lunch, happy to be observer rather than a further participant in this conversation. "You need a new baseball mitt?" she asked, or maybe was telling me. She hadn't got my drift about the bike—yet.

This was tricky. I didn't need really a new mitt, but I wouldn't have minded getting one. But a new bike was my greater goal.

"No, that old one's okay. I don't mind *some* old things."

Just to make sure she fully noted my unselfishness, I added: "My old one is fine. Don't need a new one." My mitt was a hand-me-down from older brother Simon, which under normal circumstances was a point of complaint.

But I may have been protesting in reverse too much. She eyed me with her patented funny-serious look, which meant she was about to nod, whatever that meant.

She knew more was behind my ploy. She would have to bribe me, torture me, in order to find out.

She continued, slowly: "So, um, what do you need that is—new?"

I swear: the woman could read my mind!

She went to the cupboard and fished out a cookie, maybe to soften me up. Just had to hold on a little longer. Just had to keep her going a bit more—

"A new bike!" I blurted out. "I need a new bike. Pleeease?"

Dad surfaced from his plate: "Something wrong with your old one—I mean the one you use? It's not too small, is it? I can raise the seat."

"Yeah. There's something wrong with my bike. No gears. It doesn't have hand brakes. And it has a stupid long seat. The tires are too small. It's a kid's bike. I don't even like riding it. It's too slow!"

My parents weren't all that impressed with my whine. I dug a little deeper and appealed to both peer pressure and family pride. "Well, everybody else has a bike with gears, except me. Everybody!"

Mom thought for a few seconds. "Rebecca doesn't have new bike, does she?"

Had to think for a few seconds. I drained the last drops of the juice, thinking without looking like I was thinking. Mom was more clever than I thought, which is always the case with parents: they are smarter than you think, even though they are dumb. But I got it: "Rebecca doesn't like riding bikes, and I do! She hardly ever rides her bike, but she does have a pretty well new one—her dad bought it. With streamers." Put that in your pipe and smoke it! I had one more jab: "And she gets anything she wants! From her dad." I could only repeat the new doll bribe: "Just got her this new doll. He did. Maybe two of them! With a bunch of clothes and everything!"

Mom and Dad exchanged another look. Mom started to clear up the table, which could have meant she was cornered. Would this end up being another victory for whining kids everywhere?

"Your Father and I will talk it over." She called him "Your Father" when it was a matter of official business, fiscal consultation, penal codes, or part of a warning directed at me. Otherwise, he was just "your Dad." Well, Dad was cool about such things. He knew the importance of first-rate machinery. Then she added, "Maybe for your birthday, or maybe Santa could bring you a bike for Christmas. You can write him a letter."

Santa! Christmas! That was years away! Write a letter? I hate writing.

"But I need it now. It's summer. There's nothing to do!"

"You know, we're not made of money." Yeah, yeah. And money doesn't grow on trees. Yeah, yeah. And there are starving kids all over the world. Yeah, yeah. Save it up for a rainy day. Got it. I'd heard this all before.

So I had to continue, hoping I had them on the ropes. "But Dad will say, 'Let me talk it over with your mother,' and then you two will forget about it, and then the summer will be gone. I really need a new bike! I'll do chores."

Mom flashed a scowl, so it was time to make like a banana and split. I'd made my point. There was an afternoon to kill. I grabbed the cookie, and in a wink was gone through the back door. I shouted back to her, "I'll be over at Rebecca's," and by the time I reached the road and was flying across the ditch to Rebecca's house, any thoughts of getting a new bike were erased by the voice-over in my head whenever my body carried me faster than a speeding bullet, able to leap tall buildings in a single bound—look: up in the air...It's a bird; no, it's a plane; no it's...

§

Daniel Caine was born a few years after Mr. and Mrs. Joseph Caine were married, though they wanted children right away. Or at least Mrs. Caine did.

Danny came on time into the world, but he did not come easily. At the last moment a cesarean was required. In the course of the operation and in a medical follow-up, it was discovered that something had gone wrong with Mrs. Caine, a pelvic inflammatory disease. After all kinds of tests, the new parents were told by a specialist that it was remarkable not only that Danny survived, but that he was conceived in the first place.

Not too many weeks after Danny was born, Mr. and Mrs. Caine were told that they would not be able to have any more children. While this news did not overly punish Mr. Caine's hopes or wishes, Mrs. Caine was devastated. She, Hannah, wanted a daughter—a pig-tailed cutie who would follow her around the house, take dance lessons, and wear party dresses that she would make for her or, better yet, with her. In fact, her heart quietly sank when, at Danny's birth, she asked and was told by a masked nurse, "It's a boy." "But," she thought, "I'll have another, and chances are it will be a girl."

When Mrs. Caine discovered she would not be able to have another child, for some months she fell into a darker time. That new scar on her stomach reminded her of what she wanted but could not have. And though that scar would forever mark Danny's rough, uncertain entrance into the world, and though she did her best to love her chubby boy, without knowing it, she formed an unvoiced blame for her condition not just on her husband, but, even more indirectly, on her young son. Such, it seems, is human nature.

This inarticulate, unsought-for blame became a slow-growing distancing between husband and wife. Neither could do anything about it. Neither could or would even say anything about it, though such feelings work their way over into the shaded corners of a family before eventually spilling over in unanticipated ways. Their lives continued. Their fortunes remained as veiled as those of everyone—but Daniel, that child pulled from his mother's womb, would come to know what a young son should not know. And that knowledge would break everything.

THE HEART OF A SALMON

Within about five minutes of my super-takeoff across the road and over the ditch, I was back in the kitchen where Mom was still cleaning up after lunch. Older brother Simon, still wearing his white underwear, stirred from his teenage sleeping-in to forage for grub. He seemed to be staying up later and later, reading into the night, it seemed. Probably comics.

"Mom, Mom!" I was puffing quite a bit. "Can I go down to the wharf, to Mr. Caine's boat? I'll be careful, honest. It's okay with Mr. Caine. He asked me if I wanted to come. I didn't invite myself. Can I go? They're leaving right now!"

Then I realized my mistake. "*May* I go, *please*? Please?"

I knew the conditions by heart: be good, be safe, be polite, don't get in the way, say "thank you."

Usually it was no big deal to go on little excursions with the Caines. Rebecca sometimes went out with us when we went to the beach or for afternoon outings to a park.

Despite my keen, pleading manner and the *may* and the *please*, Mom was not immediately swell on the idea. I had been down to the fishing boat once before, but Dad went as well, just to see some of Mr. Caine's new fishing gear. Danny sometimes went down, too, but not usually to help with the boat. His excursions were of a more scientific nature—checking out the sea life, gathering specimens, searching out the unusual.

"Well," said Mom, "you'll be around the water, you know, and lots of dangerous and expensive fishing equipment, so I expect you to be very, very careful. Don't play around with things or touch them unless you ask. Don't get the way. And don't run on the wharf. Be careful, you hear."

What did she think I was going to do? Jump in the water weighted with lead and fishing nets wrapped around me? What could be dangerous about going down to the wharf? After all, I was almost seven years old.

"Yeah, I will. Mr. Caine will be there all the time, and so will Rebecca—and Danny, too."

"Well, you be careful, mister—promise," she added.

This was said as both a sigh and a warning, and more: "And don't forget to say thank you!" And I was off again across the road and over the ditch to the Caine's house.

"Promise," I yelled back. Mom would probably go to the front door to watch us back out of the Caine's long driveway in their dark-blue Chev.

. . .

We drove the couple of miles to fisherman's wharf, with Mr. Caine and Rebecca in the front seat. She had her new doll with her and a bag of recently acquired doll gear. Danny and I sat in the back. As I looked out the window and the landscape passed by, I had vague, uneasy thoughts about Danny and his dad. Something not quite right. Danny didn't like talking to him all that much, or so he made out. Rebecca, on the other hand, couldn't get enough of her dad. She missed him when he was away on his fishing trips. She was, as Mr. Caine himself said a few times, "Daddy's little girl—a walkin', talkin', livin' doll."

The spots of conversation in the car were between father and daughter. Rebecca attempted to casually ask about his next fishing trip, when he was going away again, and when he'd be back, if he'd always be going away to fish, what he did up there. Mr. Caine could only respond in the vaguest of ways, but it was clear, even to me, that Rebecca wanted more of her father. There was also a reminder directed at me to tell my parents to come over and pick up a couple of salmon. "Got some Coho on the smoker." Mr. Caine, glimpsing into the rear-view mirror, also asked Danny if he had "broken in" the new baseball mitt.

"Yeah," Danny answered without blinking his eyes or looking at me. He added, lowly, "It's broken in." If only Mr. Caine knew!

As we parked, Mr. Caine let it be known that we were to keep fairly close by, and not to muck about with his equipment. Danny okayed him. I did too. Rebecca said she was going to play in the boat's cabin with her dolls.

The *Miss E. D. Pussy* was medium size boat—a troller, and not unlike many of the other boats at fisherman's wharf. Between fishing trips there was always lots of prepping, repairing, and cleaning. Lines checked, hooks secured, rigging tightened, engine tuned, the hold cleaned out, touch-up painting—generally, everything had to be in perfect order before the next trip. I learned that "ship-shape" meant something real.

These few years were pretty good times in the Pacific Northwest waters. Fish for everyone and fish forever. If you worked hard, it was a decent living despite the seasonally-intense work. When the half dozen or more "open" commercial fishing periods came up—each a couple of weeks or more—the days were long. Those few months worked were often enough to support a family for a whole year. But this would very quickly change as government policies took literal stock of the coastal salmon fisheries.

Besides the fishermen themselves, fishing life could be tough on the families. Most wives did not have jobs outside of the household. They took care of the kids, got them off to school in time, did the shopping, cleaning, and cooking, while for weeks at a time the husbands spent nights on their boats in small, sheltered fishing villages, sometimes way up the coast, following the uncertain path of the salmon.

What Danny wanted to do down at the wharf was to get his hands on some dogfish, which were plentiful and easy to catch at the deep spots off the end of the wharves. Dogfish—technically "Pacific Shark," as Danny told me—were bottom feeders with skin like sandpaper, and dark, empty eyes, and never much more than a few feet long. Though they looked like other sharks, they were not the aggressive, predator types that cruised beaches looking for wandering swimmers to chomp on. None of the fishermen minded us catching them, since dogfish were not part of the fishing industry, which around here centered around salmon, cod, sole, halibut, and herring. But unlike the east coast, salmon, not cod, was king.

Rebecca retreated into the cabin of the boat to play house with Barbie and her stuff. We stopped for a couple of minutes at Mr. Caine's boat to get some old fishing line, an old bucket, a couple of triple hooks, some lead, wire cutters, a knife, a hammer, and nails.

We also needed some bait—any fishy flesh would do, since we knew that dogfish would go after anything vaguely resembling meaty matter. Bits of salmon guts were plentiful, with some fisherman cleaning their recent catch. Danny got some from a grizzled old guy down the wharf, who definitely could have used a tooth or two—and a bath. Danny's preferred bait was salmon hearts.

"Triple hooks are best," he announced. He told me that number three stands for three hooks and all kinds of other things. "The father, the son, the holy salmon."

I quickly added my favorite grouping: "And the Three Stooges."

Danny approved of my odd connection to triple hooks, and the conversation put me in light spirits. Lucky I had cancelled my first thought: the three bears. That story was for babies.

Well, an afternoon at Fisherman's Wharf. Fishing for sharks! Could life get any better?

A few seagulls, ever-vigilant opportunists, shrieked above as we carried the innards in the bucket to the end of the wharf and sat ourselves down. Danny picked through the gory stew with same care that a miner might when picking though gravel for a gold nugget. He gave a quick anatomy lesson as he pulled out bits of salmon guts, beginning with his quick philosophy of eating, which I had heard before: "The whole world eventually goes through every creature's butt—including people."

This was interesting, but not exactly reassuring.

"See this?" Danny pulled out something long and pinkish. "The stomach, attached to the intestine, attached to the anus, which craps out the crap, that came through the mouth, that went down the throat and into the stomach, that gets pooped out again."

This, for Danny, constituted the moving parts of his Great Chain of Eating. And I did know the word "anus," which, like the word "penis," sounded goofy. We six-year-olds preferred "bumhole" or "dink." You only said "anus" when you wanted to sound weird, or when you wanted to make a joke about the planet next to Neptune. Danny had the latter in mind, and he repeated the riddle I had heard before but still enjoyed, mainly because I actually got the joke: Question: "Which planet is the butt hole of our solar system?" Answer: "Your anus. Get it? Uranus. Ha!" For a little kid, this was very clever stuff.

Danny examined the stomach, and with two hands hung it out in front of me like a gooey clothesline. He tossed the stringy glomp into the water. A shrieking seagull swooped down, scooped it out before it sank too much, and gobbled it down in one motion as other gulls closed in for a potential steal. Danny's watched the gull: "From one stomach into another—the circle of life, though it should be called the circle of death. Same difference."

He pulled out another bit. This was harder, darker, and smaller. "The liver," said Danny. "Lots of chemicals in the old liver. Strains poison. Gives out stuff called bile." Danny looked closer at the liver. "Bile has to do with being mad—nuts—you know." Danny looked at it for a few seconds more before tossing it into the water. It sank too quickly for the gathering gulls. "Too much of it—bile—and you do bad things. If you don't have the right balance of four special fluids in you, well, you go pretty well crazy."

This was something I hadn't heard before. What were the other fluids? Was pee one of the fluids, and was it a good one or bad one? What about juice? Milk? Kool-Aid? The questions never reached my lips, since Danny went straight on to pull out some smaller bits and to provide quick explanations. "Kidney. Cleans your blood. Spleen. Gives your body anti-bodies to kill the anti-anti-bodies." These too were tossed into the water with a parting comment: "Thank you very much for being an organ donor."

I listened like there might be a test on the information.

As Danny's hand waded carefully through more of the gucky bucket, I asked what I thought was a deep question: "Do fish drink water?"

Danny stopped fingering through the guts for a second. "Good question, Watson." He switched to an English accent I really liked.

"What fish eat has water, so they don't really drink it on its own. They happen to eat and drink at the same time. Very convenient."

Eating and drinking at the same time. Mom hated it when I washed down my food with what I was drinking. I'll tell her about what fish do next time she bugs me.

My stunted thoughts wandered as Danny searched through the bucket of guts—then: "Voila: the heart of a salmon."

It was a deep black-red, and about the size of a chicken yolk. He cradled it in his hand and then passed it on to me. *The dark heart of a salmon.*

"So," said Danny, "shall we—we shall—toss it into the depths and bring contestant number one to the surface?"

My cue to pass him the heart. He carefully slipped it onto a triple hook, inserting the three barbs through the heart. Now Danny used a cowboy accent: "Dinner time, get along, little doggies. Come and get it!"

Danny somehow knew we would hook something. He only hoped it wouldn't be a small rockfish or lingcod—boring and really ugly. Big, bloating eyes. But we knew, or I should say Danny knew, that there were dogfish all over the place beneath the deeper parts of the docks, scavengers that they were.

The salmon heart quickly faded into the deep green as Danny spooled out from the handline. With a small weight, it took about ten seconds to hit bottom. Danny let me hold the line while he laid out instruments for this afternoon's work, which at this point was uncertain. He gave his hands a quick wash in the salt chuck to get off the fish slime.

"Take in a bit of the slack, matey," he asked, now with a sea captain's swarthy accent. He sounded a little like the crazy old guy in the movie who went nuts after chasing the white whale around the seven seas—Dick something?

"Aye-aye," I answered, feeling good about the prospects of a fine catch, although there was the passing fear that we might hook that monstrous white whale and get yanked out to sea. I pulled in some of the loose line onto the spool until I could feel that I was directly in touch with the lead.

We sat, waiting in the warm, slightly breezy air. It was definitely a little cooler down here by the water. We knew the fish were down there on the murky, mucky bottom, while here above the sun shone down on us two, glittering off the water, its rays barely penetrating the deep. We waited. I made some comment about how cool Danny's dad's boat was. Danny just gazed into the water to the line that disappeared into the depths.

The scavenging seagulls above—some circling, some perched—kept their gaze on the bucket of innards they were determined to swipe. "Sea buzzards," Danny called them. "If I had a cross-bow," he said, "I'd shoot one."

We waited. Danny recited a little poem as I passed him the line:

Seagull seagull in the sky,
Dropped some whitewash in my eye.
I'm a big boy, I don't cry,
I'm sure glad that cows don't fly.

I thought for a moment. "Or elephants," I added.

Danny gave me a look and raised an eyebrow just a bit, which was approval enough.

We waited a few more moments. Then Danny said, quietly, standing up: "I think—I think—we've got something. Yessiree, we got us a taker. Contestant number one."

The line slowly moved out a bit. Danny let it run a little, and then when it felt firm, he set the hook with a good jerk. "Definitely a dogger. No fight. No panic. Not until it gets to the surface. All hands on deck!" That meant me.

He slowly pulled up the line. I was excited, though Danny's steady, sensible presence encouraged my cool. But it was impossible not to ask if he thought it was a big one.

"Not bad," he said. "I'm going to yank it onto the wharf. You step on its tail. I'll step on its head. Watch out for the spikes."

What? How? Step on its tail? Spikes? I worried that I might not be able to do it.

Danny continued to pull steadily for a minute or so, and we looked over the edge of the wharf attempting to get a glimpse of what we had caught. "In just a second...just a second...here it comes..."

We could see it, dark and long, and the perfect shape of a mini-shark.

"Thar she blows!" said Danny as the fish broke the surface with a flap of its tail. It allowed itself to be pulled to the surface with barely a struggle. Now it gave a few shakes and tried to run to the bottom. Danny let it go down, since he wanted to tire it out before pulling. "It's not going down without a fight, eh Starbuck."

Starbuck? Was that my name for this fishy moment?

Well, whatever moment it was, Danny liked it. "It has no idea what's going on, except that it's fighting for its life even with no thoughts about life. It can't think about such things, but its body says keep going, return to the deep." Then Danny looked at me. "And so does ours, right mate?" Danny turned to intently upon the tight line. "Vengeance I shall have."

I nodded and did something like a salute.

After the dogfish settled, Danny began again to pull it up, this time a little faster. Now when it tried to run, Danny held on. In a few seconds the fish slowed, or maybe it was tired or in shock. Then, at once, Danny yanked it up onto the wharf. The dogfish flapped around, all two feet of it. Danny managed to step, quickly but casually, and not so gently, on its head.

"The tail. Step on the tail." I had almost forgotten, but after a few floundering stomps I had it. I had it!

The fish wasn't moving much. Keeping one foot on its head, Danny quickly sorted out the messy line on the wharf.

"Touch it," he said. "Feel the skin. The skin of a heart-eating shark. No scales, not like a regular fish. See—see the spikes. Just in front of the fins. They can give a mighty sting."

I did see the spikes, but I still managed to touch the fish. Cold. Harder than I thought. Smooth when stroked from head to tail, and rough on the way back up. Like sandpaper. Its upper surface gray, its belly white. A few brown slimy bits dotted the fish. Danny flicked one off. "Parasites," Danny said. "Mind you," he added, "what isn't?"

I wasn't sure about this, but any thought was broken by Danny's eye, which gestured toward the nails. I passed him a pretty big one. He already had the hammer in his hand. Quickly, precisely, he drove a nail through the back of the fish, a few inches behind and to the left of its head. A bit of blood pooled around the entrance. The dogger barely flinched. "Another." The second nail was driven in on the right side, parallel to the first nail. Again, the fish barely reacted.

Danny explained that the fish is almost all flesh, with few nerves. "This fish, crucified, might live with these two metal nails from our bright surface world, a world that for them is hell. Heaven for them is the dark deep. Opposite for us. Or so we think."

We looked at the dogger for a few moments before Danny continued: "So, back to the deep sea with you—forgiven for your sins, honored for your suffering. And avoid magnets."

With this I lifted my foot and stepped back. The tail flapped a little. Danny took his foot off its head, but the fish didn't move.

"Oops," said Danny. "Seems it's nailed to the wharf."

Danny used the claw of the hammer to pull the nails to free the fish from the planks, and, aided by a little kick from Danny, and with two nails stuck in its flesh, it flopped back into the water, and was gone. Just like that. Danny was already looking for another salmon heart in the bucket of guts.

I was hardly calm, but wanted to be. This was more than just something new. It happened quickly and without obvious reason. There was no question of "Why?" It seemed to be pure fascination via brutal experiment, but it was not clear.

Danny had different plans for the second dogger, which we caught about ten minutes later. Danny planned to snip off one fin. "It will swim around in circles—forever. Like a cork screw, really." He then proceeded, carefully, as we pinned it to the wharf, to cut off the right-side front fins with the wire cutters.

"Will they grow back?" I asked.

"No," he answered. "Not like starfish."

Danny stood back and looked at his work.

"Let it go," he said, and at once we both pushed it over the edge with our feet. When the fish hit the water, it was stunned for a second or two, and then swam toward the depths, making, it seemed, a wide circle to the left.

The next dogger hauled onto the wharf surprised us. After we stepped on it, a little tail came out of the shark's butthole. Danny leaned forward, looking very carefully at what he saw. "Yes," he said, almost to himself. Taking out his trusty knife, he made a small slit up the shark's belly, and he mumbled something more, a word, I didn't get. Whatever it was, it was meant for him only.

Four or five tiny sharks spilled out onto the wharf along with some soupy fluid. Except for little sacs attached to their bellies, they were perfect copies of adult sharks. In fact, they were so perfect they didn't seem real. Danny looked at them, thinking. "Not the way anything should be born," he said. "No, not at all. Cut out of a mother's gut."

He continued to inspect the tiny sharks. "Hail cesarean," he said. I had no idea what this meant.

Danny, now a bit more agitated, and without acting like he was a cowboy or a sea captain, explained that sharks didn't lay eggs. He said that the little sacs attached to the babies are their food until they are ready to find their own food. "It's yolk, like the stuff you eat in chicken eggs. Salmon are different. They lay eggs and then die right away, and so they die where they were born," he added. "Seems about right."

I looked at the little creatures. They were wonderful and strange.

"This brood was close to being born—but not quite," Danny noted.

They flipped around a bit. "Not being in a dark, wet world. Forced into the wrong one—before they were ready. Unborn." Danny looked at them carefully again. "Probably not going to be great for them."

"Yeah," I said. "Too bad, huh." My words did not quite measure up to Danny's commentary, but I wanted to sound like I understood.

Danny tossed all but one back into the salt chuck. "The law: big fish eat little fish—unless the little fish can outsmart the big fish. But that would take some careful planning."

And, as if by magic, the mini-sharks slowly swam or wiggled into the depths. They seemed to know exactly what to do. Danny commented: "People are helpless when born. We'd die, taken from our mothers and just left. Slowly."

We also tossed in the mother shark, and she too, with a slit in her belly, made her way down, though she was sluggish when she hit the water.

One newborn dogfish remained on the wharf. "A leftover," Danny said. He looked at me. "And what do you do with leftovers?"

I thought. "Wrap them up?"

"Okay, what else?"

"Put them in the fridge?"

"Good." Danny almost smiled. "And later?"

"You eat them—later?"

"Right!"

What? We weren't going to eat it—now or later—were we? I didn't have to wait long to find out.

Danny baited the hook with the little shark. I was fascinated, but at the same time it was unsettling. A baby on a hook. Danny took a few breaths, which made me think this must have meant something more. "We'll see if Nature is ruthless, cruel by"—and here he paused to find one of his more special phrases—"cruel by opportunity." His words landed beyond me. "Remember: like I said, big fish eat little fish, but what about if the little fish is the same kind of the big fish—maybe even your father?"

Danny turned and looked at me. "Do you think your parents would pluck you out, yank you out, and make you into a pot roast? Or, maybe worse, turn you out into the world, damaged?"

In truth, I didn't know what to think. Bait was bait, and food was food. Maybe a codfish would go after the little thing, but not another dogfish. Picturing my parents roasting me up for dinner didn't come easily.

For Danny, however, proof came quickly: it didn't take more than couple of minutes before we pulled up a good size dogger, maybe the biggest one of the day. Around three feet, maybe. In its mouth was the dead, mutilated body of that newborn dogfish.

Danny took a good look before pronouncing, "It's a dogger-eat-dogger world." I took the statement literally.

We stood there together on this fish, and I couldn't tell what Danny was feeling, but again he seemed to darken a little. It might have been contempt for the fish. Maybe relief. As if he somehow expected as much from the way of the world. He abruptly yanked—more like tore—the hook out of the fish's mouth with the wire cutter.

He commented that the fish could be the father of the young one it just ate. "Not just cannibalism. Worse. Father eating son." Danny looked down on the helpless, sprawling fish. "Supposed to be the other way around, you know."

He thought for a few moments, and then glanced toward the *Miss E. D. Pussy*. Time to go?

His words were baffling, but my practice was not to question what he said. Danny carried the Word of Truth more than any possible tone of speculation.

Danny asked me to pass him a nail, which he drove, in one harsh blow, through the head of the dogfish. The force lodged the nail into the dock, and the fish flapped for a moment or two before remaining motionless. It must have been dead. Danny pried it from the dock and kicked the limp body back into the water. It sank, slowly, turning, into the impenetrable water.

"Maybe now—now—its children will have a chance to feed off

him." Danny stood over the end of the wharf. He had begun to sweat quite a bit.

We began to slowly pack up the fishing stuff. Danny threw the remaining fish guts into the water. The lingering gulls tore down from the pylons and the sky, grabbing and gobbling and squabbling over what they could.

After walking around the docks to kill some time and look at other boats, we made our way back to the *Miss E. D. Pussy*, where Mr. Caine was organizing things on the deck. We returned the fishing equipment and other stuff to its rightful place on the boat. Mr. Caine turned to us: "Catch anything?"

I wanted to tell him all about what we caught and what we did with it, but Danny mumbled, "Dogfish."

"I'll be finished in not too long. Then we'll get going."

Mr. Caine called out to Rebecca, who was in the cabin somewhere: "We'll be going in a bit, sweetie. Start packing up your things."

"Okay, daddy," she called back.

I sought out Rebecca to see what she was up to. Her doll stuff was spread out on the higher bunk, and she was slowly gathering it up. It looked like she had organized Barbie's considerable collection of clothing according to color. Her mom must have been making some outfits for Barbie.

Danny, meanwhile, purposefully checked around and beneath the lower bunk, like he knew what he was looking for. For a moment he stopped, and then pulled out a magazine or two. I walked over to him to see what they were, but he abruptly put them up his shirt and turned away. At that moment, Mr. Caine walked in, looking around to probably check everything was in place.

"Ready?" he asked. "Becca, got everything?"

"Almost ready, daddy," answered Rebecca, packing up the last bits of her Barbie stuff.

We left Fisherman's Wharf.

Danny said nothing on the drive back. He stared out the window, with the hidden magazines tight to his chest. Mr. Caine, noticing new houses and a few stores being built in many places along the way, made a thinking-to-himself comment about hardly being able to recognize the place anymore. "What's the world coming to?" he said. "Where are these people coming from?"

We had no idea about either of these questions.

When we arrived at the Caine's home and after parking at the end of their driveway, Danny was out of the car before the rest of us. He went out behind the garage. I said good-bye to Rebecca and Mr. Caine, and then started up their driveway toward my house, but stopped just in time to call out to Mr. Caine with my almost-forgotten appreciation: "Thanks for having me!"

"Tell your parents about the smoked salmon."

"I will," I promised, and continued up their driveway as they disappeared into their house.

I smelled my hands: fish guts. Yech. Maybe, like Danny, I would try washing my hands with toothpaste sometime. I broke off into a run—as always, like the wind, over the ditch and across the road. *Up, up, and away...*

. . .

After dinner I couldn't find Danny, though I looked in the usual places. I ran into Mr. Caine, who was outside cleaning out their car before he went back down to the boat again, which he did every night after supper. He told me that Danny was out in a hurry right after dinner. No idea where. As for Rebecca, she was helping her mom with some sewing. No doubt making more Barbie clothes, I thought.

§

Daniel Caine was a large, pasty child. He had little or no likeness to either of his parents—none of his father's hardy ruddiness, and nothing of his mother's complexion.

Even very young, Daniel was in some ways odd and inward. He was unusually focused, and satisfied to play with one toy at a time for long stretches—until, as it often happened, he had taken it apart or used it in extreme. Not by or with ruthless force, but in the spirit of discovering how it was put together in the first place, and to explore its various limits.

By the time he was in early elementary school, Danny showed without showing off an intelligence that did not so much shine as intimidate. His parents let him have his ways, not that they could stop or change him. Or understand him. They knew enough to surround him with comic books, encyclopedias, and reading material of any and all sorts, though they did little reading themselves. He liked small tools rather than large playthings. They could only watch this strange boy of theirs, bring him up the best way they knew how, yet note a disposition that kept him somehow distant. He'd grow out of it, they thought.

This distancing and Danny's edge was, though, in some ways, also a marker for how Mr. and Mrs. Caine were with each other. It wasn't just that Danny somehow may have picked up on his mother's loss and regret involving her pregnancy with him, or to the growing tensions between husband and wife that surfaced in unanticipated, brewing ways. Danny seemed to know, or at least came to know, something else—something more that gave him an inward edge that, at a certain moment, may have began to work in more outward ways.

BOOBS, BUMS, AND A QUIET WORD

The next day there were some family things—running around here and there, visiting some relatives in town, picking up some groceries. Boring, boring, boring.

After dinner, I headed out to see if Danny or Rebecca might be around. They weren't out back or behind the garage. I went to the back door and was about to knock when I heard some loud talking from inside. For a moment or two I just stood there, frozen, listening. Mr. and Mrs. Caine. But it was more than talking: Mrs. Caine was now yelling at someone—Mr. Caine, it seemed. Then a sound like something broke. And a lower voice, Mr. Caine's probably. The truth was, I really didn't want to know what was going on or what was said. I thought I could hear Rebecca in the background somewhere, but maybe not.

I finally got my body to move, and I took off down the driveway toward home. I didn't want them to know I'd been there. Needed: other thoughts to fill my head for the evening. Maybe Dad would play catch with me. Maybe watch something on TV, but there weren't any cartoons on after dinner. Maybe *Have Gun Will Travel*, or *Lassie*. It was hard thinking about these possibilities after listening to the commotion at the Caines'. It was less confusion than guilt—guilt about things heard that weren't supposed to be heard. Things best kept in families.

When I got to the front of the Caine property and slowed down, I caught what I thought was a glimpse of Danny off to the right of the top of his driveway. He was in a little area made up of some tall grass over grassy knolls as well as a little scrub bush. This land was considered part of the Caines' few acres, though technically it was probably common land between properties going up Eastfield Road. No one would probably have noticed Danny being there, except that I knew this as one of the places where we could observe goings-on without being noticed very easily. If we crouched low or got down on our stomachs, no one was able to see us. We kids sometimes crawled around there and played war or guns or hide'n'seek. We called this spot Spy Nosy Place.

My impulse was to go home, but if Danny was up to something interesting, then maybe I could tune in or, better yet, take part. As I made my way through the tall, dry grass toward him, I thought I could still hear his parents yelling, but more likely it was an echo from my imagination.

Danny was sitting on the ground, looking at a couple of magazines. He didn't greet me, and I didn't say anything more than "hi." I knew that if he were really into something, he wouldn't want to be disturbed. His actions usually indicated when it was okay to talk to him or ask questions. I plunked myself down beside him and looked at what he was looking at.

It wasn't unusual to catch Danny off reading on his own. He was often surrounded by copies of *National Geographic*, *Popular Science*, or comic books, his favorite being the series called *Strange Worlds*. He didn't like my favorite comic-book character, Superman, all that much: "A do-gooder" was his comment; "a boy scout—now, Lex Luther: at least he's got ideas." Danny even read the Bible, and told us more than once that there were some important and scary stuff in it. But the magazines before him were not comic books—and nothing like the Bible at all.

Danny, intense and deliberate, breathed heavily through his nose. I took this as a sign not to disturb him, but, when I got a glimpse of what he was looking through, I had a simple question which ended up being more of an expression of uncertainty and astonishment than a desire for information: "Where'd you get—these?" I was now leaning over quite a bit.

"On his boat," which I took to mean his dad's fishing boat.

Then I remembered Danny stuffing a few magazines up his shirt when were down at wharf and in the cabin of the *Miss E. D.*

Pussy. We kids had heard about these "girlie" magazines from older kids. Talking about them brought on giggles tinged by mysterious naughtiness and the purely forbidden. At the moment, though, there did not seem to be anything funny.

There were three magazines. Danny for some reason passed one on to me, one that he seemed to have already gone through. He slowly went through the second one. Every now and then he pulled and opened a purple-pink envelope from between the pages and put it in front of himself in a neat pile. They looked like the kind of envelopes that fancy birthday cards came it, the kind your grandma might send.

There, right in front of me, secrets from the adult world: pages and pages of smiling pretty ladies with their bums and boobs sticking right out at me. I turned the pages much more quickly than Danny. I had no idea what I was looking for or why I was hurrying. I didn't want to put the magazine down or make any kind of stupid remark, mainly because Danny's intentions were not clear, though clearly intense. Maybe research in the name of Science. Maybe he was going to pull together some astonishing truths out of all this pink skin, red lips, and glowing, flowing hair. But right now, I wanted to be doing what Danny was doing, which was looking at and turning pages. I still couldn't stop myself from turning the pages much faster than him. One after the other: a wink here, a pout there; pools, baths, beaches, beds, couches, ferns, feathers, cars. Bare-naked ladies everywhere. There was a tingle in my tummy, though it could have been the fear that comes out of forbidden knowledge.

None of the pictures showed the hairy-beard-down-below bit, but they came about as close as possible. Something was always just barely covering the most private of the private parts—a hand or a pillow or a sheet or a plant. That made me look even more carefully for what was not to be seen.

I finished the first magazine quickly, just as Danny passed me the second one. Danny now went through the third, and, once more, every now and then, he would find another envelope, pull it out, look at it for a second, and then put it on the growing pile. All the envelopes were the same purple-pink. No stamps. Every envelope had the same two words written on them in fancy printing. I couldn't make out what writing said, even though Mom had taught me to read a bit. But it did say, "To" someone, and I think it said "Joseph," but the letters were curly. It made some sense that the letters would be to Danny's father, since the magazines were from his boat.

I raced through the second magazine. More of the same: lots of writing at the beginning of the magazine, but toward the middle all photographs. These ladies were, again, pretty and, well, pretty well naked, except again for the barely covered hairy bit. For some reason, they all stuck their butts out in the same kind of way, and often they were leaning and stretching and reclining, as if were tired and ready for a nap. One or two had their eyes closed, but they definitely weren't sleeping, unless they could sleep standing up or bending over. Some were lighting candles. Some held fruit and looked like they were about to eat it. Lots of them seemed to be taking off or putting on their stockings. In a way, they slowly began to remind me of Rebecca's doll. Yes, that was it! Many of them were real, life-size Barbies! Was this on purpose?

When I had whipped through the second magazine, I put it down and waited for the third, which Danny was still going through. He found a few more envelopes to add to the pile, and then passed it on to me.

As I hurried through the last magazine, Danny began to pull letters out of the envelopes, unfold them, and put them in a separate second pile. The color of the letters matched the envelopes. When all the envelopes were empty, he began to read the letters. There seemed to be bits of dried flowers folded in with some of them. The letters somehow looked old, but maybe it was the fragile, fancy paper.

This third magazine was not at all like the other two. It wasn't just because the paper was thinner and not so glossy, and it really wasn't because there was hardly any writing at the beginning. It was the pictures themselves: they showed everything. Everything! Not just a bit of the hairy beard bit, but the ladies were bending over and sitting and leaning back. This definitely held me still for a few seconds, and as I went through the magazine, turning these thin, cheap pages, I found myself not really wanting to look at all. It was fascinating and gross and scary at the same time. Some of the ladies seemed to be biting or licking their own fingers or something. In some pictures you couldn't even see the faces of the ladies, only their clammy parts. I began to turn the pages more quickly, skipping some out.

While for some reason I was beginning to feel guiltily self-conscious, I noticed that though Danny had begun by reading the letters slowly and carefully, the more he read, the quicker he read, so that after about five or six letters of the dozen or more that he had, he began to go through them about as quickly as I had been going through the magazine. Both of us, it seemed, wanted to get to the end of our assignments. Too much information, maybe.

The more Danny read, the more agitated he became, which was not like him. He scratched off a couple of his pimples, and he just left them with a small drop of pus and blood surfacing on his face.

I put down the third magazine on top of the other two, just about as Danny put down the last letter. Danny looked at the three piles: the magazines, the envelopes, the opened letters. The handwriting was the same on the letters as on the envelopes. Danny continued to gaze at the three piles. He looked toward his house and along the driveway beside it.

What now?

Danny then said one word, a version of word I knew about, but which I hadn't heard too much. It was one of the no-no words, and we'd gathered that it was somehow the worst of all words. Danny didn't ever use it. He didn't need to. But now he said it, quietly, and I couldn't tell how he meant it: "Fucking—"

We sat there, we two. Was this a cue for me to go? Danny glanced from the three piles to his house and back again. He was silent in a way that made me, too, suddenly as inward as he seemed. He finally rendered a quiet, broken sentence that petered out: "I knew, all along—all along he..."

Danny abruptly gathered up the envelopes, letters, and magazines and stuffed them into a paper bag. A few dried flowers from the letters fell to the ground, almost like feathers. Danny said nothing, so I followed, and we set off down his driveway and past their car, a hundred and fifty feet or more away. We passed close to his house and made our way behind the garage to where we often burned and buried and dismembered things. Charcoaled remnants of the baseball mitt Danny's dad had given him were there on the ground. The rest had been completely burned. Danny walked over the charcoaled leather bits.

Danny sat on the ground, emptied the bag, and began to tear out pages from one of the magazines. Never without a lighter, he lit each page on fire, one after the other. Female body parts and smiles and pouts were licked and eaten by the flames and reduced to leafy, delicate ashes, with some floating lazily away and up through the trees, disappearing. Danny showed little expression, but his face, sweaty, slightly reflected the flames, which came and went with each new hurried blaze.

Eventually all three magazines were gone. Nothing left but a few thin, flakey ashes. Danny now took the letters and, after quickly reading a bit more of them, one-by-one he gave them over to the same flaming fate. Finally, the addressed envelopes, which I could now see and sound out what they said, were burned, one after the other. *To Joseph, For Joseph, My Joseph...*

Danny kept one empty envelope aside, and looked at it carefully. "Ashes to ashes," he said. I had heard that somewhere before.

I had to ask, though I had no idea if it mattered: "Who the letters from?"

Danny didn't answer right away. He was here but somewhere else. In a while he answered: "Someone—when he goes away fishing, on his boat." This didn't seem like much, and it didn't seem like I was supposed to ask any more. "Not the first ones, either," he added quietly.

Danny looked at his watch, and at once he said, "Let's go."

We retraced our steps out past the garage and back toward Danny's house. As we passed by Mr. Caine's car, Danny looked around, took the one envelope he had not burned, and put it beneath the windshield wiper on the driver's side, the same place they put parking tickets. Then we went back, walking quickly, to Spy Nosy Place where we had gone through the magazines. We crouched behind a grassy knoll. We could see down the driveway to the car.

I had to ask. "What we waiting for?"

"Nothing," he muttered. "Everything."

Danny scratched at his face a bit, but he said nothing. Watching, waiting. Likely picking up on my confusion, Danny finally said: "He'll be going down to the boat in a bit. Every night, as usual. Keep down."

In a few minutes we heard the back door to Danny's house close, and we could make out Mr. Caine come around to the driver's side of the car. He opened the door, got into the car, and then got back out. He took the envelope from under the wiper blade and stood there looking at it, like he was frozen. Then he just looked around. He crumpled the envelope and shoved it into his pocket. He got in the car again, wound down the window, started the engine, and backed down the long driveway, faster, it seemed, than usual. When he passed close to us, we ducked down, just in case. And then he was gone.

We stood up.

Danny spoke as he looked down the road in the direction his dad had gone. "Maybe tomorrow."

"Yeah," I said. "See ya tomorrow."

Later that night I watched *Father Knows Best* with my family. Jim, the father in the show, brainstorms and decides to let his kids work out their own problems without helping them. Of course this doesn't work. It all ends in a funny little disaster. Nothing really bad ever happened to that family, even, but especially, when the father didn't know best. Then, with my brother's prodding, we watched his favorite show, *Wagon Train*, though Mom didn't like it. "Too much violence," she (as usual) noted. "It's not good for children to watch too much violence." She was sort of right: some bad guys blew up a bank, and everyone went flying. For a moment, and for some reason, I wondered if Danny was watching, and if he liked the explosion. He did, after all, often hope for the bad guys.

That night it took a while to fall asleep. My room seemed darker than usual. And it was hot, even with the window open. I tried to ponder whether ants slept and dreamt, but I couldn't stop thinking about the way Danny had said the f-word, and about the burning magazines and letters, and all those naked body ashes floating up, up, drifting through the trees, into...

§

Almost by accident, but also with some lurking intuition, Mr. Joseph Caine figured it out, and it became a reckoning.

He did his math—he counted, double counted, triple counted. If Danny came more or less on time—being "full-term," as he heard nurses say—he would have been conceived approximately forty-one or forty-two weeks before the day he was born. Mr. Caine checked, and when he did, something at first burned in him. Danny would have been conceived somewhere right in the middle of when Mr. Caine was on one of his longest fishing trips he'd ever taken—seven weeks away. He looked at an old calendar that was still on his boat. He kept them all as a record of his past fishing trips. He always crossed off days he was away, and he made little notes about where he was fishing.

Joseph Caine had, then, doubts. And some doubts, especially those colored by personal confusion, penetrate enough so that they can become certainties. And now there was the logic of time. Dan could not be his child. Not his child! And while this explained some things and confirmed others, it was a wounding realization oddly tinged by relief. Though he cared for Dan in his own awkward way, he never felt any larger connection. Dan never felt like the kind of kid who would be—could be—his. Dan was not a robust, ball-chasing kid who let his body and physical energy do the talking. Mr. Caine had accepted this, but now he believed he understood it. Now he seemed to have found an explanation.

Questions remained: Should he tell his wife what he knew? Ask her about it—the truth in dates? Should he stay or go? How was he now to be with his wife?

But there was a stranger question that crept up on him: Was it possible that Dan knew the truth, or some version of it? Dan, he thought, sometimes had a dark, knowing look that took the place of words. He seemed to sometimes have a look that knew too much. A look that spoke with both a faint warning and with muted knowledge, a look that seemed to say, "You will see. I know. You will see."

THE MAP

The next day, after yet more grocery shopping with Mom, and then hanging around the house until after lunch, I headed over to the Caine's in order to see if Rebecca wanted to play under the sprinkler that Dad had set up in our backyard.

Danny sat cross-legged under the large cedar tree in his front yard. He was drawing or writing, and so I stopped to talk to him, in case there was something I should see. I asked what he was doing.

Danny didn't look up. "Making a map."

"Of what?"

"Of around here. This part of Eastfield."

He knew that I would wonder why.

"Maps help you carry out action. Makes you do what you need to do, in case you forget, you panic, or just freeze."

"Oh," I said, as if I knew what he meant. "What will this map make you do?"

Danny worked away with his pencil, making and re-making lines, erasing, sharpening the point, and looking around as if to see if he was getting something right. I couldn't see it.

"Here," he said, putting the map in front of me.

It was neat looking, with a few long rectangles and some bushy, round, simple shapes that looked like little trees. Some little writing with arrows. Danny started pointing stuff out by moving his finger around the map: "If you were looking down from up in the sky, this would be the view. See. These two long lines beside each other are Eastfield Road. This line—the ditch beside it. These are the properties along the road. Old Man Bryer's house, up here. This tiny circle is his big compost pile in the back of his property. This is your house. Here is where the blackbird nests are, this is where you live. This wobbly line is The Trail, leaving from your back yard, here. And this is the Ant Nest. The pond. Where Mrs. Raskolnikov lives. The fields where we get the snakes and grasshoppers. This is the garage over there, right in my yard, by my house. Here, the driveway. And—right here—is where we are sitting."

After a bit of brainwork, I could kind of get my bearings around what he had done. It was all, in a way, magical, since, yes, we were right there, almost in the center of the map. My eyed moved around and into Danny fine-lined world. It was great. We were on a map! Like we were part of some plan or story. I got it!

I had to ask: "What's that 'X' there, with like a circle around it? Buried treasure?" My extensive knowledge of pirate lore showed.

Danny did not answer right away. "No, not treasure," he clarified, but pausing again. "Part of a—the plan," he said, and added, with some strange flat, tone: "'X' marks—marks the spot."

The spot? Of what? For what? It felt like I was not to ask any follow-up question.

Danny took the map back and continued to work away. I was aware enough to know that my time was up, and so I moved on to find Rebecca in order to get her to my place and to the sprinkler.

Rebecca did come over, and under the afternoon sun we had a great time chasing each other around in the cooling spray. We only stopped when my Dad came by.

"We have to be careful with the water," he said. "Hasn't rained for a while. Water might get short. The end of summer looks like it's going to be hotter than ever. Five more minutes, then call it quits, okay?"

In a few minutes we finished up and wrapped ourselves in towels, shivering just a bit, but not for long. I wanted to tell Rebecca that we were on or in a map—Danny's map of our neighborhood—but I wasn't sure if I could explain it well enough, so I let it go.

And Dad was right about the rest of the summer. Hotter than ever.

§

Mrs. Joseph Caine was uneven and inward for most of the year following Danny's birth. As a vague distraction, the new child brought a certain kind of gain into their lives, but because of what the ordeal represented, it may have been more like a loss. Mrs. Caine was tired and silently distracted, and although she tended well enough to the needs of her new, chubby infant, she felt little interest in much else, including her husband.

Joseph felt this shift between them, but could do little. He did not understand what it was like for her to live with her new, infertile body— with its extra weight, with its stretch marks and the scar, and with an indifference that did not have words so easy to express. Joseph did come to know, however, that she had badly wanted to have a little girl, and not being able to have one counted as a large emptiness that both lurched forward into yet weighted down her life, and therefore into his. What could he do? He felt some vague responsibility for how things had worked out, but less vaguely he felt helplessness crossed over with resentment. Oddly, it was not betrayal that he felt. But he did think: What was this child doing in his family?

This made him think of his other life.

Joseph Caine had met Emily Cooday on the wharf up on that desolate fishing village, and that is when it began. It was his other life that he didn't quite consider another life. Over the next few years, he would see Emily whenever it was possible. Joseph grew to feel Emily's presence—her smell, her taste, her touch, her eyes—haunt him when he was away, and often longed for her. She could make him forget about the unspoken secrets that lurked in all directions.

Emily and Joseph were together infrequently enough that their passions were renewed with intensity each time they were together. What she had with Joseph could keep her looking forward. He would, she thought, always return. She was the reason for him to come. She was his harbor. She continued to surprise herself in the way her needs could take his and slow them down to reach a mysterious place that filled them both. It was something, and even that much—or that little—was good.

In the morning they would talk a little over the instant coffee she made on his propane stove. He would often remain on the lower bunk. Sparse talk about the sea, about the fishing season, the crabs—about when he might be back. He liked to look at ocean maps of the Pacific Northwest—tiny islands even without names. She, though, would sometimes try to talk a little about the books she was reading. He didn't say much back, though at first he wondered: Why? Why read these things? Despite that, he came to discover *some vague enjoyment in the stories that she tried to re-tell in her own way, like the story of a little girl, unloved by her parents, who die, and she then lives with relatives only to discover a secret garden as well as a crippled cousin she somehow heals. What a strange story, he thought.*

Then Joseph would be gone, though he would take some memory of these tales with him. Emily, in turn, would wander back to the decaying cedar shack of her grandparents, who knew something of what kept Emily out for those nights. Without a word, they understood a certain kind of longing. They knew much about loss, but little about hope. They worried that Emily harbored something she might not ever have. Or worse yet.

As for Emily's mother, she, randomly coming and going, took little notice of her daughter becoming a young woman, of her reading, of her longings, of her love. Emily's mother remained crippled by the loss of her husband, and from the bottom of many whiskey bottles she numbly witnessed her own passing away from whoever she might have become.

LUCKY, THE UNLUCKY WANDERING DOG

Many people who lived in and around Eastfield owned a dog, and sometimes two. We used to have one, but she had to be "put to sleep" when I was about four years old. I can't remember why; he must have been tired, it seems. Years later we got a cat. Or, I should say, a cat—a stray cat we called Gumboot—got us. But that's another story, with its own unforeseen fall from innocence.

Dogs were dogs, but our youthful collective experience—channeled, of course, through Danny's observations—allowed categorization of the Eastfield dogs as one of four types:

Type 1: Roped Dogs. Tied up outside most of the day. Barked lots and sometimes, annoyingly, into the night, as the cats and raccoons defiantly cruised along the fences and trespassed over lawns and fields. Their owners didn't seem to care much for them, which made us wonder why they had a dog in the first place. You didn't wander into their territory. Danny said that it made a dog crazy to be tied up.

Type 2: Trained Dogs. Stayed close to their owners. Happy on car rides, with their noses stuck out of the car windows like it was the best day of their lives. Clean, well behaved, walked easily on a leash, and always came when their owners called them.

Type 3: Little House Dogs. Yappy as hell. Mrs. Bryer up the street had one: a white, whiskered mop with underbite—you could hear and see it barking its brains out behind the Bryer's living room window every time we noisy kids passed by. This tiny cur was called Zu-zu or Su-su, or something weird like that. Mrs. Bryer carried it close to her, like a baby. She even baby-talked to it. Maybe that was because she didn't have kids of her own.

Type 4: Wandering Dogs. They randomly showed up at school or in back yards, chasing cars, getting into garbage cans, stealing our baseballs when we weren't looking. Wherever Wandering Dogs showed up, they were usually shooed away. When they weren't peeing or crapping all over the place, they were smelling something, including themselves and other dogs. We sometimes saw them humping, and we snickered, though we didn't know why.

The Wandering Dog that showed up most frequently around our part of Eastfield was a large, brownish mutt named Lucky. He lived about a quarter of mile down the road, in one of the smaller properties down past Mrs. Raskolnikov. He was owned by an old, retired logger and his wife. Their kids had grown up and left home a long time ago. They had three cars in their front yard, none of which seemed to run. Lucky was left to go where his nose led him.

Despite always being stinky and sometimes annoying, Lucky could be great fun. You could chase him around and try to tackle him. You could throw sticks or balls into the bush for him to fetch, though he seldom brought anything back, or when he did, he wouldn't give it up. Lucky didn't even mind if you sprayed him with a garden hose—he'd snap wildly at the water stream, and we'd all have a good laugh. Whatever you did, Lucky liked it. He seemed to enjoy the noise and activity of us kids, as if he was running with a pack of his doggy peers. No matter how many times Lucky heard the order— "Go home, Lucky! Shoo, go home boy!"—it was almost impossible to get him to leave. He simply liked hanging around if he managed to find us doing anything outside.

On occasion, Lucky would come with Danny, Rebecca, and me on our expeditions. You would think that Danny wouldn't like a dog like Lucky, especially because he was so random and unruly, but Danny—and Danny only—had a way of talking and signaling to Lucky so that he wasn't a nuisance at all. Danny could make the dog come, sit, lie down, and even roll over; and, as a reward, he would give Lucky's chest a vigorous scratching that would make Lucky's back leg start thumping. Danny would stop scratching; Lucky would stop thumping. Danny seemed to turn Lucky on and off, and we would always laugh.

Danny liked Lucky quite a bit, and he talked to him in a kind of un-Danny way: "That's a good boy, that's a really, really good boy. You'll do as you're told, won't you. Hmm, won't you, you, you."

When Lucky didn't do as he was told, Danny would go straight up to him, put his hands on Lucky's shoulders, and force him down to the ground. This always did the trick, and Lucky usually got it right next time. We were always amazed at this, since Lucky never did anything anybody else told him to do. As with most things, Danny had his way because he knew the way.

Earlier in the summer, when we walked along the upper reaches of The Trail one aimless, hot afternoon, Danny explained Lucky and dogs.

"Dogs don't quite know that people are not dogs, and that dogs are not people. When you do stuff with dogs, they think you are like them." That sort made sense. Lucky, meanwhile, circled around Danny, sniffing the ground every now and then, waiting (kind of like us) for some direction. Lucky's happy, shaking, wagging body seemed to say, *What are we doing next? Which way are we going? What should I do?*

Danny continued. "When dogs live together in the wild, like wolves or coyotes, they have a kind of order. From top to bottom. The smart and strong at top, and the weak at the bottom. Just like everything else in nature. People, too. Like with kings and presidents and generals and sergeants and stuff, and like principals and vice-principals—then teachers, and janitors." All true enough.

"So," he said, stopping to look at Lucky, "if dogs think that people are dogs, part of the pack, then dogs have to figure out who is the top dog, or else they'll think they are. They need the order. Gotta let them know you are the stronger one. Then you can train them to do almost anything if you do. Watch."

Danny sharply called Lucky over to him—"Lucky! Here! Here, boy!"—and Lucky immediately went to Danny's feet. "Down, down!" Lucky lay down.

Danny told us what was happening: "Lucky thinks I am the Alfa Dog, the Number One Dog. Leader of the Pack."

I had an immediate question: "But, like, how does he know this? When I call Lucky, he just runs by and barks, like he's making fun of me."

Danny had the immediate answer: "You haven't let him know you're stronger than him." He gave Lucky a couple of scratches on his belly.

"But I'm not really—am I? I mean, stronger than him."

"You're not. Lucky could probably rip you apart if he went nuts.

You've seen his teeth. He's basically a neighborhood wolf looking for a pack."

I looked at Lucky, and he seemed to grin my way, showing his tongue and a few of those big front teeth.

"Me too," Danny added. "He could hurt me too. But he won't. He's stronger. I'm smarter. What I did, when I met him the first few times, when he was smaller, younger, I gave him a growl and a strong pushing-down to the ground right away—held him there, then made him stay beside me, not moving, which meant—to him—this: 'Danny Boy is the Alfa Dog. Do as he says. All will be fine. He will make me feel good. If I don't, I will get clobbered.' Since then, I've taught him a few things. He does what I say most of the time. Trouble is, Lucky is just not really attached to anything or any place. He's a really good dog. Smarter than you think. Just dumb owners and dumb people. That's the problem. As usual, as always."

Lucky continued to wiggle, almost helplessly, at Danny's feet. Danny bent over to Lucky, took hold of his nose and jaw with one hand, and looked Lucky straight in the eye. Lucky ceased to wiggle. Danny said, very firmly, with a low, slow, but serious voice, "Lucky, you are a good dog. Yes. A. Very. Good. Dog."

We were impressed. Danny added a weird point: "'Dog' spelled backwards: G-O-D. Which spells 'God.' How's that?" I wasn't sure.

So, among other things that summer, Danny was also Alfa Dog. Leader of the Pack. Top Dog. And in a way, we, like Lucky, were under his control. If he told us to "sit," we'd sit; "lie down," and we'd lie down; "stay," and we'd stay. Danny didn't have to grab us by the nose or growl at us, but we too were at his feet, and his words held us captive and captivated. Danny's leash for us was invisible but very real.

Danny's last word on the subject: "Out there—out there where the wild dogs really run, sometimes the Alpha Dog gets taken out by some dog who wants its place, and then that new one takes its place. That's the Law of the Jungle, which is also Nature's law. Because you're Alpha Dog today, doesn't mean your place won't get taken tomorrow."

It seemed, somehow, that Danny had something in mind about this change in power and order.

We looked at Lucky and we looked at Danny, attempting, as usual, to make more sense of it all. Danny quickly added, "And it might not be pretty."

. . .

A day or two after I was with Danny in his front yard when he was making his map, the three of us were up to our usually rounds up The Trail. Lucky happened to be with us, trailing along and enthusiastically watching our every move. Danny had been teaching Lucky how to "heel," so that the dog would stay right beside him. Lucky was doing it real well, and Danny was quietly proud. Lucky, too, seemed pleased.

Up until this point, our outing was interesting but not exciting. We had just found a recently-deserted cat robin's nest with parts of the eggs still there, and then we gathered a big, semi-hard glob of sap from a wild cherry tree to see if it would burn (it didn't quite, though it did kind of crackle and pop), but there wasn't much else to keep us going.

We sauntered back to my backyard, and at this point Danny gave Lucky his marching orders: "Lucky. Go home. Now. Time to go home, boy!"

Danny pointed down the road as he said this. Lucky looked at Danny for a second, came up to him, wagged his tailed in a low way, and then trotted off, but not before looking back to make sure he was really supposed to leave. Danny confirmed by pointing and saying: "Go home, Lucky! Down the road! Go, boy!" And quickly Lucky was off, though hardly in a straight line.

Lucky probably needed food or water, anyway. Danny began looking at the wood siding of our house, mentioning that if we looked carefully enough, we could probably find a place where hornets had moved in without us even knowing. "They like the walls of houses," he said. "If we can find the little place they go in, we can plug the hole and they'll be trapped inside, in a coffin cask for hundreds. Or, we can just trap them for day, and see what happens."

Within what seemed like a minute or so of starting our search for a hornet entrance, we heard the sudden, loud hissing of air brakes from one the large trucks that every now and then brought gravel to the fields way down behind Danny's property. At the same time, we could hear large tires skid loudly before coming to a stop. Something was up.

Rebecca and I ran off to look down the road. Danny followed, though he walked. Down the way we saw that a gravel truck had come to a stop on the road. The driver had got out and was looking into the ditch, just about where we had started our last popsicle stick boat race.

"Lucky?" said Rebecca, looking at me. I shrugged. I hadn't thought of anything in particular except the novelty of the big truck sliding to a halt on our road, but Lucky sometimes did chase and bark at cars and trucks.

We ran to where the truck driver was down on one knee, looking into the ditch. "Must have got caught by the rear tires, or something," said the driver when he saw us arrive. He was wearing gray overalls and had the kind of sunglasses on which you could see your own reflection.

It was Lucky. Lucky! He was spread out against the side of the ditch, with his back paws just touching the water. Although at first he didn't look too wrecked up, you could begin to see that his body was limp and twisted. He was breathing quickly. You could also begin to see a bit of blood trickling out of his mouth. Lucky's eyes were open and looking around. Except for his exaggerated breathing, he wasn't moving. We didn't know what to do.

The truck driver looked at us and asked, "Is he—your dog?"

"No," we answered. "He's from down the road."

The man was relieved, and he looked back into the ditch. "That's lucky, I suppose."

"Yeah," I said. I looked at the driver. "You know his name?"

"Huh?"

"The dog—Lucky."

The man was a confused. "The dog—lucky?"

Now I was confused.

Danny arrived. He immediately saw what had happened. Rebecca was upset, and she asked him, "Is he going to die, Danny? Is he?"

Danny went down into the ditch, which surprised the truck driver, who said, "Be careful, there."

Danny looked closely at Lucky. The poor dog turned his head just so slightly toward Danny. Danny bent over and whispered, touching him on the head, "It's okay, boy. It's okay, Lucky."

Mr. Caine must have also heard the large truck and its quick, grinding stop, and he joined us at the side of the ditch. The truck driver said to him, "The dog just ran out from nowhere, barking. Got caught under the truck, sorry to say."

Mr. Caine said, "Not your fault. Darn fool dog. Runs all over the place, barking at cars and everything. Chasing 'round after about anything. Nuisance, he is. Wonder it hasn't been hit before. Should have been tied up."

"Anything I can do?" asked the driver.

"I'll take care of it," Mr. Caine said.

The driver turned away and got up into his truck. His airbrakes hissed, and the truckload of gravel rumbled away down Eastfield Road.

"Dan," said Mr. Caine, "get out—get out of the ditch. Nothing you can do for the dog now. It's as good as dead. Darn fool dog."

Danny didn't move. Rebecca started to sob a little, softly. "Can't you help him, Daddy? Take him to the animal doctor or someone?"

"Not worth it. One of you needs to go down and tell the owners what's happened. Dog needs to be put out of its misery. Sooner the better."

There was a moment of silence as this sunk in, then Rebecca questioned and pleaded, "You mean—you have—you have to—to kill him? No!"

Mr. Caine didn't answer right away. "It's—good as dead, 'Becca. Suffering, it is. You kids go away. Nothing more here to see."

Lucky's helpless eyes still followed us. This did not look good. It made me feel not very well, and somehow scared.

Danny put his words out, straight to his dad: "Lucky is not a 'darn fool' dog. He's just a wandering dog. A good dog. A smart dog. You—you don't know anything about—about anything."

Mr. Caine turned hard to Danny. Watching Danny and his father face off over the poor, dying Lucky froze the moment in a long, disturbing silence. Would Mr. Caine answer Danny? Mr. Caine knew that Danny's turf was words. *You don't know anything* held in the air above the ditch of bleeding, panting, dying dog.

Mr. Caine, though, took it to scoff at the challenge from his son: "And you do know, huh."

"I do," Danny immediately fired back. "More—more than you think."

Mr. Caine looked hard at Danny, and Danny added, "Way more."

What would happen now?

Danny said he would take him to Mrs. Raskolnikov. "She'd know what do. She's—"

Mr. Caine had had enough. "Dan! Quiet! That old hag is a crackpot. Stay away from her. I've told you."

Mr. Caine said this coldly and with authority masked in anger. "Dan. Take Rebecca away. Now! Do it now! Take your sister away."

This should have been the end of it, but Danny stood up once more: "You—you don't know anything about Mrs. Raskolnikov. Nothing about Lucky. Nothing. They don't mean anything to you, because you don't care to notice. You only care about, like your stupid boat, and that—and she's not—"

Danny stopped his words to weigh the moment.

Mr. Caine, standing on the edge of the ditch, fixed a brewing look upon Danny, waiting for him, but also wary. Danny added nothing more.

"Dan. Please take Rebecca way. Do it. Now."

Danny got out of the ditch and took Rebecca by the hand.

Rebecca sobbed as Danny took her away, "Daddy—you can't!"

Danny left with Rebecca, and I stood there beside Mr. Caine, staring down into the ditch at the poor Lucky.

Mr. Caine turned to me: "And you—you go run and tell the owners. Tell them their dog got run over by a truck. That it's bad, that I'll take care of it."

I was confused. "Do I say to them—tell them it's dead? Lucky's dead? Hit by a truck?"

Mr. Caine looked at me then back to the ditch: "Yes. Tell them. Tell 'em to call me if they want."

For a second or two I didn't move, trying to figure out what would happen next. Mr. Caine started to get down into the ditch. He turned and looked at me. "Go down, boy. Now. Tell 'em."

I started running, and I didn't turn around.

Down in the ditch, with a little water running down it, taking some of Lucky's blood away, Mr. Caine must have put poor Lucky "out of his misery," yet it was hard, maybe impossible, to imagine. There was no picture to hold on to, but maybe that was a good thing.

By the time I came back up Eastfield Road, after telling the confused owners of Lucky what had happened, everything, and everyone, was gone. The ditch was empty. Except for the skid marks left by the gravel truck, it was as if nothing happened on that dog day afternoon.

§

Mr. Joseph Caine met Emily Cooday not long after Daniel Gilbert Caine was born. They came together as the unpredictable openings in the fishing seasons permitted. Joseph found himself tied up at the wharf in Emily's tiny village as his main stopover to and from the fishing grounds he had selected, even if the take of salmon in the waters closest to her village might not have been as good as other places. He could only say to himself that her village was just as good as anywhere else, but this was a lie to what drew him.

A few years after the coming-together of Joseph and Emily, the unexpected came between them.

The opening of the fishing season had been held back for some reason, and Joseph had not been with Emily for a few months. This was their longest period apart since their first moments together. His body had a great deal to let go.

As he tied up his boat, Joseph stirred with some version of love that filled him with expectation. Emily would, he knew, come down—beautiful, light, passionately aware beyond her years—and on his boat they would hold and press each other until the ocean's bounty and the livelihood it provided once more pulled him away. They would talk. Their words would be simple and strangely innocent, and maybe she would share a story she had read. Joseph had come to enjoy these moments of Emily retelling stories, since all thoughts, commitments, and problems from beyond fell away. And for Emily, these retellings were moments of soft control over her man.

Joseph saw Emily coming from a distance, and remembered that he had a gift for her—some beauty lotion he saw in a drugstore window that he thought she might like. He returned to the boat's cabin to find it. As she stepped onto his boat, he came out and nodded to her as they moved together. But she stopped a little short.

"My Joseph," she said. "My heart."

Just being this close to Emily made Joseph warm, though before he moved to sweep her into the cabin where they would fall into each other, he gave her the lotion.

"For you," he said, eager that she would be pleased, but awkward because he had no idea if she might like it. "It's a body cream, or lotion or something," he said. "I—I thought you might..."

Emily's gaze was not fully upon him. But she took the gift, and thanked him. He noted her look seemed somewhere else, but he was not the kind of person to question the meaning of such things, so he said nothing.

They passed into the cabin and he turned to hold her. She held back, and he was confused. She sat down on the edge of the lower bunk. She toyed with the bottle. It was pinkish glass with a gold cap, which she undid. She smelled it.

"Like it?" he asked.

"Yes," she answered. "Strawberries. Strawberries and straw, it smells like." She tried a smile. "Thank you," she again said.

Those few words were withdrawn, just like her gaze. Joseph could only watch her. Look for some sign of what it meant. She continued to toy with the bottle. She smelled it again before putting the golden cap back on.

Their first moments of togetherness after periods of separation were often of few words. Their bodies were the first place where they would speak to each other.

He looked at her. She stood up. She put the bottle on the bunk, and she began to pull her bulky sweater over her head. He watched, and once more he felt his body begin to stir.

She stood there in front of him, naked from the waist up. He looked, and looked more. It was unmistakable. What had moved within him fell away. There she stood, still. And though he knew what it meant, he did not know what it might bring.

NO MAN'S LAND

The next day, around mid-morning: Rebecca and I were busy looking around in the open fields that backed on to the Caine's property. Old grass lands. Maybe old farmland. Sometimes we found interesting items, like a broken tool or bits of junk that people dumped there. Our parents would have been horrified.

The day before, under Mr. Caine's orders, I went down to tell Lucky's owners about the accident—the poor dog's death in a ditch. An old lady came to the door, followed some seconds later by her wobbly husband. I told them what happened. They didn't seem all that surprised or upset. The lady, who asked me to speak up a couple of times, was more concerned with knowing who exactly my parents were and where I lived. When she finally figured out what I was talking about, she said, "He was an old dog, he was."

And that was that. There would be, it seemed, no more said about what happened. Things would go on. A wandering dog named Lucky died in a ditch on a hot summer day, run over by a big truck.

Danny, too, this morning, after he joined us, said nothing. Maybe he got over it. But, more likely, not. He didn't often let things go. As he sometimes said, "You have to square the circle." I didn't quite get what that meant; I could only think you'd need an eraser to do that.

These fields were only partially fenced in, and most of the area was covered with tall, drying grasses. We didn't know who owned these fields. As far as we were concerned, it was all open territory. Danny called it No Man's Land. We had never been kicked out of this area, and even though the fields bordered on to a number of properties, the space was unused, except for dumping soil—and, more lately, gravel brought by the big trucks, like the one that hit Lucky. We had heard our parents discuss this area, and the conversation had something to do with plans to put some new houses or duplexes there. Some parents thought this development was good, making their own property worth more. Others said it would ruin the very reason they lived in Eastfield. But for us, what did we care? For the moment, it remained ours.

Today, though, it had become an expedition for Danny as we moved around and through these fields. Grasshoppers and garter snakes were the quarry. Danny, as usual, sent Rebecca and me to do the legwork. I was trying to catch a cracker-jack—a large type of grasshopper that made a loud cetcha-catcha-cetcha noise when it took off on its flights. A couple of them had been disturbed as we moved about. They were quick, and their jump-flights took them some distance. They were also camouflaged. Unfortunately, we didn't have nets, only a couple of jars, so we had to make do with catching regular grasshoppers. Almost every step disturbed a couple. It was just a matter of time before one happened to land at your foot, or even on your leg. You just had to grab it and stick it in the jar.

Within half an hour we had a couple of dozen grasshoppers, which we took over to Danny, who was waiting in the shade in one corner of the field. He was carving something, but he quickly put it down to inspect our jarred specimens. "Now see if you can get a snake, or maybe two."

Before Danny let us get away, he delivered some words, about where garter snakes were likely to be found, where the ground was a little rockier. We knew that they hid away at night, and that they came out with the sun as things warmed up. Mid-morning was a perfect time to catch them. As Danny told us, "They come out into the open to do their job, which is to take care of the garden, to keep the balance in seeking bugs and slugs that can harm plants."

Danny asked us to imagine what it would be like to have a cold, slow body, and then to have that body warmed and then made quick. Danny said that you'd have two lives. One in the dark and in the cold, under rocks, and the other in the light, in the open and in warmth. "Snakes don't have a great reputation," Danny added. "They get blamed for bringing death and bad things into the world in a sneaky, snakey way. Eden, it was called."

Danny looked beyond us for a few seconds, which meant he hadn't finished. "And grasshoppers don't have a good reputation either."

He then told the story of something from long ago when a mean, bragging king—some Egyptian guy—was punished with lots of things because he kept certain people as slaves. "Plagues," Danny said. "He got plagues set on him."

The story was great. As Danny told it, one punishment was that zillions of grasshoppers were sent to eat all of the food that belonged to the bad Egyptian king and his people. The skies, Danny described, turned black with the swarm. "The noise scared the begeezus out of the people. Millions of tiny helicopters with teeth coming down from the sky. They ate everything that grew. The king was stupid. Didn't do what he was supposed to do, which was to let those poor slave people go back home, where they could live on milk and honey. God ordered it and organized the plagues. The bad guys got other punishments, too, like having frogs and lice and horrid dust and stuff come down on them, with thunder and hail and darkness filling the sky. He even made them get boils all over their bodies—giant pimples that made their bodies scream with pain. Then their water was turned into thick, sickly blood, which killed the fish, too, and caused a big stink. Try drinking that water for a while."

I had heard something of this wonderous story elsewhere, but Danny told it better. He added his angle: God and Nature were the same thing. "So God is Nature. Nature, God. You otta know: God is not a forty-foot guy with a long beard, white sheets, and a big wooden stick that shoots out thunderbolts. He—he's the big balancing idea, when it works properly. Bad balance equals bad times, bad things. People say, 'Hell breaks loose.' Hell breaks loose sometimes to set up new balance. Punishments, too. New cocks to rule old chicken roosts."

Danny enjoyed what he was saying, and as he continued, his part seemed to grow.

"And so," Danny added dramatically, opening up his arms, "Go forth into the fields of Eastfield, and gather unto you the Works of Nature. Let my children go!"

Danny clearly had a little fun with this, though he also seemed a little scary, like he was in a movie or church or something. He turned away toward his own backyard and darkened: "But beware. The evil that lurks inside—there—when things get out of balance, when things fall apart, when things cannot hold. Blight. Catastrophe. Havoc. A hail of fire. And—and judgement day—when some will pay the price and some will make the price paid."

Danny could thrill with such words—*blight, catastrophe, havoc, hail of fire, judgement day*—even if their meanings pushed beyond our grasp, even if we knew that the drama was in part for us, his audience, his fold. But at this particular moment it wasn't clear what Danny meant, especially the way he said the last part—*the evil that lurks inside.* His tone stranded us—not fearfully, but enough to raise a goose bump or two, which wasn't easy on a hot summer morning. The idea of a big, bad event to come was not a cozy idea, either. We'd all heard about the mushrooming bomb.

We were about to go off and do Danny's bidding, but he had one more thing to add. "There were all those plagues, right. But then there was one more. This: that the firstborn child in the families of the bad people will suddenly die. That would be the oldest child in each family."

That sounded pretty bad. The oldest kid in each family suddenly dead, killed. Danny added a comment, "But don't worry, you two. You are both the second born. As for me—well, we'll just have to see, right?"

Danny—*the firstborn child.* Just a story, right?

Rebecca and I returned to the field of snakes, though we didn't bound back to the hunt with a spontaneous overflow of positive feelings. But if it was snakes Danny needed, then snakes we would get.

We moved slowly. Once snakes tuned into on your steps or movement, they'd be off like a slithering shot. Best if you could move them into open ground where there was little cover. The way to catch them was to step on the middle of their bodies as they tried to get away, then pick them up by their tails. We were fearless and anything but squeamish. We were used to such things. A garter snake was not much different than picking up a wiggling stick.

While conducting our snake-sweeping operation, we could just hear Rebecca's mom call out to us from their backyard. Though it seemed a bit early, it was apparently time to come for lunch. It sounded like she also called my name, which was a strange.

Rebecca's return call was a piercing "Okay, coming!", but for us it meant we had better hurry up and find a snake if we wanted to see Danny's action plan involving the grasshoppers. We considered first calls as a notice; second calls were the warning; the third was the real one, and we had to be careful.

A few sweeps through the grass rendered a snake with black grayish-brown markings and a thin, red stripe. I stepped on it firmly enough to stop its escape, but not enough to hurt it. Rebecca picked it up by the tail. It was maybe a foot and a half long, and continuously flicked its tongue as we carried it back to Danny, who gently took it from us and put it in a white cotton sack.

He asked if we knew what garter snakes and grasshoppers had in common.

Not knowing was okay, since ignorance and innocence often took us to wondrous words and demonstrations.

"When they're upset or afraid, they give out a bit of nasty brown stuff—snakes from their butts and grasshoppers from their mouths—snake poop and grasshopper puke."

We knew this from experience, but we hadn't put it together as something that they had in common. Danny picked up the jar of grasshoppers.

"Watch what happens when I give the jar a shake."

Danny shook the jar up and down a few times. You could hear the hard bodies of the grasshoppers hitting the lid, like drops of rain on a tin roof. The sides of the jars almost immediately started showing some brown, liquidy spots. We called this stuff "tobacco juice"—the grasshopper's last line of defense. It had a bad smell, and so when Danny opened the jar, he held it away from himself. A couple of grasshoppers jumped out. A few were stunned, and those he dumped out. One or two were stuck on the bottom of the jar, and more or less looked dead. "Science," said Danny, "has its ups and downs."

Danny took a Q-tip out of his pocket and mopped up as much of the grasshopper fluid as he could. He put down both the jar and the Q-tip, and picked up the snake sack.

"And now we have to take out some of the fluid that the snake poops out of its butt when it gets afraid, but we may have to be sorta rough."

At this moment, another call came across the field. This time it was Mr. Caine. "Lunch!" we could him yell out. "Get here! Now!"

Danny stopped what he was doing. We waited. There were a few patches of red around his neck—like a rash or something.

We didn't, or couldn't, really leave Danny, just like you didn't leave a classroom without your teacher's nod. We would all go back together, and then after lunch we would continue. Or so we hoped.

Danny suddenly sat down with his snake in the white sack. We weren't sure what to do.

"Sometimes," Danny said lowly, "you get freaks of nature, that go too far. They need that judgement day. Things that were not meant to be, things that—" He didn't finish.

Freaks was good topic. Monsters, mutants, zombies. But what about lunch? The call from Mr. Caine still rang in the air.

Danny looked around, though there was nothing to see. Just the sound of the dried, tall grasses crackling in the heat.

"There's a such thing as two-headed snake," he continued. "Nature makes freaks every now and then. A snake with two heads, two brains, but one body. The two-headed snake doesn't know it has two heads. It thinks it is two snakes. It fights with itself."

Danny looked around again, but once more toward his house, as if staring it down.

He continued: "The two-headed snake is against itself. If one head killed the other, the whole snake would die. But it—so it has to—has to keep fighting."

I asked Danny what it could do to stop fighting itself.

"Both sides, both heads, have to find the same thing—the same enemy—to fight against. Then it can be—with itself."

This was pretty neat and weird.

Danny gave us one more thought cradled within a question: "Can one body have or serve two masters? Both sides say, 'He who is not with me is against me'."

That didn't mean too much. "Maybe we'll might find one," I offered.

Danny sat, unmoved. He looked at his white bag with the snake. Did he have some answer? Did he know where a two-headed snake could be found? Did he have something in mind?

"Maybe we already have one."

There was no follow-up.

Danny sat there, and Rebecca and I, given Danny's silence and separation from the scene, took it as a sign to quickly head off for lunch, relieved we could get away before we got into a bit of trouble, but also disappointed that we didn't see what Danny was going to do with the snake, the snake juice, and the grasshopper tobacco juice. What did he mean? A snake with two heads? We already had one?

Rebecca and I made our way back. Mrs. Caine was around by the back door. She told me that my mom had gone down to do some shopping, and that I would be having an early lunch with them.

I'd had lunch a few times before at the Caine's place, and Rebecca had also had lunch at my house, usually when her mom had to step out for a while (she seemed to have lots of "beauty appointments"), or when Rebecca and I were in the middle of playing, and we didn't want to split up. It was sometimes more convenient for our moms to get away without having to gather up and organize their own kids. Usually we were happy not to go along. Today it meant I could probably continue to play with Rebecca and Danny right after lunch.

Mrs. Caine said to Rebecca, "Where's Dan? Did he hear us call?"

Rebecca said he would be here in a little while.

We went in and were told to wash up.

We sat down at the table at the same time as Mr. Caine came up from the basement. It looked like he hadn't shaved for a couple of days.

"Oh, we have a guest." Mr. Caine winked at me and I sort of smiled back. What could I say?

Mrs. Caine served us macaroni and cheese, which was fine. Some sliced white bread with butter was put out. Mr. Caine was also going to have some cold salmon with his meal, to which I said "no thank-you." Cold fish was not kid food. I could see by looking on the kitchen counter that we were going to have blackberries sprinkled with icing sugar, served in clear glass bowls. Kind of fancy, though blackberries were all over the place.

I watched what everyone was doing so that I knew the order of eating. Families have their own ways. Following Mr. Caine's example, I buttered some bread and put it beside my plate.

"Where's Dan?" Mr. Caine asked. He took a mouthful of macaroni, and, with some relief, I began to eat as well.

Mrs. Caine answered, "He'll be here in a second."

"He should be here, now."

Mrs. Caine returned to the table with some more bread. "He's probably just coming."

Silence. Everyone spooned in some macaroni.

Mr. Caine asked me, "So, so how's your mom and dad, there?" His actions in organizing his plate suggested he wasn't that interested in really knowing.

"They're okay, I guess."

"They liked the smoked salmon then?"

"Yeah, really liked it."

In truth, I couldn't even remember if they even had it yet. I thought I better say "thank you" on behalf of my parents, and so I did.

"You're welcome," Mrs. Caine smiled back at me. Rebecca kind of smiled at me, too. I turned to my macaroni. I felt I was doing pretty well with my p's-and-q's.

Mrs. Caine asked, "So what were you doing down in the fields?"

Rebecca answered, "Oh, looking for grasshoppers and snakes and things."

Mrs. Caine sort of shuddered a bit. "Well don't bring any of them back inside, please. I don't like snakes at all! What on earth would you want with snakes?"

There really wasn't an answer, and it really wasn't a question, so it was let go.

More silence as we ate. Mr. Caine then turned abruptly to Mrs. Caine. "You called Dan, too, right?"

"I said I did. He'll be coming."

Mrs. Caine said this sternly and fussed with her napkin. I kept looking at my food. I didn't want to see their faces while they talked to each other this way. I thought about how I heard them yelling not so many days ago.

"Well, he should be here. The food will get cold," Mr. Caine impatiently concluded. His fork clanged against a plate.

Mrs. Caine filled my glass with milk and I thanked her.

More silence and swallowing. The macaroni was good, but

at home we always had it with a vegetable or two. Mr. Caine now smothered his with ketchup. I looked over at Danny's plate, and then at Rebecca. Like her mom, she picked away at her food.

Mr. Caine suddenly stopped eating his lunch and put his fork down. "Let me call that boy. Lunch will be over. Every day he's getting more—" Mrs. Caine stopped him with a look.

Mr. Caine started to stand up. Mrs. Caine said, "Let me call him."

At that moment, Danny came in and sat down across from his dad without looking up.

More silence. I could feel Mrs. Caine watching Mr. Caine watch Danny, who started eating immediately. He grabbed a piece of bread, pulled it apart, and took a bite.

Mr. Caine started. "You should come when you're called. Lunch is probably cold. And wash up before eating."

Danny didn't look up from his plate. He just kept chewing.

"Daniel. You listening?" Danny chewed.

Mr. Caine's intensity began to spill over into unforeseen, uncomfortable territory, but for a few more moments a strained silence settled over the table.

He started again on Danny while he forked his food. "Heard you been down to that old foreign lady's place down the road. You keep away from her, you hear? She's no good, you hear." Mr. Caine chewed some more and added, "No good at all."

Danny put a piece of bread down on his plate and, without looking up, said plainly, "Her name is Anna. Anyway, what do you know—about—about her? Nothing. You don't."

"What I know, I know. Just look at her place. A mess. A communist, too, no doubt. Just keep away from her. I'm telling you."

I kept my eyes focused the plate of macaroni in front of me. It got worse. What was a "communist" person?

Danny could not wait, but he was strangely controlled, given what he was about to say: "Maybe it's you—you I should keep away from."

"Now Daniel," interrupted his mother, attempting to keep some peace. "You should not talk to your father like that."

Danny shot back immediately, but with the beginning of something that he immediately held back: "He's—"

Standing up with that one word hanging, Danny left the table, leaving the rest of us to finish our lunch. Just as he about to exit the room, he turned back. What would Danny do now? What would his father do?

What Danny did do was to take his unfinished plate of lunch from the table over to the sink, and to utter a "thanks, mom" before he left for the second time.

The sugar-coated blackberries were never served. Rebecca and I were excused after a few very long, silent minutes. I felt awkward, but also sorry for someone, but I was not sure who. As we left, I thought I could hear the voices of Mr. and Mrs. Caine rising. We eventually wandered over to my house, where we did something or other that might have involved this new play figure, Mr. Potato Head.

We never did find out what Danny was going to do, or did, with the brown stuff from the snake and grasshoppers. We never found out what he meant about the two-headed snake. *He who is not with me is against me.* We couldn't find him that afternoon. It was the last meal I ever had at the Caines' house.

§

Joseph Caine left Emily Cooday's village after getting some diesel fuel and a few supplies. That she now carried his baby unbalanced him, knocking him sideways, not forward.

Out there in the open of the ocean, with a good swell and his lines out, Joseph read the letter Emily gave him before she left his boat. She wrote about how she had talked to the priest who made rounds to her village, how she talked to him about her pregnancy. The priest, a Father Leo, suggested she put the child up for adoption. Better for the child, Father Leo said. And for her, too.

"Father Leo asked me if I knew the father of the child," Emily wrote in the letter. "I said I did not know him. I was not sure what to say. I hope you will forgive me. I pray God will forgive me."

Father Leo had seen this before with the natives. No restraint, these people, he thought. He told Emily he would make arrangements with the proper agencies, to have the baby taken away after it was born. She asked him if she would have any say in what happened to the child. Father Leo said that it was not usually the case that the mother would know where the child went. "Not good for either," he said, adding that such knowledge made for "certain complications" she wouldn't understand.

Emily ended the letter to Joseph, writing that she was going to give the child up, and once more asking for forgiveness.

Emily had thought of her drunken mother and aging grandparents while writing that particular letter, and she thought about how she herself was condemned to this no-where place and no-where life. Yes, she would give the child up. A better life, she thought. For the baby. Away from this place.

After leaving Joseph's boat that day, having shown him her swollen belly that held their child, Emily retreated to her bed in her small room up on the hill, with the few, little precious things Joseph had given her over the last few years; and there, with a small statue of Jesus overlooking all she owned, she pulled off her sweater and looked down at her belly. It was impossibly big, and would grow bigger still. A person inside her, swimming around in the dark, going nowhere, yet. She took the bottle of body lotion that Joseph gave her and rubbed it on her belly. Strawberries and straw, she thought. That's what she wanted her daughter to have. Strawberries and straw, in a place open to wide thoughts. She knew it was a girl. Her grandfather had said so after he had put his hand on her swelling stomach. He had the touch that knew.

IN HEAT

Early August slid over us like wax running down the side of a candle.

We found ourselves in the middle of what was already the hottest summer on record. Adults rattled on about the heat wave, as if noticing it for the first time. One would say "Sweltering," and the other would answer back, "A real scorcher." Nod: "Baking." Counter nod: "Sticky." Grimace: "Boiling." Wink: "Blistering." Nudge: "Another cooker." Smirk: "More like a furnace." Wells, water tables, reservoirs, water clarity, gallons per minute, and talk about bygone summers so hot that you could fry an egg on a sidewalk. And so it went. Yakety-yak. Small talk from the big people. Smokey the Bear's baritone message—"Only YOU can prevent forest fires"—interrupted TV cartoons much too often. Okay, we got it!

The unrelenting heat did have more interesting effects than all that talk. A few old cows mooed their last moos, lay down in the heat, and never got up. Some smaller ponds dried up, and, here and there, a few tiny fish in shallow pools baked in the drying mud. Yet in our brave, golden world we were protected and fortified by two magic potions, one for the outside and one for the inside: *Coppertone* and *Kool-Aid*. Our deliberate trials and toils nevertheless kept their pace and variety. Time held us captive, and we went about our business—or rather, often enough, we continued to go about Danny's business.

The heat, though, may have increasingly burdened Danny as the summer moved forward. He took more showers than usual, and it seemed like he had more pimples. There was more of an edge to his already sharp angle on things. Fewer crafty smiles and wise smirks. Less patience. Demonstrations were not always tied up with his usual eloquence and stories. Sometimes, when he was working over test tubes or magnifying glasses or specimens, sweat trickled down his temples. He didn't like it. His balance somehow seemed off, and it showed.

Some days after that lunch at the Caines', and under Danny's direction, we three found ourselves half-way up The Trail that begins my backyard. We went up as far as Stream Meadow, although it wasn't really much more than a small clearing about halfway up. There, years and years ago, my great-grandfather had planted some fruit trees, so it was also called the Old Orchard. A few old apple trees still survived, though they were knotted and misshapen.

At first we milled aimlessly around in the heat and long, brittle grass, but anything that Rebecca or I turned up for possible examination and explanation didn't interest Danny—not even the hollow, dried up, stiff carcass of a small mole, which, when we found one a few weeks earlier, Danny compared to an Egyptian mummy. Danny seemed more interested in keeping a nervous eye on The Trail.

When Danny was over at the most remote corner of the clearing, he called to us. He didn't seem to have found anything, nor did he produce anything from his pockets to suggest what he had in mind.

Danny sat crossed-legged at the base one of the old apple trees, though it gave little evidence of fruit, except a few small, wizened apples that seemed to barely hang on to the tree. They looked like shrunken, twisted faces. I thought of old Mrs. Raskolnikov, Danny's witch down the road.

Rebecca and I started to sit down, too, but Danny told us not to. Somewhere beyond was the waning, whining sound of a chainsaw— probably Old Man Bryer clearing more of his land.

Danny began, searching, it seemed, for his theme: "The Garden of Eden. Eating of the fruit. Eyes open to good and evil. The snake, the serpent."

In accordance with any direction he might set, we were ready to move our able minds and bodies, or to attend to a demonstration. No doubt Danny would come up with something for us to match or prove his words. His words were never bare.

He asked us if we knew the story at the beginning of the Bible. I, at least, wasn't sure. Sunday school had some vague merits, if only to provide fantastic and weird tales, of burning bushes that talked; like how Jonah was gulped by a whale; or how this strong guy with really long hair could kill a lion with his bare hands, but some sneak cut his hair while he was snoozing, and then he was weak. David and Goliath was my favorite: I liked the word "smote," but had never found quite the right moment to say it.

Danny began again. "Working from nothing, you know, God made everything. Light from darkness. Earth from emptiness. Water. Sky. Plants. The sun, the moon, the stars. All good. Then rested. He created a man from dust—Adam, you know. Put him a garden, Eden, and told him to eat well. He even gave him animals. Naked, he was— Adam, I mean, not God—no one knew exactly how God dressed, or even if he dressed. God told Adam to use whatever he needed there in the garden. But he should keep away from a certain tree that had fruit that helped you to—to see things."

Danny paused to look up at a couple of those shrunken apples in the branches above us.

Danny set out more of the story—Adam was lonely, so, while Adam was dreaming, God made a woman from one of Adam's ribs. "It doesn't say how God did this, but when Adam saw her—Eve—he said, 'Madam, I'm Adam.' And if you spell what he said backwards— M-A-D-A-M-I-M-A-D-A-M—it says the same thing."

What this meant was foggy, but maybe it was about beginnings or endings or something. I hadn't heard this part of the Bible before.

Danny added, "Eve was butt naked, too."

Danny explained: Adam and Eve weren't ashamed about having no clothes. "Adam and Eve weren't opposites—yet. Soon they would be. That's the beginning the trouble—of all trouble. And the beginning of interesting things, too."

Danny told us that Adam and Eve had everything they needed in Eden. "But," he added, "then a tricky, talking snake showed up. Told Eve about a tree in the middle of the garden, with fruit they weren't supposed to eat. But she did, because fruit is usually good for you, and then the snake explained nakedness and what they might do with their bodies. Eve told Adam, and then they figured they were naked and different—how they had opposite stuff. Plumbing differences." Danny almost smiled after saying this.

He continued: "After that, it didn't take them long to—you

know, to Do It. Wham, bam, thank you ma'am. Making babies. That's when men and women really became opposites. After that, clothes were invented to hide some of the naked parts. Fig leaves first, which don't cover much and don't last long."

I did remember something like that from Bible stories, and maybe even saw it in a picture, but I made the mistake of imagining my parents wearing leaves over their privates, and the picture was quickly dropped.

Danny kept on with his tale: "God thought it was okay to kill people who didn't believe in Him, which is different than his kid who came along later—Jesus, who was a humble sort, and okay with what anyone thought. That's why there are two different parts of the Bible—kinda like bad cop and good cop. Anyway, God was mad about Adam and Eve fooling around with the stuff that made them opposite—male and female—which started off good and evil. That had not been in the seven-day plan."

Danny paused before beginning again. "Okay. So. At first, after finishing the all work in six days and seeing all the stuff He had made, He said it was really good. Not sure if He said it in English, or who He even said it to. But now, with Eden, with the serpent and with Adam and Eve, maybe, not so good. Everyone makes mistakes."

Earlier summer sermons from Danny prepared us to have at least some idea of what this meant. The birds and the bees. We'd heard about "making babies" and that kind of stuff. Spermy seeds and all that. But there seemed to be a twisted repetition of these ideas, like he needed to go over them again, to make sure of something he was thinking or maybe planning or getting it right. What could that be?

Danny got to a part that worked him up.

"Then God—He threw them, Adam and Eve, out of Eden. Sent them to the fields in the east. *East field*—that sound familiar? Now, Eve was going to have a baby. They'd also have to take care of kids now, who became the punishment—punishment for parents for, you know—for Doing It. Having a baby is suffering for sin—that's what God thought it should be."

This was more confusing than unsettling. Hey, we were in Eastfield. Huh? Did all this take place here—around here? Maybe that was cool, or maybe not. Danny added something that now sounded more like a threat. "For some—for some more punishment than for others. Having kids."

"Adam and Eve," Danny continued, "they could not go back to Eden—ever—to what was a good place, that perfect place. It would be forever guarded by a twirling, flaming sword."

Now, that *was* cool. But I secretly bet that Superman could have smacked it down.

Danny's weighted breath betrayed a lack of confidence in our getting-it, but he continued on about the snake: "That's why snakes—serpents—don't have arms or legs. Why most people don't like snakes. They're blamed for starting the trouble. But human nature is the blame, as usual, as always. But more like God, too, for not getting it right. We like to think it is something else."

Danny was right. What *was* so bad about Adam and Eve, what they were doing? Just trying to get something to eat. Get kids and all that.

"And some," said Danny, even wary of his own words, "and some thought that the serpent, not Adam, was the father of the children. Serpent seed, it became known as."

Despite Danny's tale of Eden, we were beginning to get antsy, out there in the still heat, in the sparse shade of the old apple tree. Why this story of Adam and Eve? What was the demonstration going to be? The experiment? Why we were there.

Danny had a little more. "Nakedness: that's why we ended up having clothes as the opposite of being naked."

Diverting us, a small bird landed in the branches right above us before hurrying away. Danny left the moment open for us to think, or maybe for him to move to what our moment meant.

Danny's story returned. So yes, clothes. And the landscape surrounding us, complete with its failed and forgotten apple orchard, was not as perfect as Eden before Adam and Eve were sent to the east fields and away from the tree of life protected by the flaming sword. As far as us kids being a punishment to our parents, this made some sense, since once in a while we could tell our parents had just about enough of us. "Children—a curse, because men and women—got together. The serpent too, maybe. Why children sometimes—sometimes, rise up against those who made them."

Danny didn't seem much closer to what he wanted to say or do, but now he moved to something striking: "That first kid, that very, very first kid of all time—the first curse. Marked, he was, for life. Marked." That didn't sound great.

Danny added, "And you'd never guess his name, the first kid of Adam and Eve, the kid cursed first, the marked kid."

Were we supposed to guess?

Danny didn't wait: "Watch out for parents—the Bible says: 'Happy will be the one who bashes little ones against the stones'." Once more, this did not sound especially that great, especially if this had anything to do with one of Danny's demonstrations that might involve us.

With inarticulate tinges of guilt and fear and wonder, naked within our clothes, and placed within our imperfect garden in Eastfield within our imperfect world of opposites—there we were.

And Danny, beneath the old apple tree, quiet, hesitating, sweating. This was not like Danny. Hesitation was reserved for drama. This felt more like uncertainty. I knew from Sunday school that the flood and the ark bit came soon, and it too was a good story. All that rain, all those animals two-by-two on a boat. Must have been a really big boat. Was that next? Maybe Danny would get gather some pairs of bugs or something—float them on a boat. See how many he could get aboard.

At last Danny asked a question without looking at us: "What would you two be like if you took off your clothes, like in that first garden where we were meant to be?"

The question sought an answer, and so I offered: "Naked," I said, shrugging. "I guess."

I looked at Rebecca and she looked at me. There were a few pictures of us naked together when we were just toddlers, playing in one of those little wading pools.

What would you two be like?

Neither of us added anything more, which should have been the sign for Danny to jump into his own question—to show us something extraordinary. But, sitting there, only the heat crept up upon us. Danny's marked forehead seemed to be reddening. The heat, probably. He looked away, down The Trail.

Then, at once, he said, "We should find out. What happened in the Garden. Our own—try at it. Naked in the garden."

Any direction here was uncertain, but Rebecca piped in, like she had figured out where this was going: "Why? You know, daddy wouldn't like this."

In a flash, and with some quiet force, Danny replied, "Screw 'daddy.'" He looked at Rebecca for a moment, only to turn away, to look back down The Trail.

To witness Danny speak with sudden, detached anger to Rebecca—if only for a moment and for only two words, was unsettling: *Screw daddy*. For Danny, strong words—and how they were said—were connected to ideas and actions and proofs and sometimes jokes. And despite being an older brother, Danny was okay and patient with his little sister, who, as I sat there, I noticed how little she looked like her older brother. But this, his sharp tone, was not even how he spoke when an experiment went wrong, or when Nature wouldn't cooperate with his scientific theories and manipulations. There was something more—something more beneath his words but beyond the understanding of six-year-olds standing under a hot sun.

To hear him utter the name of his father was complicated— the way he said "daddy" that mocked Rebecca's warning. *Screw daddy* seemed to carry some dark, unknown promise. *Screw?* It was strange, too, because he seldom referred directly to his father, and what did that mean anyway? *Screw?* For Rebecca, it was daddy-this and daddy-that, not in a show-off way, but in a way that made it clear she was, always and forever, Daddy's Little Girl—his little girl. These things were suddenly cloudy on this clearest of days. But it was something to think about: Was Danny daddy's little boy? Why didn't that seem quite right?

Danny calmed us with a breath that hinted of resigned apology. "Just take your clothes off," he said. "It's just—just a part of the story, to act. Like a Christmas play, only here in this old orchard, not some barn with sheep and three wise guys and gifts and all that stuff."

Because we trusted Danny, or maybe because we feared him a little for what seemed his full knowledge of Good and Evil he had just preached, we began to take off our clothes.

Danny had often used us in his experiments, but never before had he used us as an experiment. We were witnesses, accomplices, assistants. Never specimens. Never actors.

In a few moments we were down to our undies. Rebecca's were

white with small berries and fruit. Mine were white with a red and yellow Superman 'S' logo splashed all over the place.

Danny looked at us. "Undies as well. You think Adam and Eve wore underwear?"

I thought for a second. Danny had seen my weenie dozens of times as we peed all over the place. No big deal. And, being Rebecca's brother, he certainly must have seen her peach place. So, with vague trust, mine came off as I pulled a face, just to ward off any possible embarrassment. Rebecca looked at me—up and down a bit—and then pulled hers off as well, maybe so that I wouldn't look so stupid being naked on my own.

And we two stood there, waiting. Butt naked as ol' Adam and Eve in the Garden of Eden, before being moved to the fields, east of Eden. No curse in sight, thankfully. No lurking serpent either, I hoped.

Rebecca began not to like this very much at all, so after a few moments she said, "So now what? This is stupid, not right, you know."

Once more, such a comment was not often put to Danny, whose purposes were usually quick and pointed.

He let it go. He began, at first uncertain: "When Adam and Eve were first together, they were like you. Didn't know much. Couldn't do much about anything—like 'Doing It,' you know. Male and female weren't opposites yet. They got into trouble only when they figured out nakedness, and good and evil—and what happened because of nakedness."

Yeah. But so? Rebecca and I were different. The sex sperm thing, which seemed to be what Danny had in mind, was vague and gross. Wasn't all this for parents in their bedrooms, teenagers in cars, and humping dogs in the schoolyard? Danny didn't want us to, like, Do It, did he? We couldn't, could we?

Danny read the uncertainty: "You two are too young for that kind of knowledge. You're innocent, like Adam and Eve were before badness came along. If God created all things, he must have created the serpent, too."

Did Danny just want to see us naked standing out there beside each other? It was quickly beginning to feel fuzzy. I covered myself up without trying to look like I was covering up. I thought of the fig leaf. Hurry, I thought.

He gathered himself. "Tasting the forbidden fruit—what got those two into all the trouble. What it said. Just like that: opposites made. Eve gave her fruit to Adam, for him to taste. The serpent directed. The serpent. And when Adam tasted Eve—well, that's when all Hell broke loose. The rest is history. The Fall and all that. The curse. The cursed child then came."

Danny looked down at his hands and turned them to look at his palms. They were very white, as if somehow they had been hidden from the sun for the whole summer. How could they have stayed so white? And his face, so red. My thoughts ended with Danny saying, "Eating fruit."

I glanced at the few old apples on the tree stretched out above Danny. Eat one of those wizened apples? Was that it? Danny's point had become as blinding as the sun. He was sweating even more now.

"The Bible says that the fruit Adam tasted just didn't come from Eve. It was Eve."

Adam ate her? This made no sense.

Danny now spoke more quickly, since we knew this had to end quickly. "That was the fruit. The part different from his part. Tasting her. The beginning of things going wrong. Like children. Like parents sacrificing their children. Like the very first murder. Of Abel. Abel, murdered by— Like children turning on their parents. Like death. Like balance. Things falling apart." Danny was getting worked up and, it seemed, mixed up, which was not at all like Danny.

Trying hard to stay with the moment, I asked, "So what should we do?" Everything shimmered, reflecting the ever-reaching sun as it rose above us.

Danny looked at me with firmness. "Taste the fruit. Rebecca's fruit. Taste her there. Tell her the taste, out here in the garden. While you are still—before it's too late."

Late? For what?

Things seemed to fade, and then returned as Rebecca and I awkwardly began to focus on each other. We turned. What could happen? In the old garden under the apple tree, and in the moment and for a moment, we were together in its heated arms, moving together without, it seemed, moving at all. What was she down there? I knelt. And then I quickly tasted her, my eyes closed for that split second.

When I looked up at her, and she down at me, I said, "Summer straw. That's the taste like down here. Like straw. Maybe, strawberries."

I stood up. And now?

Danny had got up and begun to make his way down The Trail, without any signal for us to follow him. As he turned away, he stopped to say one last thing. "Flaming sword. Yeah. That's it. Oh, one more thing—that first kid ever to be cursed, his name—the first born and the first murderer and the first to be marked and cursed? His name: Cain."

Together, in the silent heat, and feeling some kind of loss, we quickly dressed and went back down The Trail. Danny was out of sight. We quietly agreed to see each other later, though usual enthusiasm was weakened from our scene in the Old Orchard, our Eden, which could have been nothing or everything. Who was to know?

As we separated, I wondered if we were any different now. Opposites made? Hell broken loose? Was there a curse? On who? Danny? He was the "marked" one? What did that mean?

But then the questions and the wonder shifted in the way childhood attention can so easily jump from one thing to the next: the hope that Mom was making something good to eat. I was hungry.

§

When Joseph Caine pictured Emily Cooday standing there, naked to the waist, showing that she had their child inside of her, he fell into a fog. Yet the image of her was so clear, and he could do little to push it out of his head. Even pregnant—very pregnant—she was still something wonderful, he thought. Strangely, maybe even more so. But what could he do? Was it his problem?

At home, Joseph slid into his domestic routine—tending to the garden, diddling with repairs around the house, sometimes even trying to have some kind of brief conversation with young, strange Daniel, going down to his boat to prepare for the next trip every evening, same time. Yes, the boat: his retreat, his world, though now it was also a world with more than a piece of Emily Cooday in it—his thoughts could not resist wandering to Emily, holding their child within her. She would be giving birth in not too long. It was, he felt, best she give the child up, like she said in one of her many letters. Like the priest said. It would not do for a child–his child–to be brought up like her, trapped, stuck in that place. No father. Not much at all. A good home could be found, he thought. Would be found, he thought.

Lost in this helpless reflection that straddled vague hope, and while there in his living room chair, he looked to his wife. She was sewing something, which was one of her few pleasures. She made many of her own clothes, which also saved money. He watched her, and sorrow settled upon him. He felt her heaviness. The sadness that had sunk into her she when she found out she could not have any more children. The sadness that she would never have a daughter. The sadness in the unspoken uncertainty and tensions between them, of what each knew but could never say.

And then–and then a thought, impossible and unannounced...

A few weeks later, when his wife was out, he made a number of long-distance calls. After a few dead-ends, he managed to speak with a worker in the social services in Emily's district. Without revealing his part in things, he eventually found out what he needed to know, and some weeks later he got a letter that told him what he had to do. Would he now move forward in some way? Go the right way, do the right thing–but an impossible thing? Maybe it would somehow make things right, things better. For everyone.

AN INSTRUMENT OF INFINITE DESTRUCTION

My family left on a four-day camping vacation the next afternoon. The timing was good, since it further distanced that hot, strange afternoon in the Old Orchard.

Even though it was a short camping trip, it involved all the attendant paraphernalia, activities, and behaviors, including testing discussions over where to pitch the tent, gas station restrooms, and who wanted their photograph taken at places with signs in the background saying "National Park." Even with my brother bossing me around every now and then and calling me a pest, the trip was fun, especially getting the campfires going at night and roasting marshmallows. Cheeky chipmunks scrounging around the campsite. Whiskey jacks unafraid to steal from your plate. At night, the surrounding darkness was, though, always a little scary: the fire sent sparks into the night, while its hectic shadows enticed the weird shapes of the trees and stumps to lurch forward into our camp. Brother Simon's attempts to unnerve me with ghost stories about campers being spooked out of their skins didn't help, though he did (and still can) tell a good tale, with the annoying habit of seeming to know everything.

My parents were probably more relieved than we kids were when we returned and pulled into our driveway. It was nice to get home. We all had things to attend to immediately:

Dad's line: "The garden needs watering."

Mom's line: "I hope the milkman remembered not to leave any milk."

Simon's line: "I'll unpack later."

My line: "I'll be over at Rebecca's!"

Within seconds of getting out of the car I was off and down the driveway, over the ditch, seeking out Rebecca or maybe Danny, or both. I went around and knocked at the back door. I wanted to tell them about the dead bear we saw in the park, as well as how one of those chipmunks made its way into our tent, and then how it bit my brother's thumb when he tried to grab it. Mrs. Caine told me that Rebecca was over at her girlfriend's house for a sleepover, which was a brand new thing. Danny, she said, might be somewhere in their backyard. Mr. Caine was cleaning out their car at the end of their driveway.

It took a while, but I knew Danny's various places and found him out back behind his house sitting in the shade of a large maple. His chemistry set, which was a pretty good one, was set out on some planks supported by a couple of old red bricks. He had some beakers and bowls with powdery stuff in them.

He greeted me with the somewhat eccentric "How, Tonto," which may have made him the Lone Ranger, or Lone Stranger, as Danny was fond of calling the masked man. He asked about my trip: "Any road kill?"

I told him about the dead bear, and added, "And my brother got bit by a chipmunk."

"That's good."

"But I did get some porcupine quills. They're not super sharp. Well, a little sharp. They've got little hooks on them."

Danny almost looked impressed, and I said I would bring some over to him when I remember. He nodded and returned to his work.

I plunked myself down and sat quietly, knowing that when Danny worked with his chemicals, stillness and attention was called for. His set included two Bunsen burners, beakers and test tubes of all sizes, tongs, spoons, cups, rubber and glass tubes, some black rubber stoppers, and of course chemicals—lots and lots of chemicals. He was always adding to it with stuff from the local hobby shop. His chemistry set was definitely hands-off for us.

I asked what he was making.

Danny kept working, measuring and mixing. "Finishing something. Mixing a few things we may get a little bang out of."

Using a wooden spoon, he crushed together three kinds of powder, separately in their dishes, remeasuring every now and then.

He said he was going to combine them—"Carefully. Very carefully."

"What do you get when you mix them up, I mean together?"

He stopped his crushing and looked at me, closely, in the eye, which he didn't often do. "A bomb."

I gazed at the three dishes. "You mean, a bomb that goes, like, boom? Or the kind like a stink bomb?"

"The boom kind," he said.

"Oh," I said.

I watched and thought. "Bigger than a firecracker?"

"Yes, bigger."

"Oh," I said.

I watched and thought some more. "Much bigger?"

Danny thought: "We need to do some testing," he said. "Then you'll have your answer. Big boom or little boom."

"Oh," I said again.

This was really cool. I wanted details. This wasn't your regular chemistry set stunt, turning a clear fluid into a green fluid with a drop of some chemical. Or disappearing ink or fizzing powder. Or even stuff that would put insects to sleep or dissolve them into a gooey, acid mess. This was heavy duty. A bomb!

I had to ask. "How'd you make it?"

Danny looked around, like he was revealing a secret formula.

"Depends on how powerful you want your bomb to be. And how you mix it."

I nodded. Danny continued: "You need four things to make a bomb. First: take two spoonfuls of the charcoal. Two: a bit more than one spoonful of sulfur. You mix the two together by smushing them into each other."

He did this as he spoke, and he took his time to make sure they were mixed well.

"Third: take about seven spoonfuls of saltpeter. Put it together with the other stuff. Mix them together carefully, really well, with a wooden spoon—not with a metal one, because you don't want any sparks, otherwise *you* might be the object of total devastation. You might end up being not much more than pair of smoking running shoes with parts of you up dripping from the trees."

Danny mixed. I moved back, just a little.

After a few more minutes, he pronounced it was finished. A fine, silver-black powder was before us.

"There—one-hundred-percent gun powder, capable of making hell break loose. Take your breath away"—he looked at me once more—"permanently." I might have backed up even more. "Capable of—of rendering justice—judgement—upon pestilence. Getting balance back, maybe."

Despite not quite getting it, it sounded pretty good, if not vaguely dangerous.

I took note of the little pile of powder. But then I remembered something was missing, and so I asked: "What's the other thing? Number four. I think you only said three, maybe." I was a humble about asking this, since Danny didn't usually leave things out.

I was relieved when Danny said, "Glad you asked. Well," he said, "the fourth thing is—what we need, is something to blow up. But vee ave not ka-vite completed za task. Vee must putz it in za form uv za bomb."

I liked it when Danny did this voice, which was a little like a vampire or a mad scientist or something.

"Vee moost pack it, shhtuff it, very tightly, very tightly, into za small place, like zis test tube."

Danny produced a large test tube, and proceeded to spoon the gunpowder into it through a little red funnel, a bit at a time, frequently stopping to pack it tightly with a tiny cork plunger. When the test-tube was almost full, he added: "Und now vee need za fuse to lead into za powder to bring to it za shhpark to make za kaboom go kaboom."

For his stink bombs, Danny had made fuses by wetting narrow strips of newspaper and then rolling the newspaper strips up into what looked like crumply pieces of thick string. When the newspaper dried, it was a fuse. I knew there was something rolled into the newspaper, but until now I didn't know what. Gunpowder.

Danny explained how to make a different kind of fuse from a spark. Tape a piece of rough steel against a flintstone. When you hit a flintstone with a piece of steel you get a spark. He said you then surrounded this sparking device with lots of tightly packed gunpowder. Then you get the steel and flintstone to rub together or get forced together somehow—but, Danny made clear, you didn't want to be around when it happened. He said you could set off this kind of bomb by just dropping it, or, he said, thinking, "Say, by—by having something hit it or run over it to make the friction spark. Works just like a lighter."

He showed me his piece of steel and a flintstone. "They used to use a flintstone to fire old fashioned guns, you know—flintlocks. A little hammer makes a spark and then a boom, like a little cannon!"

How cool was that? Like carrying a cannon around with you.

Before he went further, Danny paused. He finally produced a black rubber stopper with a small hole in it, into which he threaded the fuse, which stuck out a couple of inches. He put the stopper into the test tube and forced it in until it was tightly lodged, tightening it by wrapping some black tape around the stopper and the tube.

He held it out for me—for us—to behold: "Ladies und gentleman: za kaboom-bomb!"

It looked quietly efficient, even though it was just an ordinary test tube filled with black powder. My imagination raced. Visions of mushroom clouds danced through my head. An instrument of infinite destruction. Danny passed it to me and let me hold it for a moment or two. It was cool, and scary, and heavier than I thought it would be.

"But like all za bombs," Danny added, "it needs to be tested, to zee vhatt kind of devastation it can make."

Danny was content to look at his bomb a little longer. He dropped his accent. "If you pack bit of metal around something like this, or place it beside gasoline, then you have something very—." Danny stopped here, clearly thinking about the right word—"you have something serious." I believed him.

This was really going to be neat. Danny packed up some of his things together from the chemistry set. I thought about the prospect of blowing a little something up.

"Now?" I asked.

"Now?"

"I mean, are you going to blow something up?"

Danny replied, "Why not?"

"What? Ka-boom what?"

Danny, it seemed, already had plans, so he might have been sort of teasing me. "That big, heavy pile of compost and stuff out behind Old Man Bryer's. That big pile of rotting straw and grass and clippings that he's always adding to. That."

I didn't have any deeper questions to ask. *Why not?* became a statement of intent rather than a question. Danny finished tidying up his chemistry set, and told me to wait where I was until he came back from his house. He passed me the test tube bomb.

"Stay here. And don't move. I'll be back in a minute. You are the official bomb holder. Try not to blow yourself up into bits."

Danny walked off, and I suddenly found myself alone in the quiet heat. Alone with the bomb—a bomb! It wasn't a time bomb, but it felt like one, with my stomach ticking away for a few long minutes. What if he didn't come back? Where would I put it? What if someone found me here holding a bomb? What if I dropped it? If I squeezed it too long—or too hard? Would it go off? Would my hand heat it up too much? What if—

Thankfully, Danny came back, and my stomach returned to churn with excitement rather than worry.

We were off and away, but not before Danny said, "And besides, Bryer is a genuine one-hundred-per-cent jerk-off." I could only take his word for it.

Old Man Bryer—he wasn't really that old—lived on the same side of the street as I did, but a couple of properties up. He didn't have quite the biggest strip of land, but he did have the tidiest. He painted his front fence every year. The colors were always the same: white with a little green trim, to match, it seemed, his house, which was green with white trim. When he wasn't washing his car or his truck, he was mowing his lawn with the only driven lawnmower we knew of—and no doubt about it: his lawn was the greenest and most closely trimmed lawn in all of Eastfield.

Mr. Bryer also put up the most elaborate outdoor Christmas decorations for miles around, and on December evenings, people, even from Silverford, our nearby town, would drive by just to gaze upon his prancing, flashing reindeer, giant sparkling north star, and winking Santa, not to mention the twinkling, rocking elves and hundreds of colored lights that outlined his house and garden and front fence. We imagined his smug pride as he sat there in his house on those holiday evenings, knowing that just beyond his green and white fence were ogling fans of his shimmering display that played homage to confused Christmas excess. We neighborhood kids, though, weren't all that impressed with Old Man Bryer—nor him with us.

Despite this electrified gesture of yuletide goodwill, Mr. Bryer was not the most friendly guy. In fact, he was a grouch. He made it clear by his intimidating glances and always-closed front gate that he was kid-intolerant. He also openly sneered at those in the neighborhood who didn't approximate his standards. I'd heard my parents say that Mr. Bryer let it be known to the one official at the Eastfield Municipal Hall that houses like Mrs. Raskolnikov's and the Slough's further up the road should be torn down and the property redeveloped to fit in with the changing "ambiance" of the area. His only possible redeeming quality was that he apparently had a large gun collection in his rec room, so Dad once said.

Old Man Bryer and his pretty wife did not have kids. Like his property, she somehow looked too neat and tidy, though she, at least, occasionally smiled shyly at us. She seemed to spend a lot of time in her house with that little yappy white dog, vacuuming almost every day; Mom on a few occasions had mentioned the lovely knickknacks all over her house. One of the older kids in the neighborhood once conjured a nursery rhyme to capture Mr. and Mrs. Bryer:

Peter Peter Pumpkin Eater
Had a Wife and couldn't keep her.
Kept her in a Pumpkin Shell
And there he kept her very well.

The name stuck: we called her Mrs. Peter Pumpkin Eater. But we had to admit that at Hallowe'en she did give out pretty good stuff in perfect little bags. Old Man Bryer didn't hand out anything. He was probably downstairs, polishing his guns and practicing his aim.

Bryer didn't like us kids because he no doubt thought we might mess up his yard or scratch his cars or make marks in his lawn. I could tell my own parents didn't especially like all him that much, but they vaguely defended him and his view that "good fences make good neighbors." Well, for kids, there is no such thing as a good fence, and we had made sure that, in the back reaches of his property, a hundred yards or more from his house, where the fencing was older and harder for him to patrol, we had secret access to use his property, mainly as a shortcut on our outings.

So, Danny and I found ourselves back in the furthest reaches of Bryer's property. We could partially see his place through a sparse stand of trees.

Bryer was nowhere around, but as we crossed over the fence into his property, we stayed on the far side of the target of our quest—the big compost pile. Danny muttered a few words I'd heard before somewhere: "Forgive us our trespasses."

Keeping low, we moved like soldiers on a search-and-destroy mission. The pile was about three or four feet high, and maybe a bit more in diameter, maybe six feet or more. It was mostly compacted rotting grass clippings and stuff from his neatly trimmed hedges that may have been through a shredder—no one else but Mr. Bryer had such a thing. Danny once said he'd like to toss that little yapping dog of theirs into it: "Nabisco Shredded Meat," he joked.

When we were close, Danny pulled the test tube bomb out of his shirt.

"We'll put it as deep inside of the pile as we can. The noise will be muffled. No one will probably notice it—much." Danny kept his voice down, and I nodded.

We started carving out a little tunnel into the center of the pile with our hands and then with a stick. The pile was warm—almost hot—inside. And moist, too. Danny told me why: "Living stuff rots. Dead plants and leaves and stuff. Little bacteria break it all up. That's the heat. There's the gas that comes out." He stopped digging for a second. "Methane, I think, sometimes. When not enough oxygen in the rotting." He briefly expanded: "Methane. Think cow farts."

I quickly considered this as we worked on our tunnel. Danny once said that digesting food was just composting. Almost surprising myself, I repeated his lesson to him: "We eat food. We give out gas farts, and it smells like something rotten, right? A compost pile inside our butts."

I seldom said this much to Danny, so maybe his summer

tutoring was paying off. I may, in fact, have sounded a little like him. And like most six-year-old boys, I liked talking about farts.

He added, "Same gas."

I nodded.

"And flammable."

I had just come to know the word *flammable*—once more through Danny—and felt good about that.

Now, this had me thinking. Flammable farts?

"Less talk," Danny said. "More action."

We were almost done tunneling. Danny made sure it was a deep enough and not loose.

"We don't want it to cave in—extinguish the fuse," Danny said quietly. "Need to make sure enough air is in the tunnel so the fuse will burn."

Danny carefully slid the test-tube bomb inside the tunnel, and then took it out. He seemed to be checking how far it would go in. He paused.

"Ready," he said.

I nodded and took a breath. Danny placed the glass-cased bomb back into the tunnel. He produced a box of wooden matches from his pant pockets, and from it, a match, which he lit from the side of the match box.

"You ready?" he asked again and looked at me.

"I guess so."

The match had burned down a bit, and so Danny put his hand with the match into the tunnel, carefully, where the end of the long fuse could just be seen.

"You should always name bombs," he said quickly, adding, "Little Boy."

That would be me, though I didn't get it. "Me? What?"

Danny pulled his hand out. The match failed.

"The name of the atomic bomb. Dropped on Japan. Torched one hundred thousand people. Just sitting around. They called the bomb 'Little Boy'."

"Oh," I nodded.

Danny struck another match and put his hand back into the tunnel.

Oh indeed! The fuse caught the match and was fizzing down.

We quickly retreated behind a large stump, some thirty or so feet back, just in case it actually did something. We didn't, or I didn't, know that to expect. A big bang?

We waited a second or two more. For some reason I mumbled, "Old Man Bryer's Butt."

"What?" said Danny, trying to concentrate on the bomb.

"Old Man Bryer's Butt. For the name of the bomb."

Danny quickly thought of something else: "If we named it 'The Buttbomb of Old Man Bryer,' the initials would be 'B.O.M.B.' Bomb. That's how you spell 'bomb.' Good coincidence."

I tried to work out the spelling, but Danny's satisfaction was enough to silence any worry about the weird, silent "b" in "bomb."

Back to the pile. Nothing.

A few more seconds. Danny's frustration surfaced: "Rats," he said. "Probably not enough air—oxygen—down inside the tunnel. Maybe the fuse got wet. When I put it down inside."

Danny began to stand up, resigned to the fact that the bomb was not going to go off. But as he did, *ka-WHOOMP!* The bomb indeed went off, not with a loud bang, but with a deep, thick, heavy thud! The ground under us seemed to jump a little. The large pile of compost vibrated, lifted, and shifted its place before flattening out. Then silence. What was once a big compost pile now looked sunken, with some smoke or vapors rising from it! Almost like a crater, or a large pie that had fallen in.

"Whoa," whispered Danny. Surprise, fear, and wonder flashed across our brows. "The power and the glory!" he added.

"Wow!" was about all I could muster, followed by the unintentionally appropriate "holy smokes."

"We better vamoose!" Danny said. I still gawked. Somewhere we could hear Mrs. Bryer's stupid little dog yapping.

We were out of Bryer's property within seconds. I wanted to run. Danny walked, though quickly. When you're in control, you never have to run—Danny always said.

As we were about to split up and go our ways, Danny looked me in the eye: "Say nothing, nothing about this—to anyone." He got even closer. "Nothing! Pinkie swear."

"Pinkie Swear," I said, and we hooked our baby fingers.

We were about to part, but I said, "We smote it."

"What?"

"The pile. We smote it, right?"

Danny looked at me, a little confused, until he got whatever idea I thought I had. "Yeah, we smote it." He smiled. "Maybe the same sound as Goliath hitting the ground. After David *smote* him."

I felt oddly relieved not just that Danny knew what I was talking about, but that I was witness to the bomb test. It wasn't loud, but it felt, somehow, heavy—yes, like Goliath hitting the ground, bloodied by the stone from a boy's sling.

As a final act, Danny reminded me of our pinkie swear before disappearing toward his place.

Within a few minutes I was back to the safety of my own backyard, and then in the house, where Mom was fixing something to eat. Dad was still unpacking the remaining camping stuff from the car. He was probably the safer choice to be with, so I went back outside. Mom always seemed to know when something was up.

Breathy, I asked, "Can I help?"

Dad looked at me like he wasn't sure what he heard. Volunteering to help was not usual behavior.

"Uh, yeah. Okay. Pull the rest of the sleeping bags out of the car. Unzip them and put them out over there, so the sun can get to them, air them out."

"Sure," I said.

The thump of the Bryer butt-bomb could still be felt inside my almost guilty head. The noise had been muffled by the weight of all the wet, rotting grass and clippings, but still, it was a wallop. Wow! If caught, I knew we would be in big trouble, or, as my older brother put it when Mom and Dad were out of range, "In Very Deep Shit." But how cool was that! We blew something up. We *smote* something. I was trying to imagine what Mr. Bryer would be like when he saw his neat pile flattened, caved in, like it had been leveled by some giant falling on it. He'd have a big hairy conniption. Ha!

And then I asked my Dad: "What'd you want me to do again?"

§

Joseph Caine called his wife over to where he sat. She looked okay, maybe a little tired, a little sagging. Some heaviness in her shoulders. She expected something quick from him, something to do with domestic issues.

"No, sit down," Joseph said.

She did.

"I been thinking, Hannah," he said, but then hesitated.

She looked at him.

He began again, awkwardly. "Been thinking. I know you–you wanted another child after Dan was born. I know–like, a little girl. But–it couldn't, you know, happen."

Hannah had no idea what her husband wanted to say. She didn't like to think too much about her lost hopes, though they too-often weighed upon her. This loss stayed only barely hidden, yet it worked away in thoughts too deep for tears.

Hannah had nothing to say. Why would he bring this up?

"You know," Joseph continued, stammering forward. "There are–I been looking into–if you think it's okay–I been looking into, thinking about maybe if you want to adopt a little girl. I mean, 'we'."

Joseph looked to his wife to collect her reaction. She didn't know what to say. But after the words sunk in, something light began to come up in her.

"Adopt? A little girl?"

"Yeah. I been looking into it. A baby girl. Brand new."

She had never really thought about it. She looked at her husband carefully. He was being real. Honest. This much she could tell. Gaps of silence and hidden life had grown between them, but they knew each other.

"And," she asked, "you found out–what?"

"Well, there's a little girl. Just born. Young mother. Up north. Healthy baby, I been told. And she can be adopted. She's only a couple of months old."

Hannah felt lighter still, giddy almost, but confused. "How? But how?"

"I phoned around. Heard. She's part native. Maybe not even half. A good-looking baby, I been told. Healthy. Pretty little thing."

"And–we can get her?"

"Yes. I been told yes. Just have to make a few more calls. Fill out some things, forms."

"And–and she can–could–be ours?"

"She can."

Hannah stood up and went over to her husband and knelt beside him. Uncertainty and hope crossed back and forth within her. She put her hands on his lap. "I never thought," she said. "I never!"

Joseph was surprised how open his wife suddenly felt, how buoyant she suddenly seemed. At best, he expected suspicion from her. At worst, he would not have been surprised by scorn or even anger. Blame, even. Joseph looked into her eyes to what seemed like swelling tears, and he felt some sympathy, some sadness, and even a sense of tenderness. Maybe, he hoped. Maybe.

A month or two later, after a flight and a load of paperwork, Mr. and Mrs. Joseph Caine brought home a new little daughter. A tiny, round baby. They named her Rebecca. She was olive-skinned, robust, and, as the new mother said, "Cute as a pin." And for a while, a form of happiness crossed into family life.

From the start, Hannah noticed with some wonder how her husband took to and loved this new addition to their family, since she had detected a holding-back in his attentions toward their firstborn, Daniel, who never seemed easy. She, of course, had no idea that Rebecca was Joseph's daughter. And she had no idea about Emily Cooday.

As for Daniel Caine, he grew to have many ideas.

A DOLL'S HOUSE

There were only a few, fleeting moments with Danny over the next couple of days. "Old Man Bryer's Butt" remained big. Danny had made a real bomb, and he blew something up! I was there! I thought I heard my parents say something about Mr. Bryer's asking around about something that had happened. Maybe even calling the police about it. No specifics, though Bryer apparently said he found some evidence or some clue or something. I guessed what this might be about, but wasn't sure. Bryer was often cross or complaining about something or other. I knew better than to ask about it, though I was surprised my parents didn't ask me if I knew or heard anything about it.

I did see Danny pacing around his driveway, and I also saw him slipping in and out of Spy Nosy Place. Normally, he was easy to find, and he often stayed in one place for a while as he carried out his various activities.

Even though I didn't have the words, I mustered a few simple thoughts about how, over the last while, Danny was at moments unsettled or uneven, despite having directed some booming focus upon Mr. Bryer's compost pile. Unlike the beginning of summer, he hadn't finished off some of the lessons, parables, and demonstrations. Proofs were left in the air. The orchard Eden scene, which I would like to have forgotten about, was also not right. He did nothing with a frog after he filled it with air. Nothing with the sky-blue robin eggs we found, except break them. The termite nest we discovered in an old stump was simply pulled apart without even a story, with just the remark that "termites are white because they hate the sun." Then, for some reason, he repeated, "hate the sun," as if it had a new meaning. Danny's showers became more frequent still, and sometimes he didn't return from them, though we waited.

Maybe he was leaving us, his captive audience, with the final word. Maybe he wanted us to boldly go off on our own. Maybe he thought we weren't up to his standards. Maybe he had a new secret focus. It certainly couldn't be—could ever be—that his pronouncements and stories didn't hold anymore. We had come to believe that certain truths—the truths of the Balance in Nature that Danny transformed into Gospel, with Good and Evil as different sides of the same coin—were constant and incontestable: his lectures, lessons, labs, sermons—from on high—that all things break down to become new again. You could depend on his words and proofs like you could depend on the buzzing fury of a trapped wasp.

Maybe Danny's disappearing acts and odd behavior had to do with the recent death of Mrs. Raskolnikov, just a week or more ago. Danny was standing there when the ambulance pulled away from her house. Rumor spread that she had died a few days before she was found. We also heard that she seemed to have dressed for her own death, and had put on her best clothes, that she had set herself down on her favorite chair, an old wicker rocker beside her stone fireplace. I heard my parents say that she held some old photographs and drawings in her hand, tied together with a ribbon. That's how they found her. I remembered her darker predictions—her fortune-telling—as told to us by Danny. She, then, was part of her own prediction. And the next?

Meanwhile, I made do with hanging around with a few of the other kids who lived around Eastfield, though none too close by. They might have been fine for throwing rocks, riding bikes, hide'n'seek, snakes'n'ladders, and other low-level kinds of play, like catching a few tadpoles, but they didn't provide the wide world and the wise word that Danny offered. For them, the bushes and the fields and the streams were for crashing and splashing through; for Danny, these places were realms of scientific miracles and mythological conflicts, places to stop and look and act upon in order to learn about the meanings behind all those surfaces and in those holes, in places where those words and worlds moved together to transform each other.

For some days, I hunted with the unthinking pack, waiting for my guide and teacher to return, if ever he would.

. . .

After a few days of not having much direct contact with Danny, I went around to the Caine's house and knocked at the back door. Mrs. Caine answered. She had her housecoat on and was wearing slippers. I asked if Rebecca or Danny could come out and play. Mrs. Caine said that Danny was not home. She added that Rebecca was busy doing something with her father. I thought that she might call out to Rebecca that I was there, but she didn't—like she had forgotten what usually happened when I called by.

"Okay," I said. "Maybe I'll see 'em later. Thanks."

I started to leave, but Mrs. Caine decided to stop me. "Oh, just hang on," she said, like she had a realization. "Come on in. I'll see if Rebecca wants to play. She hasn't been out of the house for a while."

Mrs. Caine went to find her. I waited in the kitchen. It was mid-morning. The place was messy. Dishes all over the place. A few empty beer bottles in various places. Some empty packages on the floor. I had never seen our own kitchen look like this— Mom would never permit it—and neither had I ever seen the Caines' kitchen in this state. For a six-year-old to even notice a mess meant it was much more than the regular untidiness that can take over a family kitchen in a couple of busy hours.

Somewhere at the end of the house I could hear a strained discussion going on between Mr. and Mrs. Caine. A minute or two later, Rebecca came through the kitchen.

"Hi," I said.

"Hi," she said.

Rebecca too looked untidy. Normally, before she ever went out, Mrs. Caine would brush back her jet black hair; Rebecca often had perfect braids or a neat, tight ponytail.

"What you wanna do?" I asked.

"Don't know. What you wanna do?"

I didn't have any plans. She didn't have any plans. Unless we were with Danny, Rebecca and I usually divided our playing. Sometimes we did what she wanted to do, and sometimes she did what I wanted to do, and then we went from there, hedging our differences. Because Rebecca looked a little lost, and because I was happy just to get her to play, I made the noble suggestion of doing something with her dolls.

Now, while that might sound odd for a kid whose growing idols included baseball players, cowboys, professional wrestlers, superheroes, and monsters, to play dolls meant playing in such a way that was okay for me. Playing anything could be stretched into other things.

Rebecca perked up. "I'll get my Barbie stuff."

"I'll go home and get my army men. Meet you 'round the front of your house."

And I was off, with passing confusions brushed aside.

In a few minutes we were both on our knees in the shade of single, tall cedar tree that towered over the front yard of Caine's house. Rebecca had her Barbie and some outfits. She also had a shoebox and some smaller things in it that looked like furniture. I brought a bag of green and tan plastic soldiers, most with rifles, but also some posed with pistols, machine guns, and grenades. Although the army men and Barbie were not close to being on the same size scale, nothing could stop them from being in the same imaginative realm.

Barbie, meet the Wolf Platoon. Wolf Platoon, this is Barbie.

Danny mentioned Rebecca's new Barbie once, noting that it did not have private parts. He added, though, that this would make things a lot easier. "Less to worry about. Plumbing can be a problem—it was, from the beginning."

Quick wit that I thought I was, I answered, "Like going to the bathroom."

Danny clinically addressed my observation: "You only need holes for that."

Rebecca began to define our play world geography: "Barbie's house is over here. The beach is there. The shopping place is right behind you."

I named and made claims about the rest of the landscape: "Over here will be the jungle"—where a couple of the cedar's low, sweeping branches touched the ground—"and the army base will be over here"—where the grass came up against some exposed soil.

Rebecca didn't pay too much attention to the placement of my sites, since it wasn't likely that Barbie would be paying a visit to either the jungle or the army base in the near future. Rebecca was more concerned that Barbie was appropriately preened for the beach. It appeared that a black and white bikini, beach coat, and high heels were the afternoon's dress code. Barbie was forever up on her toes. Barbie's long hair also needed some work. Perhaps a ponytail.

Just for a second, while Barbie was being undressed for a change of clothes, I thought of the magazines Danny had taken from his dad's boat, with those pouting, naked women with long legs. I'd thought it before: they were kind of like—well, a lot like—Barbie. But what did I know?

While Barbie prepared for the beach, Wolf Platoon made their way through the jungle on an impossible mission. Enemies everywhere. They shot, ran, fell, threw grenades, and jumped, with appropriate sound effects from me. Nothing could stop them, though they did take some hits. They finally made it back to base, where they could rest and make further plans.

Rebecca worked away with Barbie, brushing her hair, trying clothes on her, posing. Rebecca half whispered little phrases like, "There you go. There. That's nice, isn't it." She was, for the moment, a Barbie girl in a Barbie world.

Suddenly distracted from my exhausted troops, and perhaps even a little intrigued—jealous?—with how Barbie fully took Rebecca into that world, I asked about Barbie's personal life: "She married?"

"No. She has friends. She shops with them. They meet at the beach."

"She have a friend who is a boy?"

"Maybe."

Then I'd tried my best to be cheeky: "They kiss and stuff?"

Rebecca stopped preening Barbie and thought for a moment. She turned her gaze to Barbie, and Rebecca turned Barbie so that the doll looked back at her with those huge, unblinking eyes. "When they go out, like on a date, they take one kiss when they're finished, when they say good-night."

"Will they get married?"

I was thinking about what this make-believe boyfriend might be like. Maybe he was a soldier.

"If he asks her, they'll get married." She thought a little more. "And they will always be together. And he will never leave her by herself and go away. Always."

"But what if he has to go away, like, for a long time. To do more work or something." I was thinking that if he were a soldier, he'd have missions. Wars and battles don't take an afternoon, and they don't stop for supper.

"He won't, doesn't, go away. Except to go shopping for her. To buy her presents and lots of nice things for her."

"But what if he really had to go? Like a secret mission. She wouldn't know where he was."

"Well, it would only be for a very little while." Rebecca thought a little more on this. "She might go, too. They want to be together all of the time, or go to the same places and meet. If not, they could talk on the telephone all night, if they want, you know."

Rebecca's tone became sharper with my insisting comment that Barbie's boyfriend may need to go away sometimes.

For a second or two, my motives became selfish, mainly because I liked the story of a dangerous mission running through my head. I pushed one part further: "Well, sometimes this guy will just have to go away and just leave her. They can't be together all the time, or be on the phone all the time. He may have some secret stuff—some job away. Other people he has to see that he likes, and things to do, so there." I was thinking of my army guys.

Rebecca said nothing.

I repeated what I said, so that it appeared even more true: "They don't need to be together all of the time, for sure. He'll go away, see others."

I looked at Barbie. Rebecca held the doll in her hands, and I waited for her to answer. My soldiers rested.

Rebecca was still, and then her shoulders shook a few times. A drop of water fell on Barbie's chest. I looked at Rebecca. Was she—was she beginning to cry? Yes. A few more tears rolled down her cheeks and fell to her lap. She put down Barbie, stood up, turned, and walked swiftly into her house up the front stairs, closing the door behind her.

I sat there under the cedar tree for a few minutes. What happened? Should I go and see what was the matter? I didn't get it, whatever it was. Did she get stung by a bee or something? In a while, I gathered up my soldiers and headed home, leaving Barbie and all her stuff behind, scattered on the ground beneath the solitary cedar tree.

§

Emily Cooday brought a little girl into the world, and she gave that little girl up for adoption. At least giving birth was something out of the ordinary, though the two nurses who attended her at the birth of her child seemed something like masked robbers on business.

Emily signed lots of papers, and was asked if she understood what was going on. She said she did, though her head and her body fought each other. Emily asked if she was allowed to give the little girl a name. No one seemed sure, and so she picked the First Nations name her grandfather gave to her. "That's her name," Emily said, looking around. It didn't seem that anyone wrote it down.

Father Leo, to whom she had first confessed her pregnancy, and who had convinced her to give the child up, told her that others in her situation had done the same thing. This was a dull, sad thought, and she had nowhere to put it. The thought of all those children, not knowing where they came from, not knowing where they were going. Not knowing their secret names.

With the child taken, loss and relief fused as she moved back to her enclosed life in the tiny village and at her grandparents' broken-down house below the hill. Her own mother, always pinned under the bad side the bottle, could barely tell what had happened. She only muttered, hopelessly and resigned, "The baby? Gone? They're all gone." And that was all.

Emily Cooday had no idea where her little girl would end up, but at some point she was told by Father Leo that a young couple was very keen, and that they would give the child a good life. "She'll have an older brother," he added.

Emily was barely listening. "A good life," she reflected. "What did that mean?"

THERE IS A HOLE IN EVERYTHING

"**D**o the wings of a soul bleed?"

This was the kind of impossible question Danny conjured during much of the summer as we witnessed him perform his secret, scientific ministry. He would pause, lift his head, and turn to us—as well as to a place out there. Somewhere was a greater, larger audience. Or another purpose. We two, six-year-old Rebecca and I, had front-row seats, but the show seemed to be coming to some kind of an end. We hadn't always been capable of taking in the full scope of Danny's lessons and all those interconnections, but we could at least witness the details laid before us. As Danny seemed to warn a few times, "The devil is in the details," though once he made a slight revision: "The details are in the devil."

Danny's endings—and his questions that often seemed at once strange and essential—were not always clear to us, but now, as the summer smoldered on, they seemed to be becoming less so. But if our ants-in-the-pants restlessness could be held in check, there was often a wondrous point somewhere at the end of his parables, fables, evidence, and conclusions—at the tip of his tongue and the touch of his deft fingers, at the snip of some scissors and under the power of his ever-ready magnifying glass. Danny was at the switch, and he knew how to turn on our lights. But whatever it was, poetry or proof, Danny managed to balance Truth and Beauty, Good and Evil, Dark and Light, and Life and Death, so that all were part of the same plan, the same story, the same struggle back and forth and in between. That was all we really needed to know, even when, on few occasions, he said that being in a little mystery, doubt, or uncertainty could end up being good thing—if your mind was big enough.

So now, as usual, we waited—not so much as a virtue, but as a reward. And the waiting now meant something more than it did even just weeks ago, more because Danny had become evasive, somehow distant—and the lessons less frequent. Maybe all it meant was that this hottest of summers was coming to some kind of end.

"Do the wings of a soul bleed?"

The soul? The soul has wings? Angels have wings? How could you tell if something that you can't see bleeds? Our faith in Danny held us for an answer. Truth would no doubt be furnished with evidence, but where would he find a soul to prove it?

This particular day Danny had Rebecca and I had running around the neighborhood with our pillowslip butterfly nets fashioned over coat hangers, working up a hormoneless sweat, calling out to each other, "There's one! Over here, over here!" To and fro, we fluttered around each other, not unlike the butterflies themselves that tumbled about and through the air, sometimes in tangled twos.

We had become good at catching butterflies. We learned that white and black Cabbage Butterflies tended to gather and fan themselves on potato plants. The more highly prized but skittish Monarchs hid among the lower flowers. Then there were the magnificent and rare Swallowtails, which were larger and had teardrop extensions to the bottoms of their wings. They spooked easily. Danny said that Swallowtails were "aloof," which sounded like it had something to do with flying lightly and highly.

After netting and jarring two Cabbagers, and having caught only one battered-looking looking Monarch after a hectic chase, Rebecca and I decided to employ more stealth than strain. We knew the Monarchs often sunned themselves at the rockery around the front of my house that bordered one side of the driveway. We looked up and down the rock wall, keeping about ten feet away, which would be close enough to spot a butterfly without disturbing it.

At first we didn't see it, but—but there it was, perched right in the middle of one of the larger flowers that sprung out between the rocks: a Swallowtail! A big one! Its black and yellow markings glistened under the white sun, with the two tiny spots of blue and red on the inside edge just visible. We gulped, stopped, looked at each other, and mirrored shushes. We knew enough to make our move quickly, before it became "aloof."

Rebecca whispered, "I'll go from this side," which meant I would approach from the opposite direction. We parted, and began to form the first part of our u-shaped approach. Our strategy—choreographed earlier in the summer by Danny—was well rehearsed. If, during our slow dance to the butterfly, it happened to take off, it might come directly at one of us before gaining height.

Slowly, steadily we started to come together. The Swallowtail was now between us, its wings together, but every few seconds it fanned itself slowly on the heated rock, shimmering, almost still.

We were within reach. Our hearts stopped as the Swallowtail briefly rose before settling back down again. The dangerous time would come when we raised our nets, since the movement, even slight, might alert the butterfly. An unexpected breeze could cause the pillowslip nets to flutter, which might also alarm the Swallowtail.

Now, together, in a moment of truth, we raised our white nets into the clear blue sky...slowly, slowly above our shoulders. Our eyes met before we turned back to the butterfly. Time stopped, and then moved fast. The Swallowtail opened its wings, like hands coming apart after prayer. Our nets fell upon it in a flash. We had it! It was ours! It was Danny's!

As it turned out, it was my net that came down first on the Swallowtail, with Rebecca's on top of mine. I didn't make a point about it right there—teamwork was the key to the capture. But inwardly, and with a tinge of guilty pride, it felt like it was my catch. Danny might ask who was responsible. He might commend, and that commendation, even a smile or nod or a few words, was like receiving a medal for outstanding service, especially now that our contact with Danny was more and more rare.

We hoped our Swallowtail was not damaged during capture. It was a large one, easily the largest one we'd seen this summer, and we knew we would have to be careful jarring it, so as not to harm its wings. Danny liked his specimens in tip-top shape. He told us that "damaged goods" are not good at all.

Rebecca looked at me, "I think we need the bigger jar."

She was right.

Rebecca held the butterfly nets steady as I grabbed the larger of the two jars we had with us—a wide, old peanut butter jar, and, though clean and without a label, it still had that unmistakable smell. Removing the lid and giving it a quick sniff, I was barely conscious that I was quietly chanting a peanut butter song driven in by relentless ads....*S-K-I-P-P-Y, you will love it when you try Skippy Peanut Butter...*

Rebecca, meanwhile, hadn't moved. "Yeah, good," she said, then added, "You singing something?"

"No," I said.

"You were."

"Weren't."

We let it go, and tuned to the important work at hand: transferring the Swallowtail to the jar. One slip and it would escape to the skies. Too much hurry and there could be damage. We slowly lifted the net to look beneath. The butterfly was there, holding on to the inside of the pillowslip. We moved the opened jar into the pillow slip, and slowly, carefully, cupped it around the Swallowtail. It barely fit, but it was in. We could turn the jar upside down while holding the outside of the pillowslip. All we needed to do now was slide the lid under the jar. This was easy, since the Swallowtail had shifted slightly more toward to the top of the jar, which was really the bottom since it was upside-down. We carefully screwed on the lid. We had it! Yes! Rebecca took the jar.

We gazed through the clear glass, which slightly magnified the butterfly. It was beautiful and strange and perfect: a rare, unearthly creature. Its body was even larger than the yellowish, bulbous, egg-laden termite queen that we fed to the Ant Nest in early summer. "Feeding the unborn to the undead" was Danny's comment when the helpless queen was dragged underground by the devilish red and black army, probably to feed the Ant Queen herself.

The Swallowtail did not move. Its limiting glass surroundings seemed to freeze it. Maybe it was somehow above panic, like Danny. It seemed to get bigger and better with every moment.

"Danny won't believe it!"

And we were off with our glittering prize.

We found Danny near the base of The Trail, where he was crouched and bent slightly forward. With the powerful magnifying glass he always carried around, he was focusing the heat of the mid-afternoon sun on the opening of one of the small holes that black ants made in the dry dirt. We'd seen him do something like this before. He would aim the heat-ray just beside the hole, and, the moment an ant came out, he would adjust the aim and zap the ant with blazing light. The result was a little sizzle and a barely visible little puff of smoke, and voila: an immediately-crumpled dead ant. Rebecca kept the jar behind her while Danny finished.

"That smoke: his little soul rising to ant heaven," Danny said. "*Animula*," he added, like it was something secret and mysterious—or even magical. Danny would not harm the next ant to come out of the hole. It would usually find its burnt up fellow worker, explore it a bit with its antennae—tenderly, quickly, efficiently—and then take it underground. Meanwhile, back at the hole, another ant would come up, perhaps informed about possible further brethren bounty. It too would get sizzled. Then the next ant would be left unharmed to take away the new, crispy corpse. So it went: one up, one burnt; another up to fetch the burnt ant...

"Dear, dear," Danny said. "Ants these days—they toast and roast so easily." Danny's tone was almost playful, which lately hadn't been the case. He cooked another in the blink of an eye, then turned to us.

Rebecca proudly handed Danny the jar. He stood up. He looked at it. He looked at us.

"Very, very nice. Good work."

Returning his gaze to the jar he asked, "So, who caught this beauty?"

I wanted to say that I did, since my net had come down first. Rebecca beat me to an answer: "We both did."

I looked at Rebecca. She didn't look at me. Pride and bragging rights were quickly swallowed by the moment.

Danny concentrated his attentions on the Swallowtail. "Know the difference between moths and butterflies?" he asked, still gazing upon the supreme catch.

We didn't, though I knew that moths liked to eat sweaters and that butterflies didn't. Danny mentioned their different antennae, how they held their wings differently when they landed, and how moths were night creatures. But according to Danny, there was more to the story of butterflies and moths than facts.

"Moths are fallen butterflies. They live in the dark. They can't get into heaven. They want the thing that doesn't want them—the light, heaven. They circle 'round it, going nowhere. The light they want often burns their wings and bodies, and then they die—back into the darkness—back to hell—again."

We liked this, even if it was confusing. Hell, heaven, death, darkness, burnt bodies...there were always dead moths at the base of a street light, or caught in ceiling lights. It made sense, and fell right into one of the larger truths that Danny provided all summer: attraction and harm, reward and punishment, often become the same thing.

"Butterflies—they soak up the sun. Every time a butterfly goes to heaven, it is a soul returning to where it comes from."

Danny returned his gaze from the blue sky and looked at the Swallowtail with new interest. "Butterflies and moths are related. More similar than different, but opposite. That happens—in families."

After a few more moments of looking at the Swallowtail, Danny posed a half-question: "In very old stories and old languages, when the soul leaves a body, it does as a butterfly—when you die, you know." Of course we didn't know. We didn't even know there were old languages.

Then, with explorative intention, Danny asked that question: "Do the wings of a soul bleed?"

Whoosh.

The wonder of such a question is that little kids don't distinguish the physical from the metaphysical, and Danny went from one to the other and back again just like that. Wings, soul, blood. Danny's words were often like rocks skipping across the surface of water: impossible, yet real. The distinction between material world and the imagination hadn't scarred and divided our experience—not yet, anyway. Within and under the teachings of Danny, there were never unconnected categories of being. In a world that kept marking out differences, borders, and breaks, Danny's crusade was to make them one, to show that, in all things, difference does not mean division, and that with connections there had to be conflict to move the connections. Innocence and experience had to play together and off each other at the same time. Life and death and good and bad all revolve on the same circle, chasing each other, yet sometimes changing direction to necessarily crash into each other, to become new again. All causes were effects of other causes. All things break down to become other things. These, then, were the components—the moving parts—of Daniel Caine's enacted themes. But now, thinking back, some drifting change was coming about: Danny seemed more anxious or uncertain, about conflict and action without connections, about incomplete circles. So yes, easy to say now, but impossible to understand then.

So when were heard "wing" and "soul" in the same sentence, we never for a moment believed these could possibly be two different, uncoupled orders. Butterflies have wings. Butterflies are souls. Souls have wings. And then: Do they bleed?

Danny screwed the lid off the jar carefully. When he finished, he held the lid so that he would be able to lift it off at the right moment. He shook the jar lightly a couple of times to get the butterfly in the right position. When it was, he dropped the lid and pulled the butterfly out by holding on to its folded wings between his thumb and index finger.

And there—there it was before us, under the sun and in the hot, open air. It was big. It was beautiful. It was faultless. And it was helpless. We were amazed, and the huge Swallowtail was amazing.

"Let's find out."

Danny's plan wasn't clear, but it seemed to involve using the magnifying glass. Surely he wasn't going to burn the Swallowtail to death! This was too high and perfect a prize to waste for such a quick, easy act. Ants were a dime a dozen—sure, fine, toast 'em up. But for this rare creature from light and heaven, Danny must have had something special in mind, something more wondrous. But did he—or was it a blurred exercise in destruction?

First Danny examined its wings with the magnifying glass. He told us that butterfly wings are made of hundreds of tiny perfect scales, just like the skin of snakes and dragons. We got a glimpse through the magnifying glass. It was true. Overlapping, shimmering scales, almost like the shingles on houses. We gurgled our usual "wow" and "neat." Danny didn't like to repeat information unless he was going to use a completely different example to make the same point.

"So, we'll see. It will be a—it will be a sign."

Danny knelt down and focused the sun on the ground through the lens of the magnifying glass, and he produced a white dot of smoldering heat on the dirt, which smoked a bit with the intense temperature. A sign of what? For whom? Danny looked across our backyard and down our driveway toward his house.

When he felt it was somehow right, he took the magnifying glass away and glanced toward the overhead sun. We waited. It was hot, and we were in the direct sun. Danny's brow produced a little sweat.

He took the Swallowtail and, still carefully holding on to its wings between his thumb and index finger, he held it sideways to the ground where he had just focused the needle of heat. Oh, no! But he drew the magnifying glass precisely down onto the wing of the butterfly. The spot of light began as large and soft, but quickly got smaller and brighter as Danny concentrated the beam and the heat. Then he held the magnifying glass and the butterfly still. I had a vision of the butterfly bursting into flames. Then, in a second, a heat ray, like an invisible, glowing pin, pierced the butterfly's two wings in a flash almost too quick to see. Danny quickly pulled away the magnifying glass, and we gazed. There was a small, perfect hole where there was once a black spot. The Swallowtail did not move. We two did not move. And Danny, for the moment, did not move. No blood! The wings did not bleed. The butterfly did not burn up.

Danny inspected the hole he had made. He held the Swallowtail up for all of us to see, and a tiny ray of sunlight flashed through it.

Danny finally spoke, slowly, but without revealing much: "Everything has to have a hole. How light gets in." He added, still looking carefully at the butterfly, "To meet the darkness, its twin."

We all stood up. What was Danny going to do? We had to shade our eyes from the sun, which bore down. Danny, who had been steady, now teetered there in front of us. The butterfly was held up to the sun and sky in one hand, with his magnifying glass at his side, in the other. Anything could have happened. Anything in this moment seemed possible.

He turned to us. "Can a damaged soul rise to heaven? A soul— now not perfect. With a hole it in, with a hole burnt through it. That's what I—what we—need to know." Danny looked in the direction of his home and said, "The killing sun." It might have been a question, but it was hard to tell what he meant.

Danny released the Swallowtail, and for a long, quiet moment it appeared to fall like a dry leaf from a tree. Then, slowly, it began to flutter—flutter away from us and toward The Trail and into the shadows of the tall evergreens. It seemed to rise momentarily on the lightest of breezes, and then fall—but it was impossible to say if it then went up or down, whether it was finding its way to heaven or struggling against some downwards pull.

We lost sight of the soul with a perfect hole through its wings, but we kept on looking and moved forward to see just in case it might return or drop from the sky by flying too close to the sun. It didn't. It was gone.

When we turned to figure out what we had seen with Danny, he too was gone. He was disappearing down our driveway and across the road toward his house, and he was walking a little more quickly than usual, his magnifying glass tucked into his back pocket.

Rebecca, somewhat randomly, said, "It's his birthday."

"Oh," I said. "How old is he now?"

"Thirteen," she said.

"Oh," I said. I remembered what he said about the number at the beginning of summer.

§

Over the few years and fishing seasons after the birth and adoption of little Rebecca, Joseph Caine continued to see Emily Cooday, but not as frequently, and not with the same intense, explorative passion they once shared. He now kept condoms on the boat. Not gonna happen again, he thought. He hated these rubber things for the awkward moments they created, for putting even something so thin between him and Emily, and for the need to handle and dispose of those limp, sagging sacks. Emily, too, somehow resented them. It was no longer his skin inside her. Once out on the open ocean, Joseph threw the used ones overboard, and he would watch them float away, slowly. Seagulls sometimes swooped down to eye them, but would at the last moment turn away.

Emily and Joseph began to speak less about their feelings for each other, and more about the weather, the passing seasons, the salmon stocks.

She had fewer if any stories to re-tell him. Emily, Joseph thought, was less balanced, less flowing, less coy—still beautiful, still gentle and warm, but somehow heavier in heart and body. The child of which they could not speak both gave and took away. Should he tell her?

On one occasion he almost did. Emily had noticed a small, bright wax crayon drawing, obviously done by a very small child, pinned up on one of the walls of the boat. It pictured a green hillside with a little red flower, a yellow sun hanging over a mountain, with a blue sea below. "It's beautiful," Emily said. Not really thinking, Joseph said she could have it; he unpinned it from the wall, folded it up, and gave it to her. Words almost came to him, to tell her the truth. But then, instead, it became some kind of secret repayment for all her letters, and maybe for more. Emily would take the drawing and place it with the other treasures given to her by Joseph, another obejct added to her closed hopes.

Emily continued to give Joseph letters to take away when he left her, and in them she tried to describe in unfindable words some of her feeling, some of what happened between them, as well as things they did with each other—even their passions. He would read these letters while rolling out on the sea. And though one part of him wanted to simply toss them into the ocean, he kept them all, half hidden on his boat, like he had to keep a part of himself. The letters at moments mentioned her cloudy, confused feelings for her lost child, and Joseph could fully read its presence when her words stumbled through thoughts of loss. Emily expressed, then, a few passing thoughts about where her little daughter might be, imagining what she might be doing, who her parents and friends might be.

Joseph decided that he could not tell Emily that he had adopted her daughter—their daughter. The shared loss between them that became a gain for only one of them sat heavily and silently, without, it seemed, any possibility of ever joining them.

Yet Joseph could only have fantasies of telling Emily about Rebecca: how Rebecca grew, how pretty she was, how adventuresome and smart; about her friends; about the skinny blonde-haired boy across the road she often played with; her love of dolls; about her older brother whom she often followed around. But something inside offered a warning, that if he told Emily about Rebecca, Emily might become greedy to have more of him, perhaps even wrestle some deep guilt from him, and this did not sit well. He also feared the unknown: What else might Emily do if she knew about where her daughter was? About her new mother and new older brother? Would she try, somehow, to see her daughter—get her back, even?

All Emily and Joseph could do now was to vaguely rehearse the way they had come to know each other over the years since they first fell together on his boat. And that was their life, or a part of their life, passing—closer than either could really ever say or know, though now, after some time passing, at the same time somehow moving apart. They both felt this slow drift, but for Emily it was also a sinking. What did she have? What did she really have?

For Joseph Caine, he had gained a daughter, yet he seemed to somehow be losing a part of himself that once felt as vital as the sea itself.

As for young Daniel Caine, at six years old, he gained a little sister. You might think that the arrival of a new baby adopted into a family might make the older, single sibling jealous, especially with the attentions so suddenly demanded by an infant; but instead, Daniel Caine was curious—curious to watch and study his new little sister grow and move and reach out into the world. Daniel quietly waited for the moment, that came in about six years, when he could teach and show Rebecca some of things he had learned about the world and nature, and he knew much. Some would think that he grew to know too much.

THE RISING, YELLOW FLAME

Just as my family finished up supper on the day of the butterfly, our doorbell rang. I bolted up from the supper table—"I'll get it!"—and went to the front door. Any excuse to escape vegetables. It was Rebecca.

She asked, as if communicating someone's frustration, "Is Danny here—did you see him?"

"Danny? No."

"He's supposed to be home for supper. I was sent over to ask."

This didn't seem like a very big deal. Parents often sent out their kids in order to locate their other children who are late to show up for scheduled events, like meals, music lessons, shopping trips, or homework—and play-ending bedtime.

Rebecca thought for moment, as if she was confused. "Okay, then. Bye."

I added before I closed the door, "See you after supper, maybe. At the Tarzan swing." Mr. Caine had recently tied a thick rope to high limb of an old tree in their yard, knotted the end of it, and we hadn't really tested its potential yet.

Without answering, Rebecca walked off toward her house, seeming to be a little upset.

I closed the door and returned to the dinner table. I looked at my plate again, staring down at what remained. Mom asked who it was.

"Huh? Oh, Rebecca."

"Well, what did she want?"

"If Danny was here. He's supposed to be home for dinner."

Like about a million other kids that night, I was told that

vegetables were good for me and that there were lots of starving kids all over the world. By the time I got to the peas, they were cold and even more disgusting. I spread them out over the plate in order to make it look like there were fewer of them.

Vaguely eyeing my strategy, Mom asked, "Weren't you with Danny just a while this afternoon? Out back?"

"Yeah. Thought he went home." I chewed what I hoped would be my last bite. "We caught a big Swallowtail. Huge." My parents took a passing look of vague interest. "Then we let it go." I thought this was the right thing to say. Mom did not like any cruelty to creatures big or small.

Dad cut in. "They're pests, you know. Their eggs turn to caterpillars that do crops damage—they like vegetables. Not like—ahem—certain people."

Ever the realist, Dad didn't have Danny's way with words, but his point was clear. It was strange that something like a butterfly did have such a different form in the cycle of its life. Danny said that living things change, with stages, and some you couldn't recognize after the change. Same for people, too, he said—and then they do things you wouldn't recognize. Danny taught us the word, and he used it a couple of times in our outings. For reasons not clear, I blurted it out between chewing and swallowing: "Metamorphosis."

The table fell still for moment, and even my brother, Simon, who was usually too busy wolfing down anything put in front of him to comment at all, looked up from his plate at me.

I looked around at everyone looking at me. "What?"

"Well," Mom said, as the table's proceedings began again, "that's a big word." I could tell she was impressed. Learning and education were high on her list of good things.

Simon piped in with a double-sided compliment: "Pretty smart—for a pea-brain."

Mom checked Simon gently for his sarcasm: "Enough of that." And turning to me, "Now eat your peas." I gave my brother a smirk, which he probably missed.

Mom asked, "So where did you learn such a big word? School?"

I bottomed-up the last of my milk and was only too happy to answer, "From Danny."

For some reason, this unsettled my parents just enough for me to take advantage. "May I be excused, please. I'll get some dessert latter."

Dad gave me permission, but not without a provision: that I clean up a mess I had made the day before. During a lull when I couldn't find anything else to do, I mixed a potion just outside the backdoor on the sidewalk. I got completely carried away and used small quantities of anything I could find around the kitchen that Mom would tolerate letting me take out and put into an old, stainless steel bowl: cooking oil, food coloring, floor polish, Drano, window cleaner, vanilla extract, vinegar, Worcestershire sauce, baking soda, sugar, salt, syrup, pepper, shoe polish, detergent, ammonia, molasses, chili powder, lemon juice, flour, mayonnaise, milk—and one egg. Unfortunately, some of the containers were left outside, and I was told in no uncertain terms that if I wanted to go outside and play after supper, I had first better "clean up the mess."

At the time of mixing the potion, I had mad-scientist visions of poisons or creating new life forms, or maybe even a liquid explosive— maybe something like what Danny conjured when we blew up the compost pile. Now, a day later, my concoction just looked like an unnamable, brown, sticky mess. I clearly did not yet have Danny's delicate or explosive touch.

Where to even begin cleaning all this stuff up? I thought I better check out the state of the potion before blasting it out with the garden hose and washing the goo into the grass.

I inspected it as carefully as a six-year-old might, just in case any new life forms had somehow evolved. A few small, dead fruit flies and a bee were stuck on the surface. A very small victory. Perhaps the invention of a new insect attractor-killer? Attraction followed by destruction was a principle Danny drummed in with one of his more simple maxims: "Life's a rat trap. It's the cheese."

After a couple of trips to the kitchen, all of the containers were returned. The hosing worked pretty well, but there was still a kind ring around the steel bowl that wouldn't wash off, even with the battering force of the water. The bowl was brought into the kitchen and given to Mom, who was at the sink washing up the supper dishes that my brother was delivering from the table.

"Can I go now? I've cleaned up everything. Please?"

I whined a bit in saying this, and I wanted to sound like I was more in a hurry than I had to be. There was no specific urgency, except the desire to fit as much play as possible within the ever-shrinking time. Rebecca or Danny or both were bound to be around somewhere. I'd check the Tarzan swing first.

"And you sprayed off the sidewalk with the hose?" Dad asked at the last moment.

"Yeah. Well, most of it, anyway, I think." I made a mental note to look on the way out, but of course this intention would fade in an instant.

Mom looked at the mixing bowl and wooden spoon I handed her; she then looked at me. I looked at the mixing bowl; then looked at her. After a slightly deeper breath than usual, she gave me her patented scowl-smile, and said, "Okay, go."

And I was off out the back door, bolting right over top of the still-sticky sidewalk without a thought. I only slowed down when I rounded the corner of our house at the top of the driveway and was certain I wouldn't get called back.

Now out of the shade of the back of the house, I could feel how hot it still was. The afternoon heat that was absorbed by the ground seemed to radiate back as early evening approached. The kind of heat that stills things. The kind that echoes even the smallest of sounds. There was little traffic on Eastfield Road in the evenings.

Was I supposed to meet Rebecca at the swing? She must be finished her supper by now.

On the way to the Caines', I also wanted to check out the rock garden, just in case there was a Swallowtail like the one we caught this afternoon. Not that there would ever be another like it. Not by a long shot. Nothing there, except a few bumble bees and the two nets that we had left behind when we jarred the huge butterfly. I could count on being asked to clear them away from the side of the driveway.

I walked by slowly and replayed the event: how we spotted the Swallowtail; how we caught it so perfectly and so carefully jarred it; how perfect and big it was; how butterflies never made any noises. And then Danny's awe of the butterfly, yet the chance he took by burning a perfect, small hole through its wings. Fears about the possibility of the butterfly bursting into flames. And the way Danny let it go into the sky, and how, just for a moment, he didn't seem to have the knowledge we had come to expect. Then the butterfly disappearing into the shadows up The Trail. Danny, somehow agitated and uncertain, leaving us to wonder, leaving without an explanation to tie things up. The soul: Did it rise or fall, live or die? Heaven or hell? It was a scene hard to let go, maybe because it felt in some ways both striking and incomplete, a magical mystery.

As I came to the front of our property, looking for Rebecca. I could see the Caines' car parked, as usual, in the shade way down at the end of their driveway, beside their house but not quite in the garage, which was really just an open-ended shed. I couldn't spot Rebecca over by the swing or in her front yard. Eastfield felt at rest, stilled, as if taking a break from the heat and the cares of the passing day.

I crossed the road and was going to go down Caines' long driveway and around behind Rebecca's house, when I decided to take a slight detour on the left through Spy Nosy Place, just in case she or Danny might be around. Because of the knolls among the scrub brush, it was sometimes hard to spot anyone playing there from the road or from the Caines' driveway. I entered from the road side. Not even a slight breeze this evening. The long grass was brittle from the heat and sparse rain over the last few months.

I almost missed him, but just ahead I saw Danny on the upside of a grassy knoll, crouched, looking toward his house and down his driveway. He wasn't too far from where we had looked at the magazines with the naked Barbie-doll types, where Danny stacked those letters, and from where we secretly watched his dad discover that envelope he placed on the windshield of the car. He didn't seem to hear me coming from behind. He wasn't doing anything except watching his house.

When I was a few feet away behind him, he turned, startled. His shirt was wet with sweat, his face blotchy and red, his hair strangely scattered, and his clothes dirtier than usual. It looked like he had been there a while.

He immediately pulled me down to the ground slightly behind him. "What you doing here?"

This took me back. Normally, if I came across Danny, he would be doing something that he would show or tell me about, like he was waiting to be found, offering an invitation to watch and learn—

the teacher waiting for the pupil, the actor for an audience. Now, suddenly, my presence was questioned. And Danny had never grabbed me like that. In fact, I couldn't remember him ever hardly touching me.

I didn't know what to say. Before he let me go, Danny looked again down the driveway toward his house.

I answered, uncertain: "I was just looking—for Rebecca, I guess."

Danny's trusty magnifying glass half stuck out of his back pocket, and, on the ground in front of him, was the map of Eastfield he made earlier in the summer, the one with the 'X' on it—but now with an extra 'X' beside it. The map looked worn out. Beside it was that old card he had been given by Mrs. Raskolnikov. He had showed us the card after he had been in her old house—guys with wings, angels, looking down from sky, blowing down from some long trumpets. Those below, sort of naked, were looking up, like they needed to rise or be taken up, or something. Danny had told us. I tried to remember what it meant—the word Danny said—and it came back, though still holding mystery. *Judgement*. That's what the card meant. *Judgement*. The card also had 'XX' on the top, which Danny said meant twenty—card number twenty—but I couldn't understand the weird writing below.

A few seconds passed. The silence in that evening heat suddenly wasn't pleasant. I felt I had to say something: "Rebecca was looking for you to come home for dinner a while ago."

Danny answered straight, but his voice was tight and low: "I'm not going—I'll never, so long as he—" Danny stopped, but then added, like he was whispering to himself, "This will be it," he said. "A last supper."

What would? Would be what?

Being late for dinner was one thing, but it was something else not to show up at all. Who Danny meant by "he" wasn't clear right away, but it must have been his dad.

"Waiting. For him—to go. No more."

It was about now that every evening after dinner that Mr. Caine went down to his boat to ready it for his next fishing trip, or just to find his peace. Danny must have been waiting for him to leave before he went home to get his supper.

I stayed, waiting for something—but what? Mr. Caine might leave—so? Danny would go home?

I felt unneeded, and so I said, "Well, maybe I'll go see if Rebecca is around back. See if she wants to play or something."

I stood up, but, before I took more than a step, Danny once more grabbed and pulled me—this time harder—back to the ground. He held my eye to tell me straight: "Don't look for her. Don't go to our house. Go home. Now. You hear? Go. Don't look back."

I could only look at Danny, shaken by his tone, remembering his warning story about the pillar of salt.

Then, yes then.

The next moment unrolled, and this summer stopped and split into a thousand pieces. Pieces that, years and years later, still don't fit. That have yet to land.

We both heard the car door shut. Danny froze, and then he let me go as he turned toward the car, straining. I sat up and looked as well. The low light of the sun reflected off driver's side window. The engine started. Danny leaned forward. The engine barely revved.

"For thine is the kingdom, and the power," he whispered. Then, "Judgement. My card." Yes, that was the word on that old fortune card, picked by Daniel from our witch.

The driver's side window wound down. I could just make out Danny's mom at the wheel—not his dad, like I expected, and I guess what Danny expected. Where would she be going, I vaguely wondered.

Danny at once stood up and tottered. I stood up beside him and brushed the dirt off my pants. Maybe now I could go look for Rebecca.

But, with barely a breath, Danny said, "No." And then, just a little louder, "No." Then he shouted, "No!"

Danny stepped—no, lunged—in the direction of the car, and, as he took off, his magnifying glass fell to the ground beside the map and the old card. He immediately stumbled forward, hit the ground, scrambled up, and kept going. I wanted to call him back to get his magnifying glass, the old card, and his map—his map with the 'XX' on it, the 'XX' marked on his driveway, to where he was heading right now. 'XX': that marked the spot and the Judgement card.

"Mom! Stop!" he shouted, wildly. He ran a few more steps and fell yet again and kept going. I had never seen him run before. He never had to. He never fell.

"No!" he shouted one last time. Danny closed in on the car, and then it backed up a few feet.

The car exploded once, then twice, and everything else that summer was swallowed up by the rising, yellow flame.

§

After the death of Daniel Caine and his mother, Hannah, on that hot, late-summer evening, Mr. Joseph Caine sold the house on Eastfield Road. He could not altogether register what happened, or even fully why. It was too much. Too much to think about, too much to lose, too much to remember. Too much to think about his place, his role, in what happened. All dark. His mind whispered words he did not want to hear. His only remaining certainty that pointed forward was his little girl, his darling Rebecca. She would come first. She was all. That would have to be it. And what loss did she feel? What could she know? Joseph Caine could not think of this.

What would or should he do?

Joseph Caine's hesitant, brewing thoughts at last gave him a possible path, one that surprised him in its sudden clarity. He would return to Emily Cooday's village with Rebecca, and then take Emily away with him. Like Emily always wanted, what she seemed to dream about. Bring daughter together with mother. A loss returned. Marry Emily. It could be right. It would be right, he thought.

The sale of the Caine property on Eastfield Road went quickly. Joseph Caine just wanted to get rid of it. There was even a little life insurance. He could always make a living from the sea, too—the sea which held the fisherman's secret. It would all be okay, somehow. He remembered one of his own mother's proverbs: Life is not a map.

With his little girl, now just turned seven years old, he took his boat up the coast to Emily's village. Emily was still young. She would, he felt, make a good mother. She would read with her daughter, tell her all those stories she had herself read. Yes, yes: the last few times with Emily, things had not been very good. Emily had been down, and she did not cover him with her body like she used to. She did not seem to be there, in a way. They drank tea together, mainly in silence, on the deck of the boat. Joseph felt, then, some regrets, though he was not sure why. He wanted to say sorry to her, but he did not know what the right words might be, and even what he might be sorry for. But now he would try. He would. He had something. He would now try for Rebecca, too. His daughter. Their daughter.

So, with plans steeped in hope, Joseph felt better as his boat made its way north toward Emily's village, there on the boat with Rebecca, who also badly needed some hope. Yes, the three of them would start again.

EPITATH

I found myself clinging to the upper branches of an evergreen on our property, an old Douglas fir I was not supposed to climb. It was a few days after the—what was it supposed to be called? the accident? the incident? the explosion? the deaths? the murder? the tragedy? the nightmare? What word was there? It was all of these and none of these. Danny, though, seemed to have the word, and that word was *Judgement*. But of what? Danny had told us that Nature doesn't really judge things—it just does things. But now, with this, what did it mean?

Here, for once, memory of the end of that summer fails just a little. It was cooling, and a wind from the west made the top of the tree sway slightly. Rain was coming. You could smell it. It was overdue, and the land was dry and waiting.

Danny was dead. His mother was dead.

Danny always said that death was a taking back into life, a return, that any time was all time. But any reasoning about the Circle of Life at this moment failed—and still fails. And maybe, as it brewed over the hot summer, it had begun to fail for Danny. Or, was it possible, that his act was a way to complete a circle?

Danny had just turned thirteen, which, only a month or two ago, he said was the unluckiest of all numbers.

Something became hollow, yet hard. I held the tree tightly. Danny's magnifying glass, the crumpled map, and the old tarot card were in my back pocket, as well as the silken label from the sliced up baseball mitt, buried even deeper within the same pocket— "Something to remember me by"—that's what he said. Shivers mixed with a quiet sob and with the taste of salt somewhere in the back of my throat. I was afraid I might never stop. And, for the first time ever, I was afraid I might fall.

Across our yard and over to Danny's house was the driveway that the police had cordoned off with yellow ribbon that rippled lightly in the gathering wind. The grotesque, burnt-out wreck of the car was still there. Over to the left: my own backyard, the woodpile, those apple trees cleared of caterpillars, Dad's garden, and the rock border beside our driveway where we captured that perfect swallowtail. Further back, The Trail made its way into the bush and through the trees, past the Ant Nest and up to the small meadow and the Old Orchard where Danny's staged us in his attempt at a new Eden. And somewhere, back further, just where our property ended, the Sperm Tree, decorated with the last of our limp findings. And further up still, Lovers' Lane. I had no idea that, six years later, being up there in Lovers' Lane would, once more, one October night, change everything—with a different kind of flash. Again, another moment of innocence and guilt, of being at the wrong place at the wrong time.

From my forbidden perch I could just see the ocean's inlet, where salmon would soon gather to spawn up the river that bordered the southern end of Silverford City. Danny told us that Pacific salmon return to the exact gravel beds where they were born. He told us that they—both mothers and fathers—die after the new eggs were ready, which Danny thought was a good idea: "Should be a rule," he said. "It would make things more simple." Even while they are still alive, the bodies of the salmon begin to fall apart and drift down the rivers, like pieces of rotten bark. I thought of the dogfish on the dock. Crucified dogfish. Danny's dogfish hauled up into the sun, unblinking fish that seemed to feel no pain, swimming around in endless circles in the dark waters. The dogfish that ate its own young.

I could also see to the fields behind the Caines' house, to where we did some of Danny's bidding and hung on to his every word. The captured snakes. A two-headed snake named, but never found. What was Danny's plan that day? A dump truck was parked there now, like the one that ran over poor Lucky, the wandering dog, and which Danny's father somehow dispatched in a ditch. There were now some flag posts in the fields that marked out how the ground might at some point be levelled and subdivided.

There was talk of Mrs. Raskolnikov's old, decaying house being torn down, but no one seemed to know how to contact her relatives, if she had any. Her animals were gradually taken away, although, for quite a while after her death, her cats could be seen wandering around her property. Out there kittens would be born from these cats, and one of them would later come our way and change everything. All Mrs. Raskolnikov's predictions that she passed onto Danny came true—now, and then one six years later: a light in the forest.

As for Old Man Bryer up the road, to this day he's still probably wondering how his compost pile was flattened. What a thing that was! Was it—had it been a test? A test for the unthinkable?

Mr. Caine soon had their yard cleaned up, and all the stuff from the house and the garage taken away. He had gone somewhere up the coast, it was said, with his Rebecca. But no one was quite sure.

Rebecca and I would not be walking to Eastfield Elementary School together. She wouldn't get the new teacher who, even when it was freezing outside, kept opening all the windows and telling us that fresh air was good for us. Rebecca wouldn't be there to see an astonishing beetle collection from one of her classmates, and she wouldn't hear what happened to that boy's pet rabbits, about what his dad did with them. She wouldn't be there to see if I got a new bike that Christmas. I probably would have let her ride it, if she asked.

I still have the photographs of Rebecca and me at Christmas holidays, birthday parties, days at the beach, and just plain goofing around in basements and backyards. Our parents always thought we were a cute pair—salt and pepper, my Mom once said. I can hear Rebecca's voice shout out when we chased butterflies and ran from wasps. I can remember the strange taste of late-summer straw and strawberry. Danny exists in just a few photographs, usually in the background and to the side, cut off by the photograph's edge. He managed to avoid being directly in the line of the camera's fixing stare. "Cameras," he once said, "are very good liars."

And so, I found myself clinging to that old, tall evergreen, with clouds, rain, autumn, and the uncertainty of a school year coming much too quickly. Mom would soon be calling me in for supper. There was pitch on my hands, but she would remove it with butter, like she always did. I would probably be a little late, but they wouldn't start without me.

§

Isolated First Nations villages like Emily Cooday's had, for too long, suffered from the cruel legacy of colonial abuse. Some of this was the product of the church, which, with blessings from the governments of the day, often had the power to take children from their families and communities and place them in residential schools, where speaking their own language, holding their own culture, meant a beating. The names of children were changed, their identity stripped, and hidden pains put upon them. Some of these children who fell upon illness or accidents were buried in unmarked graves. Emily had heard her mother mention some of this, but only once, as if it was their own shameful secret. When these schools were eventually disbanded, generations were set up for sadness and failure. Such was the cheerless inheritance passed into Emily from her grandparents and parents.

When Joseph Caine docked in Emily's village with his young daughter Rebecca, he at first waited for Emily on his boat, thinking that she would, as always, notice his coming. He began to look for her. Taking Rebecca by her hand, he went to the house of her grandparents, where Emily lived with them. Rebecca carried her doll. Joseph had never been up to the old place before, though he could just make it out from down on the wharf.

Up close, the house was more destitute and fragile than he thought. The cedar shakes were brittle and peeling away. All was uneven. It was less a house than a shack. Joseph kept thinking about how he would introduce Emily to his daughter, to their daughter. He was afraid but also hopeful in carrying the faith that this was a good thing—the right thing, the only thing. Maybe he would ask her to go on a walk with him and Rebecca. Tell her slowly.

Joseph knocked on the door. Joseph's mouth went dry. He hoped he could say the right thing and that she would understand.

An old man, Emily's grandfather, the one who fondly called her "Witch of the Sea" for enticing crabs into the traps she set, eventually answered.

The old man, bent with age, looked at Joseph, and did not say a word. He held on to the door frame. Joseph wondered if the old man knew who he was, if he knew about his secret life with Emily, that maybe it wasn't much of a secret after all. The old man glanced at the little girl, who now shied away behind her father with her doll.

"I'm looking for Emily."

The old man once more looked Joseph over, and then looked squarely at

Rebecca, who was peeking out from behind her father. The look held the two of them together—somehow fixed, if only for a moment or two. Did he know? Could he guess who this little girl was, his granddaughter? No. That was impossible.

The old man at last lifted his eyes to say, "She's gone."

"Gone?"

Joseph thought for a second and questioned again.

"Gone? Where?" Joseph asked. His mind raced. Gone for a walk? Gone away to live in another place? Gone to look for her long-lost father? Or for her abandoned child, who was now here, here on her doorstep?

The old man looked past Joseph toward the sea.

Joseph repeated the question, "Gone?"

"It tried to take her," the old man said, returning his gaze to Joseph, his head slightly trembling. "Like it took others. Slow. Then, sudden like."

The old man again looked past Joseph. Was he smiling a bit, or biting down on his toothless gum?

Joseph waited, and Emily's grandfather tried a few more words, but they were slow and broken. "She's—the past. It tried to. No. She didn't let it—no. She wouldn't. She did it, did it herself, her way, to stop it going longer. Brave and nowhere. Now she's gone. Better, too. Oh, now," he muttered, "Oh, now."

Joseph felt sickly warm, standing there with his daughter. The old man spoke once more, pointing behind him.

"Around back. Up the hill. With others. She's there. You find her. It's the new one."

Joseph waited, but he knew there was nothing more for him to say.

The old man bent a little to once more meet Rebecca's eyes. He looked at her carefully, then reached out and touched her head. Rebecca did not shy away from his hand, though she hid the doll behind her back. "Híntu Nakws'aatí," the old man said. "I see. I see you, little one." He backed away a bit, then closed the door slowly.

Father and daughter stood for an uncertain moment.

"What'd he mean, Daddy?" Rebecca asked.

"Don't know," he said.

Joseph walked around the old house and headed up the hill, pulling Rebecca by her hand. A wind from the sea was beginning to come up from behind them. The kind of wind that whipped up the open waters, and that sometimes drove fisherman to find safe harbor.

What he had begun to think went through his body, but also numbed it. The past took her. The past. He thought of the storm that took him here, to her, those years ago. And now, again? To her again?

There it was. A crooked wooden cross, a bare mound with no grass or weeds yet covering the exposed soil. The name "Emily," barely recognizable, was scratched onto the wood, below some other name he could not read.

Joseph looked around. A few other grave markers. Older. Here and there. No rows. No enclosed area. He remembered: Emily told him that here, on this hillside, was where she used to sometimes sit and look for his boat coming up the small inlet to her village. Where, in the spring and summer, she picked wild flowers that she put in those letters, letters in which she tried to tell him everything that was so little and so much. She had written about this place on the hill more than once. And here she was.

He pulled out a little bottle with a gold cap from his pocket, and placed it on Emily's grave, beside some bleached crab shells that had been scattered around the base of the fragile cross. There was also a pen, a fancy one, among the shells.

Little Rebecca watched him place the gift offered to the grave. She looked to her father. "Who was it, Daddy?"

He tried to find that most simple of answers. It rose up in him, then fell away. He picked up the pen, looked at it, and gave it to Rebecca. "Here," he said. "She'd want you to have it."

But then, too, passing through Joseph, was the darker mystery of what had happened to those letters hidden on his boat, written with this pen, and to what those letters held. No, he thought.

Rebecca held the pen, and could only wonder.

"Did you know her?" she asked.

Looking at little Rebecca, and seeing how her eyes were so much like those of her mother, Joseph Caine remained silent on the hillside, wondering about the best place for secrets to rest.

READERS GUIDE

1. What are the secrets in the novel, and how are they connected? In what different domains do these secrets exist? When is a secret also a lie?

2. What are the different roles of the two narratives—the central one provided by the narrator, and the one delivered by Simon, the narrator's older brother? Are these narratives competing or complementary or mixed? How would you describe the relationship between the narrator and Simon?

3. What are the emerging tensions in Caine family? What is the first sign? What are the hidden (yet in plain sight) origins of these tensions?

4. Existing as the backdrop to the story are two families who live across the road from each other. How do they compare?

5. What is Daniel's view of nature, and how is or isn't it tied to his portrayal of selected Biblical stories? Do Danny's two chief narratives—one via the Bible, the other via, say, Darwin—work together, and what do the kids (the narrator and Rebecca) make of them?

6. What role does Rebecca play, and how does her identity become increasingly important?

7. What is the relationship between Daniel Caine and his father? How do the secrets between them hold key tensions in the story?

8. What role does Mrs. Raskolnikov play? What does her relationship to Danny represent?

9. What do we take or learn from the incident with Lucky?

10. At what point do you begin to get hints that Danny's view of a balanced world is beginning to change or become unbalanced? What kind of change is it, and what goes into causing the change?

11. Describe the life and situation of Emily Cooday. Does Joseph Caine take advantage of her, or is their relationship in some ways natural, mutual, or even honest? What does each get or not get from the relationship?

12. What role does Mr. Byrer play? In particular, what does he represent in terms of values, beliefs, and judgments relative to others in the story?

13. What, do you think, did Danny want out of the Garden of Eden scene?

14. The "gaze" or perspective in this narrative comes via an adult looking back to moments in his past. What perspectives determine or control this "gaze"? Describe it in various ways as determined by, for example, gender, family, socio-economics, ethics, nostalgia, trauma, place (Pacific Northwest), and time (late 1950s/early 1960s). Do you trust the narrator?

15. How, in the end, would you describe the narrator's view of Danny? Is this a coming-of-age story?

16. How, in the end, does Simon's narrative "leave" the story of Emily Cooday and Joseph Caine?

Printed in the USA
CPSIA information can be obtained
at www.ICGtesting.com
LVHW032106090624
782653LV00005B/18

9 781632 936639